Something About You

Something About You

JULIE JAMES

BERKLEY SENSATION, NEW YORK

THE BERKLEY PUBLISHING GROUP
Published by the Penguin Group
Penguin Group (USA) Inc.
375 Hudson Street, New York, New York 10014, USA
Penguin Group (Canada), 90 Eglinton Avenue East, Suite 700, Toronto, Ontario M4P 2Y3, Canada
(a division of Pearson Penguin Canada Inc.)
Penguin Books Ltd., 80 Strand, London WC2R 0RL, England
Penguin Group Ireland, 25 St. Stephen's Green, Dublin 2, Ireland (a division of Penguin Books Ltd.)
Penguin Group (Australia), 250 Camberwell Road, Camberwell, Victoria 3124, Australia
(a division of Pearson Australia Group Pty. Ltd.)
Penguin Books India Pvt. Ltd., 11 Community Centre, Panchsheel Park, New Delhi—110 017, India
Penguin Group (NZ), 67 Apollo Drive, Rosedale, North Shore 0632, New Zealand
(a division of Pearson New Zealand Ltd.)
Penguin Books (South Africa) (Pty.) Ltd., 24 Sturdee Avenue, Rosebank, Johannesburg 2196,
South Africa

Penguin Books Ltd., Registered Offices: 80 Strand, London WC2R 0RL, England

This is a work of fiction. Names, characters, places, and incidents either are the product of the author's imagination or are used fictitiously, and any resemblance to actual persons, living or dead, business establishments, events, or locales is entirely coincidental. The publisher does not have any control over and does not assume any responsibility for author or third-party websites or their content.

SOMETHING ABOUT YOU

A Berkley Sensation Book / published by arrangement with the author

ISBN-13: 978-1-61664-088-0

BERKLEY® SENSATION
Berkley Sensation Books are published by The Berkley Publishing Group,
a division of Penguin Group (USA) Inc.,
375 Hudson Street, New York, New York 10014.
BERKLEY® SENSATION and the "B" design are trademarks of Penguin Group (USA) Inc.

PRINTED IN THE UNITED STATES OF AMERICA

*To the jokers in the room next to me
at the JW Marriott San Francisco—
As you kept me awake with your antics,
this is the book I wrote in my head.*

Acknowledgments

To my amazing editor, Wendy McCurdy, for her input and wisdom, and for knowing what I wanted to do with this book before I fully realized it myself. Thanks also to Kathryn Tumen, Katherine Pelz, and the entire team at Berkley for all their support.

To my agent, Susan Crawford, for her encouragement and unflagging enthusiasm, and to Christine Garcia for all her great ideas and dedication.

A special thanks to Kati Dancy, for her fantastic insight and feedback on the manuscript. Even if she is off her rocker when it comes to Mr. Reynolds.

Thanks to John Mehochko, for answering my questions about the daily life of an Assistant U.S. Attorney, and to my father-in-law, for his knowledge of the technical aspects of criminal investigations.

I've been very blessed to have met, both in person and online, the greatest group of reviewers, bloggers, readers, and fans an author could ask for. You ladies—and you know who you are—truly rock.

To my friends and family, for all their love and support. And to my son, who always puts a smile on my face and who is too darn cute for words.

And lastly, thanks especially to my wonderful husband, Brian, who honestly seems to know just about everything (boy, am I going to regret putting *that* in writing), and for his never-ending encouragement.

One

THIRTY THOUSAND HOTEL rooms in the city of Chicago, and Cameron Lynde managed to find one next door to a couple having a sex marathon.

"Yes! Oh yes! YES!"

Cameron pulled the pillow over her head, thinking—as she had been thinking for the past hour and a half—that it had to end *sometime*. It was after three o'clock in the morning, and while she certainly had nothing against a good round of raucous hotel sex, this particular round had gone beyond raucous and into the ridiculous about fourteen "oh-God-oh-God-oh-Gods" ago. More important, even with the discounted rate they gave federal employees, overnights at the Peninsula weren't typically within the monthly budget of an assistant U.S. attorney, and she was starting to get seriously POed that she couldn't get a little peace and quiet.

Bam! Bam! Bam! The wall behind the king-sized bed shook with enough force to rattle her headboard, and Cameron cursed the hardwood floors that had brought her to such circumstances.

Earlier in the week, when the contractor had told her that she would need to stay off her refinished floors for twenty-four hours, she had decided to treat herself to some much-needed pampering. Just last week she had finished a grueling three-month racketeering trial against eleven defendants charged with various organized criminal activities, including seven murders and three attempted murders. The trial had been mentally exhausting for everyone involved, particularly her and the other assistant U.S. attorney who had prosecuted the case. So when she'd learned that she needed to be out of her house while the floors dried, she had seized on the opportunity to turn it into a weekend getaway.

Maybe other people would have gone somewhere more distant or exotic than a hotel three miles from home, but all Cameron had cared about was getting an incredibly overpriced but fantastically rejuvenating massage, followed by a tranquil night of R&R, and then in the morning a brunch buffet (again incredibly overpriced) where she could stuff herself to the point where she remembered why she made it a general habit to stay away from brunch buffets. And the perfect place for that was the Peninsula.

Or so she had thought.

"Such a big, bad man! Right there, oh yeah—right there, don't stop!"

The pillow over her head did nothing to drown out the woman's voice. Cameron closed her eyes in a silent plea. *Dear Mr. Big and Bad: Whatever the hell you're doing, don't you move from that spot until you get the job done.* She hadn't prayed so hard for an orgasm since the first—and last—time she'd slept with Jim, the corporate wine buyer/artist who wanted to "find his way" but who didn't seem to have a clue how to find his way around the key parts of the female body.

The moaning that had started around 1:30 A.M. was what had woken her up. In her groggy state, her first thought had been that someone in the room next door was sick. But quickly following those moans had been a second person's moans, and then came the panting and the wall-banging and the hollering and then that part that sounded suspiciously like a butt cheek being spanked, and somewhere around that point she had clued into the true goings-on of room 1308.

WhaMA-WhaMA-WhaMA-WhaMA-WhaMA-WhaMA . . .

The bed in the room next door increased its tempo against the wall, and the squeaking of the mattress reached a new, feverish pitch. Despite her annoyance, Cameron had to give the guy credit, whoever he was, for having some serious staying power. Perhaps it was one of those Viagra situations, she mused. She had heard somewhere that one little pill could get a man up and running for over four hours.

She yanked the pillow off her head and peered through the darkness at the clock on the nightstand next to the bed: 3:17. If she had to endure another two hours and fifteen minutes of this stuff, she just might have to kill someone— starting with the front desk clerk who had put her in this room in the first place. Weren't hotels supposed to skip the thirteenth floor, anyway? Right now she was wishing she was a more superstitious person and had asked to be assigned another room.

In fact, right now she was wishing she'd never come up with the whole weekend getaway idea and instead had just spent the night at Collin's or Amy's. At least then she'd be asleep instead of listening to the cacophonous symphony of grunting and squealing—oh yes, the girl was actually *squealing* now—that was the current soundtrack of her life. Plus, Collin made a mean cheddar and tomato egg-white omelet that, while likely not quite the equivalent of the delicacies one might find at the Peninsula buffet, would've reminded her why she'd made it a general habit to let him do all the cooking when the three of them lived together their senior year of college.

Wheewammawamma-BAM! Wheewammawamma-BAM!

Cameron sat up in bed and looked at the phone on the nightstand. She didn't want to be that kind of guest that complained about every little blemish in the hotel's five-star service. But the noise from the room next door had been going on for a long time now and at a certain point, she felt as though she was entitled to some sleep in her nearly four-hundred-dollar-per-night room. The only reason the hotel hadn't already received complaints, she guessed, was due to the fact that 1308 was a corner room with no one on the other side.

Cameron was just about to pick up the phone to call the front desk when, suddenly, she heard the man next door call out the glorious sounds of her salvation.

Smack! Smack!

"Oh shit, I'm cooommmminnggg!"

A loud groan. And then—

Blessed silence. Finally.

Cameron fell back onto the bed. *Thank you, thank you, Peninsula hotel gods, for granting me this tiny reprieve. I shall never again call your massages incredibly overpriced. Even if we all know it doesn't cost $195 to rub lotion on someone's back. Just saying.*

She crawled under the covers and pulled the cream down duvet up to her chin. Her head sank into the pillows and she lay there for a few minutes as she began to drift off. Then she heard another noise next door—the sound of the door shutting.

Cameron tensed.

And then—

Nothing.

All remained blissfully still and silent, and her final thought before she fell asleep was on the significance of the sound of the door shutting.

She had a sneaking suspicion that somebody had just received a five-star booty call.

BAM!

Cameron shot up in bed, the sound from next door waking her right out of her sleep. She heard muffled squealing and the bed slammed against the wall again—harder and louder than ever—as if its occupants were *really* going at it this time.

She looked at the clock: 4:08. She'd been given a whopping thirty-minute reprieve.

Not wasting another moment—frankly, she'd already given these jokers far too much of her valuable sleep time—she reached over and turned on the lamp next to the bed. She blinked as her eyes adjusted to the sudden burst of light. Then she grabbed the phone off the nightstand and dialed.

After one ring, a man answered pleasantly on the other end. "Good evening, Ms. Lynde. Thank you for calling Guest Services—how may we be of assistance?"

Cameron cleared her throat, her voice still hoarse as her words tumbled out. "Look, I don't want to be a jerk about this, but you guys have got to do something about the people in room 1308. They keep banging against the wall; there's been all sorts of moaning and shouting and spanking and it's been going on for, like, the last two hours. I've barely slept this entire night and it sounds like they're gearing up for round twenty or whatever, which is great for them but not so much for me, and I'm kind of at the point where enough is enough, you know?"

The voice on the other end was wholly unfazed, as if Guest Services at the Peninsula handled the fallout from five-star booty calls all the time.

"Of course, Ms. Lynde. I apologize for the inconvenience. I'll send up security to take care of the problem right away."

"Thanks," Cameron grumbled, not yet willing to be pacified that easily. She planned to speak to the manager in the morning, but for now all she wanted was a quiet room and some sleep.

She hung up the phone and waited. A few moments passed, then she glanced at the wall behind the bed. Things had fallen strangely silent in room 1308. She wondered if the occupants had heard her calling Guest Services to complain. Sure, the walls were thin (as she definitely had discovered firsthand), but were they *that* thin?

She heard the door to room 1308 open.

The bastards were making their escape.

Cameron flew out of bed and ran to her door, determined to at least get a look at the sex fiends. She pressed against the door and peered through the peephole just as the door to the other room shut. For a brief moment, she saw no one. Then—

A man stepped into view.

He moved quickly, appearing slightly distorted through the peephole. He had his back toward her as he passed by her room, so Cameron didn't get the greatest look. She didn't know what the typical sex fiend looked like, but this particular one was on the taller side and stylish in his jeans, black corduroy blazer, and gray hooded T-shirt. He wore the hood pulled up, which was kind of unusual. As the man crossed the hallway and pushed open the door to the stairwell, something struck her as oddly familiar. But then he disappeared into the stairwell before she could place it.

Cameron pulled away from the door. Something very strange was going on in room 1308 . . . Maybe the man had fled the scene because he'd heard her call Guest Services and was abandoning his partner to deal with the fallout alone. A married man, perhaps? Regardless, the woman in 1308 was going to have some serious 'splaining to do once hotel security arrived. Cameron figured—since she already was awake, that is—that she might as well just sit it out right there at the peephole and catch the final act. Not that she was eavesdropping or anything, but . . . okay, she was eavesdropping.

She didn't have to wait long. Two men dressed in suits, presumably hotel security, arrived within the next minute and knocked on the door to 1308. Cameron watched through the peephole as the security guards stared expectantly at the door, then shrugged at each other when there was no answer.

"Should we try again?" the shorter security guard asked.

The second guy nodded and knocked on the door. "Hotel security," he called out.

No response.

"Are you sure this is the right room?" asked the second guy.

The first guy checked the room number, then nodded. "Yep. The person who complained said the noise was coming from room 1308."

He glanced over at Cameron's room. She took a step back as if they could see her through the door. She suddenly felt very aware of the fact that she was wearing only her University of Michigan T-shirt and underwear.

There was a pause.

"Well, I don't hear a thing now," Cameron heard the first guy say. He banged on the door a third time, louder still. "Security! Open up!"

Still nothing.

Cameron moved back to the door and looked out the peephole once again. She saw the security guards exchange looks of annoyance.

"They're probably in the shower," said the shorter guy.

"Probably going at it again," the other one agreed.

The two men pressed their ears to the door. On her side of the door, Cameron listened for any sound of a shower running in the next room but heard nothing.

The taller security guard sighed. "You know the protocol—we have to go in." Out of his pocket he pulled what presumably was some sort of master key card. He slid it into the lock and cracked open the door.

"Hello? Hotel security—anyone in here?" he called into the room.

He looked over his shoulder at his partner and shook his head. Nothing. He stepped farther in and gestured for the second guy to follow. Both men disappeared into the room, out of Cameron's view, and the door slammed shut behind them.

There was a momentary pause, then Cameron heard one of the security men cry out through the adjoining wall.

"Holy shit!"

Her stomach dropped. She knew then that whatever had happened in 1308, it wasn't good. Uncertain what she should do, she pressed her ear to the wall and listened.

"Try CPR while I call 9-1-1!" one of the men shouted.

Cameron flew off the bed—she knew CPR—and raced to the door. She threw it open just as the shorter security guy was running out of 1308.

Seeing her, he held up his hand, indicating she should

stop right where she was. "Ma'am—please get back in your room."

"But I heard—I thought I could help, I—"

"We've got it covered, ma'am. Now please step back into your room." He rushed off.

Per the security's guard order, Cameron remained in her doorway. She looked around and saw that other people in the nearby rooms had heard the commotion and were peering into the hallway with mixed expressions of trepidation and curiosity.

After what seemed like forever but what was probably only minutes, the shorter guy returned leading a pair of paramedics pulling a gurney.

As the trio raced past Cameron, she overheard the security guard explaining the situation. "We found her lying there on the bed . . . She was nonresponsive so we began CPR but it doesn't look good . . ."

By this time, additional staff had arrived on the scene, and a woman in a gray suit identified herself as the hotel manager and asked everyone to remain in their rooms. Cameron overheard her tell the other members of the staff to keep the hallway and elevator bank clear. The thirteenth floor guests spoke amongst themselves in low murmurs, and Cameron caught snippets of conversations as a guest from one room would ask another if he or she knew what was happening.

A hush fell over the crowd when the paramedics reappeared in the doorway of room 1308. They moved quickly, pulling the gurney out into the hall.

This time, there was a person on that gurney.

As they hurried past Cameron, she caught a glimpse of the person—a quick glimpse, but enough to see that it was a woman, and also enough to see that she had long red hair that fanned out in stark contrast to the white of both

the sheet on the gurney and the hotel bathrobe she wore.
And, she saw enough to see that the woman wasn't moving.

While one of the paramedics pushed the gurney, the
other ran alongside it, pumping oxygen through a hand-
held mask that covered the woman's face. The two security guards raced ahead of the paramedics, making sure
the hallway was clear. Cameron—and apparently several
of the other hotel guests as well—overheard the shorter
guard saying something to the other about the police being on their way.

At the mention of the police, a minor commotion broke
out. The hotel guests demanded to know what was happening.

The manager spoke above the fray. "I certainly understand that all of you have concerns, and I offer you our
sincerest apologies for the disturbance." She addressed
them in a calm, genteel tone that was remarkably similar
to that of the man from Guest Services who Cameron had
spoken on the phone with earlier. She wondered if they all
talked that way to each other when no customers were
around, or if they dropped the charm routine and that
vague, quasi-European-even-though-I'm-from-Wisconsin
accent the minute they hit the lunchroom.

"Unfortunately, at this point I can tell you only that the
situation, obviously, is very serious and may be criminal
in nature," the manager continued. "We will be turning this
matter over to the police, and we ask that everyone remain
in their rooms until they arrive and assess the situation.
It's likely the police will want to speak with some of you."

The manager's gaze fell directly upon Cameron. As the
crowd fell back into their murmurs and whispers, she
walked over. "Ms. Lynde, is it?"

Cameron nodded. "Yes."

The manager gestured to the door. "Would you mind if

I escorted you back into your room, Ms. Lynde?" This was Polite-Peninsula-Hotel-speak for "You might as well get comfortable because your eavesdropping ass isn't going anywhere."

"Of course," Cameron said, still somewhat shell-shocked by the events that had transpired over the last few minutes. As an assistant U.S. attorney, she'd had plenty of exposure to the criminal element, but this was different. This was not some case she was reviewing through the objective eyes of a prosecutor; there were no evidence files neatly prepared by the FBI or crime scene photos taken after the fact. She had actually *heard* the crime this time; she had seen the victim firsthand and—thinking back to the man in the blazer and hooded T-shirt—very possibly the person who had harmed her as well.

The thought sent chills running down her spine.

Or, Cameron supposed, maybe the chill had something to do with the fact that she was still standing in the air-conditioned hallway wearing nothing but her T-shirt and underwear.

Classy.

With as much dignity as one could muster while braless and without any pants, Cameron tugged her T-shirt down an extra half-inch and followed the hotel manager into her room.

Two

SOMETHING WASN'T RIGHT.

Cameron had been trapped inside her hotel room for nearly two hours while the Chicago Police Department supposedly conducted their investigation. She knew enough about crime scenes and witness questioning to know that this was not standard protocol.

For starters, nobody was telling her anything. The police had arrived shortly after the hotel manager escorted her back into her room. A middle-aged, slightly balding and extremely cranky Detective Slonsky introduced himself to Cameron and took a seat in the armchair in the corner of the hotel room and began to take her statement about what she had heard that night. Although she had at least been given two seconds of privacy to throw on yoga pants and a bra, she still found it awkward to be questioned by the police while sitting on a hastily made hotel bed.

The first thing Detective Slonsky noticed was the half-empty glass of wine that she had ordered from room service still sitting on the desk where she'd left it hours before. That, of course, had prompted several preliminary questions regarding her alcohol consumption over the course of the evening. After she seemingly managed to convince Slonsky that, no, she was not a raging alcoholic and, yes, her statement at least had a modicum of reliability, they moved past the booze issue and she commented on the fact that Slonsky had introduced himself as "Detective" instead of "Officer." She asked if that meant he was part of the homicide division. If for no other reason, she wanted to know what had happened to the girl in room 1308.

Slonsky's sole response was a level stare and a curt, "I'm the one asking the questions here, Ms. Lynde."

Cameron had just finished giving her statement when another plain-clothes detective stuck his head into the room. "Slonsky—you better get in here." He nodded in the direction of the room next door.

Slonsky stood and gave Cameron yet another level stare. She wondered if he practiced the look in his bathroom mirror.

"I'd appreciate it if you would remain in this room until I get back," he told her.

Cameron smiled. "Of course, Detective." She was debating whether to pull rank in order to start getting some answers, but she wasn't quite at that point. Yet. She'd been around cops and agents all her life and had a lot of respect for what they did. But the smile was to let Slonsky know that he wasn't getting to her. "I'm happy to cooperate in any way I can."

Slonsky eyed her suspiciously, probably trying to decide whether he heard a hint of sarcasm in her voice. She got that look a lot.

"Just stay in your room," he said as he made his exit.

The next time Cameron saw Detective Slonsky was a

half hour later, when he dropped by her room to let her know that, due to certain "unexpected developments," she would not only have to remain in her room longer than anticipated, but that he was posting a guard at her door. He added that "it had been requested" that she not make any calls from either her cell phone or the hotel line until "they" had finished questioning her.

For the first time, Cameron wondered whether she personally was in trouble. "Am I considered a *suspect* in this investigation?" she asked Slonsky.

"I didn't say that."

She noticed that wasn't officially a "no."

As Slonsky turned to leave, she threw another question at him. "Who are 'they'?"

He peered over his shoulder. "Excuse me?"

"You said I can't make any calls until 'they' finish questioning me," Cameron said. "Who were you referring to?"

The detective's expression said that he had no intention of answering that question. "We appreciate your continued cooperation, Ms. Lynde. That's all I can say for now."

A few minutes after Slonsky left, Cameron looked out her peephole and—sure enough—was treated to the view of the back of some man's head, presumably the guard he had stationed outside her door. She left the door and went back to sitting on the bed. Cameron glanced at the clock and saw that it was nearly 7:00 A.M. She turned on the television—Slonsky hadn't said anything about not watching TV, after all—and hoped that maybe she would see something about whatever was happening on the news.

She was still pushing buttons on the remote, trying to figure out how to get past that damn hotel "Welcome" screen, when the door to her room flew open once more.

Slonsky stuck his head in. "Sorry—no television either."

He shut the door.

"Stupid thin walls," Cameron muttered under her breath. Not that anyone was listening. Then again . . .

"Can I at least read a book, Detective Slonsky?" she asked the empty room.

A pause.

Then a voice came through the door, from the hallway. "Sure."

And indeed the walls were so thin, Cameron could actually hear the faint trace of a smile in his answer.

"THIS IS GETTING ridiculous. I have rights, you know."

Cameron faced off against the cop guarding the door to her hotel room, determined to get some answers.

The young police officer nodded sympathetically. "I know, ma'am, and I do apologize, but I'm just following orders."

Maybe it was her frustration at being cooped up in her hotel room for what was now going on five—yes, *five*—hours, but Cameron was going to strangle the kid if he ma'am-ed her one more time. She was thirty-two years old, not sixty. Although she'd probably given up the right to be called "Miss" somewhere around the time she had started thinking of twenty-two-year-old man-boy police officers as kids.

Deciding that throttling a cop was probably not the best way to go when presumably dozens more stood right outside her door (she couldn't say for sure; she hadn't been permitted to even look out into the hallway, let alone step a toe out there), Cameron tried another tactic. The man-boy clearly responded to authority, maybe she could use that to her advantage.

"Look, I probably should've mentioned this earlier, but I'm an assistant U.S. attorney. I work out of the Chicago office—"

"If you live in Chicago, what are you doing spending the night in a hotel?" Officer Man-Boy interrupted.

"I'm redoing my hardwood floors. The point is—"

"Really?" He seemed very interested in this. "Because I've been trying to find somebody to update my bathroom. The people who owned the place before me put in this crazy black and white marble and gold fixtures and the place looks like something out of the Playboy Mansion. Mind if I ask how you found a contractor to take on a job that small?"

Cameron cocked her head. "Are you trying to sidetrack me with these questions, or do you just have some weird fascination with home improvement?"

"Possibly the former. I was under the distinct impression that you were about to become difficult."

Cameron had to hide her smile. Officer Man-Boy may not have been as green as she'd thought.

"Here's the thing," she told him, "you can't keep me here against my will, especially since I've already given my statement to Detective Slonsky. You know that, and more important, I know that. There's clearly something unusual going on with this investigation, and while I'm willing to cooperate and give you guys a little leeway as a professional courtesy, I'm going to need some answers if you expect me to keep waiting here. And if you're not the person who can give me those answers, that's fine, but then I'd like it if you could go get Slonsky or whoever it is that I should be talking to."

Officer Man-Boy was not unsympathetic. "Look—I know you've been stuck in this room for a long time, but the FBI guys said that they're gonna talk to you as soon as they finish next door."

"So it's the FBI who's running this, then?"

"I probably wasn't supposed to say that."

"Why do they have jurisdiction?" Cameron pressed. "This is a homicide case, right?"

Officer Man-Boy didn't fall for the bait a second time. "I'm sorry, Ms. Lynde, but my hands are tied. The agent in charge of the investigation specifically said I'm not allowed to talk to you about this."

"Then I think I should speak to the agent in charge. Who is it?" As a prosecutor for the Northern District of Illinois, she had worked with many of the FBI agents in Chicago.

"Some special agent—I didn't catch his name," Officer Man-Boy said. "Although I think he might know you. When he told me to guard this room, he said he felt bad for sticking me with you for this long."

Cameron tried not to show any reaction, but that stung. True, she wasn't exactly buddy-buddy with a lot of the FBI agents she worked with—many of them still blamed her for that incident three years ago—but with the exception of one particular agent who, fortunately, was miles away in Nevada or Nebraska or something, she hadn't thought that anyone in the FBI disliked her enough to openly bad-mouth her.

Officer Man-Boy looked apologetic. "For what it's worth, I don't think you're so bad."

"Thanks. And did this unknown special agent who allegedly thinks he knows me have anything else to say?"

"Only that I should go get him if you start acting fussy." He looked her over. "You're going to start acting fussy now, aren't you?"

Cameron folded her arms across her chest. "Yes, I think I am." And it wouldn't be an act. "You go find this agent, whoever he is, and tell him that the fussy woman in room 1307 is through being jerked around. And tell him that I would appreciate it very much if he could wrap up his little power trip and condescend to speak to me himself. Because *I* would like to know how long he expects me to sit here and wait."

"For as long as I ask you to, Ms. Lynde."

The voice came from the doorway.

Cameron had her back to the door, but she would've recognized that voice anywhere—low and as smooth as velvet.

It couldn't be.

She turned around and took in the man standing across the room from her. He looked exactly the same as he did the last time she'd seen him three years ago: tall, dark, and scowling.

She didn't bother to mask the animosity in her voice. "Agent Pallas . . . I didn't realize you were back in town. How was Nevada?"

"Nebraska."

From his icy look, Cameron knew that her day, which had already been off to a most inauspicious start, had just gotten about fifty times worse.

Three

CAMERON WATCHED WARILY as Jack, aka FBI Special Agent Pallas, looked over at Officer Man-Boy.

"Thank you, Officer, I can take it from here," he said.

The police officer made a hasty retreat, leaving her alone in the hotel room with Jack. His gaze was stone cold.

"This is quite a mess you've gotten yourself involved in."

Cameron straightened up. Three years had passed, and he still managed to put her immediately on the defensive. "I wouldn't know. Thanks to you, I have no clue what I'm involved in." She paused, hating being out of the loop on whatever was going on. "What happened to the woman next door?"

"She's dead."

Cameron nodded. The presence of CPD detectives had pretty much given that away, but the confirmation of the woman's death shocked her nevertheless. She suddenly felt an overwhelming urge to get out of that hotel room. But she forced herself not to show any reaction in front of Jack.

"I'm sorry to hear that," she said simply.

He gestured to the chair in front of the desk. "Why don't you take a seat? I need to ask you some questions."

"Do you intend to interrogate me, Agent Pallas?"

"Do you intend to be uncooperative, Ms. Lynde?"

She laughed hollowly. "Why? Are you going to get rough with me?"

His eyes remained steely and dark. Cameron swallowed and made a mental note to be careful when taunting a man who carried a gun and blamed her for nearly wrecking his career.

She remembered the day three years ago when they'd first met to discuss the Martino case. She'd never worked with Jack before; at that point she'd only been a prosecutor for a year and he had been working undercover that entire time. She had been surprised—but eagerly so—when her boss assigned her the Martino investigation, one of the most high-profile cases in the district. Rob Martin (aka Roberto Martino) was widely known by both the Bureau and the U.S. attorney's office to be the head of one of the largest crime syndicates in Chicago. The problem had always been getting enough evidence to prove this.

Which is precisely where Special Agent Jack Pallas came in. Prior to their meeting, Cameron learned from her boss that Jack had worked undercover for two years to infiltrate Martino's organization, until the FBI had been forced to pull him out when his cover was blown. Her boss had not told her much about the extraction other than that Jack had been cornered in a warehouse by ten of Martino's men, had fought his way out, and had been shot in the process. She'd learned one other thing—by the time FBI backup arrived, Jack had already managed to kill eight of Martino's men.

He made quite an impression on her the first time he and his partner walked into her office. Cameron suspected nearly everyone who met Jack Pallas had the same reaction: with predatory brown eyes, nearly black hair, and dark facial scruff, he looked like the kind of guy that women—and men—should avoid in dark alleys. He had a cast on his right forearm, presumably an injury inflicted by Martino's men, and he wore a navy T-shirt and jeans instead of the standard-issue suit and tie most agents were expected to wear. From the look of him, she was not at all surprised the FBI had chosen him for undercover work.

And three years later—as he stood across from her in that hotel room that suddenly seemed far too small, with his eyes glittering with a low-simmering anger, and, yes, even despite the standard-issue suit and tie he wore this time—he looked not one bit less dangerous.

"I want to talk to a lawyer," Cameron said.

"You are a lawyer," he said. "And you're not considered a suspect, so you're not entitled to one, anyway."

"What am I considered, then?"

"A person of interest."

This was bullshit. "Here's the deal: I'm tired and not in the mood to play games. So if you don't start telling me what's going on, I'm walking," Cameron said.

Jack eyed her yoga sweats and Michigan T-shirt, looking unconcerned with her threats. Thank God she wasn't still hanging out in her underpants.

"You're not going anywhere." He pulled the chair out and gestured. "Take a seat."

"Thanks, but no. I think I'll just stick with the plan where I walk out." Before he could call her bluff, Cameron grabbed her purse and headed for the door. The hell with her stuff, she'd get it later. "It was nice catching up with you, Agent Pallas. I'm glad to see those three years in Nebraska didn't make you any less of an asshole."

She threw open the door and nearly ran into a man standing in the doorway. He wore a well-cut gray suit and tie, appeared younger than Jack, and was African American.

He flashed Cameron a knock-out smile while precariously balancing three Starbucks cups in his hands. "Thanks for getting the door. What'd I miss?"

"I'm storming out. And I just called Agent Pallas an asshole."

"Sounds like good times. Coffee?" He held the Starbucks out to her. "I'm Agent Wilkins."

Cameron threw a knowing glance over her shoulder. "Good cop, bad cop? Is that the best you're capable of, Jack?"

He stalked across the room and stopped in the doorway, towering over her. "You have no idea what I'm capable of," he said darkly.

As he reached over and took one of the coffee cups from Wilkins, Cameron made a mental note to be careful when taunting a man who carried a gun, blamed her for nearly wrecking his career, *and* who was over a head taller than she was. She internally said a few profanities for her earlier decision to put on gym shoes; she needed at least three-inch heels to face off against Jack Pallas. Although that still would have only put her at his chin level. Not to mention that she would've looked like a major jackass wearing Manolos and yoga pants.

Wilkins gestured with the coffee cups. "Do you two know each other?"

"Ms. Lynde and I *almost* had the pleasure of working on a case together," Jack said.

"Almost? What does that mean?" Wilkins turned to Cameron with a look of realization. "Wait a second—*Cameron* Lynde? I knew that name sounded familiar. Of course, from the U.S. attorney's office." His light brown eyes lit up as he laughed. "You're the one that Jack said had—"

"I think we all recall just fine what Agent Pallas said," Cameron interrupted. Three years ago, his words infamously had been broadcast all over the national news for nearly a week. She didn't need to hear them again, particularly not with him standing right beside her. The experience had been embarrassing enough the first time around.

Wilkins nodded. "Sure, no problem." He looked between her and Jack. "So . . . this is awkward."

Changing the subject, Cameron pointed to the coffee. "Is that regular or decaf?"

"Regular. I heard you had a long night."

She took one of the cups from him. She'd been up for twenty-three hours and adrenaline wasn't cutting it anymore. She took a sip, sighing gratefully. "Thank you."

Wilkins took a sip of his coffee. "See, that's all we are, just three people having coffee and talking. So what do you say—think you might want to stay and chat with us about what happened last night?"

That almost got a smile out of Cameron. Wilkins, at least, appeared to be a pleasant, reasonable man. Too bad he'd drawn the short stick in his partner assignment.

"That's not half-bad," she told him.

Wilkins grinned. "The coffee or the good-cop routine?"

"Both. If *you* would like to ask me some questions, Agent Wilkins, I'd be happy to cooperate." Cameron brushed past Jack as she turned and headed back into the room. He and Wilkins followed her as she took a seat in front of the desk. She crossed her legs and faced the two FBI agents head-on.

"All right. Let's talk."

IF IT HAD been anyone other than Cameron Lynde, Jack probably would've found her attitude amusing.

But since it *was* Cameron Lynde, he wasn't laughing. In fact, there wasn't anything about the situation that he found even remotely funny.

He decided to let Wilkins take the lead in questioning her about the events of the night before. Not because she very clearly wanted nothing to do with him—he could care less about Cameron Lynde's wishes—but rather because, not surprising given their history, she responded better to his partner than to him. The investigation was his focus, and he was not about to let personal issues get in the way.

When he and Wilkins had first arrived at the Peninsula and Detective Slonsky told them the name of the witness in room 1307, for a split second Jack had thought the whole thing was a setup, some sort of welcome-back prank for his return to Chicago. And he still had considered this a possibility when they entered the crime scene. There was no body, after all—Slonsky said the paramedics had taken the victim to Northwestern Memorial in an attempt to revive her.

Then he saw the videotape.

After that, it was pretty clear to Jack that the call he had received at 5:00 A.M. from his boss, asking him to check out CPD's claims of what they thought they might have stumbled into, was indeed not part of some elaborate joke. And his first priority at this point was to determine whether the FBI had jurisdiction over the matter.

Cameron Lynde was the key to answering that question. If Jack believed her story, the FBI would have no choice but to conduct its own investigation. For that reason, as much as he might've wanted nothing more than to pawn her off onto Wilkins, as the senior agent on the scene he knew that wasn't an option.

From his post in the corner of the room, Jack studied her. Not surprisingly, she looked exhausted. And for some reason, she seemed shorter than he remembered. Probably because all the times he'd seen her three years ago had been during work hours and she'd been wearing heels.

Yes, he remembered Cameron Lynde and her high heels . . . In fact, despite the fact that it had been three years since he'd last seen her, Jack was surprised at how accurate—and detailed—his memory of her had been: the long chestnut hair, the crystalline blue-green eyes, the attitude that he'd once—very briefly—found admirable.

Then again, he shouldn't be surprised he'd remembered those things. After all, he was an FBI agent and it was his job to remember details.

And, he supposed, it didn't hurt that Cameron Lynde was—some men other than him might say—fucking gorgeous.

Which, to Jack, only made it that much more annoying that she also happened to be a total bitch.

Thankfully, the long chestnut hair currently was pulled back into a ponytail, and the blue-green eyes had dulled a little given her lack of sleep. The yoga pants and Michigan T-shirt she wore were actually kind of cute, but because of the aforementioned bitch factor, he ignored this.

"So when they woke me up the second time," Cameron was saying, "that's when I decided to call Guest Services."

"I want to step back for a moment." Jack's interruption from the corner of the room startled Cameron; it was the first time he'd spoken since she'd begun giving her statement.

"Tell me what you heard right before you fell asleep. Before the noises next door started up again," he said.

Cameron hesitated. He knew she didn't want to answer *his* questions—she probably didn't want to say anything to him at all, in fact—but now that she'd started cooperating, she didn't have much choice.

"I heard the door shut, as if someone was leaving the room," she said.

"Are you sure it was the exterior door you heard?" Jack asked.

"Yes."

"But you didn't check to see if anyone left at that time?"

Cameron shook her head. "No. Then the room went quiet for a while. For about a half hour or so."

"Tell me about the noises that woke you up."

Cameron turned to face him now that he had taken over the questioning. "What would you like to know, Agent Pallas?" she asked mock-politely.

"I just told you. I'd like to know what you heard."

"Pretty much the same things I heard coming from the room the first time," she said with an air of defiance.

Jack cocked his head. "Really? You said the first time around you heard the people next door having sex."

"Yes, I think the ass slapping and the screams of 'I'm coming' gave that away."

Jack stepped out from the corner to approach her. "So when you woke up the second time, did you hear any asses being slapped?"

"No."

From her expression, he could tell she didn't enjoy being on the receiving end of a cross-examination. "How about the 'I'm coming' screams? Any more of those?"

"I heard squealing."

"But no proclamations of impending orgasms?"

She glared. "You made your point, Agent Pallas."

He drew closer and stared down at her. "My point, Ms. Lynde, is that I know you're tired, but that's no excuse for getting sloppy."

Cameron's eyes filled with anger. But then she paused for a moment, and nodded. "Fair enough."

She looked over at the wall she shared with room 1308.

"When I woke up the second time, I heard the bed banging against the wall, louder than before. But only a couple of times. Then like I said, I heard squealing."

"A man or a woman's voice?" Jack asked.

"A woman. The sound was muffled, as if her face was covered by a blanket or pillow." Cameron turned back to him with a look of sudden realization. "She was suffocated, wasn't she?" she asked softly.

Jack debated whether to answer this but knew he eventually would have to fill her in anyway. "Yes."

Cameron bit her lip. "I just thought they were trying to be quieter about it. I didn't realize . . ." She took a deep, steadying breath.

"You couldn't have known," Wilkins assured her.

Jack threw him a look—enough with the good-cop already. She was a big girl, she could handle it. "You told Detective Slonsky that you called security and the room went quiet again?"

"And then I heard the door open, so I ran and looked out the peephole," Cameron said.

"Just being nosy?"

The sarcasm seemed to reinvigorate her. "And thank goodness for that," she said. "Otherwise you wouldn't have whatever information I know that I don't yet *realize* I know." She smiled ever so sweetly. "Besides, if I hadn't been so nosy, Agent Pallas, you and I never would've had this lovely chance to reconnect."

Wilkins coughed while taking a sip of his coffee. It sounded suspiciously like a chuckle.

Jack found her sarcasm laughable. Back when he was in Special Forces, before he'd joined the FBI, he'd interrogated foreign operatives, suspected terrorists, and members of various guerilla militias. He could certainly handle one cheeky assistant U.S. attorney. "I'm glad to see the coffee's put a little fire back in you," he said dryly. "Now why don't you tell me what you saw when you were doing your civic duty and spying though the peephole?"

Wilkins held up his hand. "Um, I'm thinking maybe I should pick back up with this."

Cameron and Jack answered simultaneously. "We're fine."

"I saw a man leave the room, which I'm sure you know," she told Jack.

"Describe him."

"I already described him to Slonsky."

"Do it again."

Jack saw her eyes flash. She didn't like being told what to do. Too bad.

"Five foot eleven, maybe six feet tall," she said. "Medium build. He wore jeans, a black blazer, and a gray hooded T-shirt pulled over his head. He had his back to me the entire time, so I never saw his face."

"Didn't you think the hooded T-shirt was a little odd?" Jack asked.

"I heard butt cheeks being slapped and walls that were banged so hard my teeth nearly rattled. Frankly, I've found this whole evening to be a little odd, Agent Pallas."

Out of the corner of his eye, Jack could see Wilkins glance up at the ceiling while fighting off another smile.

"Are you certain about the man's height?" Jack continued.

Cameron paused, thinking. "Yes."

"How about his weight?"

She sighed. "I'm really bad at guessing that kind of thing."

"Make an effort. Pretend this is something important."

Another glare.

Cameron glanced over at Wilkins. "How much do you weigh?"

"Wait—how come Jack doesn't have to answer that?"

"The man I saw seems closer to your build."

"Oh, so he's a smaller guy, then?" Jack suggested help-fully.

Wilkins turned around. "A smaller guy? I'm an inch above the national average. Besides, I'm spry."

"Let's try to narrow this down," Jack regrouped. "I weigh one-eighty-five, Agent Wilkins is about one-sixty. Given that, where would you say this guy falls?"

She looked between the two men, considering this. "About one-seventy."

Jack and Wilkins exchanged looks.

"What?" Cameron asked. "What does that tell you?"

"So just to make sure we're clear on this, the man you saw leave the room right before security arrived was about five-eleven or six feet tall, and around one hundred and seventy pounds. Is that what you're saying?"

"That's what I'm saying," she agreed. "And I see that you've gotten whatever information it is you wanted out of me. So I would like some information in return." She looked to Wilkins first, who looked to Jack.

After debating a moment, he leaned against the wall. "Okay. Here's what I can tell you."

"AND JUST SO we're clear: everything I'm about to tell you needs to be kept confidential," Jack told her. "In fact, if you weren't with the U.S. attorney's office, I wouldn't be telling you anything."

Cameron got the message: he didn't want to tell her jack-shit, but his boss had ordered him to share informa-tion as a professional courtesy.

"Crystal clear, Agent Pallas," she said.

"You've obviously put a few things together, so I'll speed through the preliminaries," Jack began. "You called hotel security, they found the dead woman next door, so they called the paramedics and the police. CPD arrived at the scene, saw there were signs of a struggle, and began their investigation."

"What signs of a struggle?" Cameron asked.

"To save time, you should assume going forward that anything I don't tell you is a deliberate decision on my part."

Cameron looked up at the ceiling, biting her tongue. Of all the murder and she-had-no-friggin'-clue-what-else-but-something-that-apparently-involved-the-FBI crime scenes in all the hotels in all of Chicago, Jack Pallas had to walk into this one.

"While CPD was conducting their sweep of the room, they stumbled onto something hidden behind the television across from the bed. A video camera."

"Do you have the murder on tape?" Cameron asked. If only all crimes came to prosecutors so neatly wrapped up.

Jack shook his head. "No. What's on the tape is the stuff that took place before the murder."

"Before the murder?" Cameron thought about the raucous sex noises she'd heard through the wall. "That must be quite a tape."

"It is," Jack agreed. "Especially since the man on the tape is a married U.S. senator."

Cameron's eyes widened. She had not expected that. She asked the obvious next question. "Which senator?"

Agent Wilkins pulled a photograph out of the inner pocket of his suit jacket and handed it to Cameron.

She glanced at the photograph, then back at Jack. "This is Senator Hodges."

"So you recognize him?"

"Of course I recognize him," Cameron said. Bill Hodges had represented the state of Illinois in the U.S. Senate for over twenty-five years. And lately she'd seen his face in the news more than usual—he had just been appointed the chairman of the Senate Committee on Banking, Housing, and Urban Affairs.

Cameron thought back to the redheaded woman she had seen on the paramedics' gurney. "That wasn't the senator's wife in room 1308, was it?"

"No, it wasn't," Jack said.

"Who was she?"

"Let's just say that Senator Hodges was paying to have a lot more than his hardwood floors done last night."

Nice. "A prostitute?"

"I think women at her level generally prefer to call themselves 'escorts.'"

"How do you know this already?"

"We have the escort service's records. The senator had been seeing her regularly for almost a year now."

Cameron got up and paced before the bed, working the scenario like a new case she'd been handed. "So what's with the camera? Don't tell me the senator was stupid enough to think he could keep a sex tape secret." She stopped, thinking quickly. "No . . . of course. Blackmail. That's why CPD called you guys."

"Having reviewed the tape, it's obvious that Senator Hodges had no clue he was being filmed," Wilkins said.

"You're the one who got stuck reviewing the tape? Lucky you," Cameron said.

"Not exactly. But Jack was busy playing bad-cop with Senator Hodges."

"And here I thought that was special for me."

Wilkins grinned. "Nah—he likes to break that out with everybody. It usually works, too, with that whole dark and glowering thing he's got going on."

Cameron peeked at Jack, who was back at his post in the corner of the room. "Glowering"—she liked that description. It was certainly more insightful than the generic "asshole" she'd been going with for the past three years.

She wondered if Jack Pallas ever smiled.

Then she remembered that she frankly didn't give a damn whether he did or not.

"Given the content of the tape, Senator Hodges would normally be CPD's primary suspect," Jack said to her. "In fact, the police probably would've arrested him already, if it wasn't for you."

"Is that so?"

Jack pushed away from the wall and stormed over. He yanked the photo out of Cameron's hands and held it in front of her face.

"Let's cut through the crap. The guy you saw leave the room five minutes before hotel security found the girl dead—is there any possibility it's this man?"

Cameron hesitated, momentarily caught off guard by the suddenness with which Jack had gone into attack mode.

He shoved the photo even closer. "Come on, Cameron— is there any possibility it was this man?"

Cameron felt an odd flip in her stomach, hearing Jack say her first name. They'd once, very briefly, been on a first-name basis before. She brushed this off and focused on the photo he held before her. Really, she didn't even need to look. Senator Hodges was not only a shorter man, but if she had to guess—and apparently she did—she'd say he weighed at least two hundred and fifty pounds. She might not have gotten the best look through her peephole, but she knew enough to know one thing.

"It's not him," she said.

"You're sure?" Jack asked.

"I'm sure."

Jack stepped away from her. "Then Senator Hodges owes you one hell of a thank you. Because your word is the only thing keeping him from being arrested for murder."

A silence fell over the room. "Doesn't he have some sort of alibi?" Cameron asked.

Jack remained silent. That clearly fell into the I'm-not-answering-no-stinking-questions category.

"I'll take that as a no," Cameron said. "How about if instead of questions, I just see if I can fill in the blanks? So this escort who's been sleeping with Senator Hodges, the married senior senator from Illinois—"

"Who just happened to be appointed the chairman of the Senate Banking Committee," Wilkins threw in. When he caught the look of death Jack shot him, he shrugged. "What? I don't have your issues with her. Besides, I heard what Davis said—we're supposed to *share*, remember?"

Much glowering ensued.

"So this escort decides to get the senator on tape and use it as blackmail," Cameron continued. "He meets her tonight, they do the deed—many times—I'm still going with the Viagra theory on that, by the way—and the senator leaves. Twenty minutes later, our mystery man shows up. There's a struggle, and he kills the woman. And since there's no sign of forced entry, we can assume the girl knew the murderer and let him into the room. How am I doing so far?"

Wilkins nodded, impressed. "Not bad."

"What I think," Jack told her, "is that you've had a long night, and we don't want to take up any more of your time. The FBI appreciates your cooperation, Ms. Lynde. We'll be in touch if there's anything further we need."

Cameron watched as he turned and headed toward the door, apparently with the mistaken impression that there was nothing left for them to discuss.

"Actually, I do have another question, Agent Pallas," she said.

He looked back at her. "What might that be?"

"Can I *finally* get out of this hotel room?"

Four

WHEN AGENT WILKINS suggested that he and Jack drive her home from the hotel, Cameron reluctantly accepted. As much as she was eager to put some distance between herself and Jack, she didn't want him to think that his attitude was getting to her.

Sitting in the back of Wilkins's car—at least she assumed it was Wilkins's car since he was the one driving and she couldn't picture Jack owning a Lexus—she rested her head against the cool leather seat and looked out the window. She'd been stuck in that hotel room for so long that the brightness of the daylight had been jarring and surreal when she'd first stepped outside. It was nearly noon, which meant she now was going on almost thirty hours without sleep. She doubted even Starbucks had a fix for that.

Fighting the lulling motion of the car, she turned away from the window. With her head against the backseat, she observed the man sitting in front of her through half-lidded eyes.

Jack Pallas.

She might have laughed at the irony of the situation, if she wasn't so damned tired. And also, as a general rule, she found it prudent to refrain from strangely laughing to oneself while sitting in a car with two FBI agents—one of whom already distrusted her with an intensity that was palpable.

Not that Cameron was surprised Jack still felt that way. She recalled all too well the look on his face when she'd told him they weren't going to file charges in the Martino case.

It had been three years ago, late on a Friday afternoon. Earlier in the day, she had been called into a meeting with her boss, Silas Briggs, the U.S. attorney for the Northern District of Illinois. He'd told her that he wanted to talk about the Martino case, and she assumed they were going to discuss the charges she planned to pursue against the various members of Martino's organization. What Silas told her instead came as a shock.

"I've decided against filing charges," he declared. He said it as soon as she sat down, as if wanting to get through the conversation quickly.

"Against Martino's men, or Martino himself?" Cameron asked, assuming at first that Silas meant he'd made an immunity deal with somebody—or several somebodies—in exchange for their testimony.

"Against everybody," Silas said matter-of-factly.

Cameron sat back in her chair, needing a moment to process this. "You don't want to file *any* charges?"

"I realize that you're surprised by this."

That was the understatement of the year. "The FBI has been working on this case for over two years. With all the information Agent Pallas gathered while undercover, we have enough evidence to put Martino away for the rest of his life. Why wouldn't we prosecute?"

"You're young and eager, Cameron, and I like that about you. It's one of the reasons I snatched you away from Hatcher and Thorn," Silas said, referring to the law firm she had worked at prior to coming to the U.S. attorney's office.

Cameron held up her hand. True, she was new to the job, and she definitely was eager, but she'd had four years of trial experience as a civil litigator before becoming a prosecutor. Nevertheless, if Silas didn't think she was ready, she wouldn't let pride get in the way. "Hold on, Silas. If this is because you don't think I have enough experience to try this case, then just give it to somebody else. Sure, I'll be a little testy, I'll probably mope dramatically around the office for a day or two, but I'll get over it. Hell, I'll even help whoever you reassign to the case get up and ru—"

Silas cut her off. "No one in this office is going to file charges. Period. I've been around long enough to know that a trial like this will quickly escalate into two things: a media circus, and a black fucking hole for the United States government. You think you have enough evidence now, but just wait: after we openly declare war on Martino, you'll have witnesses flipping on you—or worse, mysteriously disappearing or dying—and before you know it, you'll be two weeks into trial without a shred of hard evidence to back up all the promises you made to the jury in your opening statement."

Cameron knew that she probably should've just backed off at that point. But she couldn't help herself. "But Agent Pallas's testimony alone will be enough evidence to—"

"Agent Pallas saw a lot of things, but unfortunately his cover was blown too early," Silas interrupted her. "And while I certainly appreciate the two years he spent investigating this case, if we go forward with pressing charges and we don't get a conviction, the fallout will be on us—

not Agent Pallas or anyone else at the FBI. I'm not willing to have my office take that risk."

Now Cameron did fall quiet. Roberto Martino and his minions were responsible for nearly one-third of all drug trafficking in the city of Chicago; they laundered their money through more than twenty sham corporations; and they extorted, bribed, and threatened anyone who got in their way. Not to mention, they killed people.

Going after criminals like Roberto Martino was the reason she had joined the U.S. attorney's office in the first place. In the dark time surrounding her father's murder, that decision had been the one thing—in addition to Collin and Amy's support—that had kept her driven and focused.

Generally, she had liked working at her old firm. With her father having been a police officer, and her mother having worked as a court reporter until she divorced Cameron's father and married a pilot she'd met during a deposition she was transcribing (in *his* divorce case, no less), her family had gotten by reasonably well. But they certainly hadn't been wealthy. Because of that, Cameron had appreciated the independence and security that had come with the $250,000 salary she'd been earning by her fourth year in private practice.

Her father had been proud of her success. As Cameron had learned again and again from the police officers who offered their condolences at her father's wake and funeral, he'd apparently bragged incessantly to his partner and other cop friends about her achievements.

She'd remained close to her father and his side of the family after her parents' divorce—particularly after her mother moved to Florida with her new husband, who retired from the airline shortly after Cameron entered law school.

His death had hit her hard.

One late afternoon during Cameron's fourth year at the

firm, the captain in charge of her father's shift called her
at work with the grave words anyone with a family member in law enforcement dreads hearing: that she needed to
come to the hospital right away. By the time she'd burst
frantically through the doors of the emergency room, it
had been too late. She'd stood numbly in a private room
as the captain told her that her father had been shot to
death by a drug dealer while responding to what they had
believed to be merely a routine domestic disturbance call.

Those first couple of weeks after her father's murder,
she'd felt . . . *gray* was the word she'd used to describe it
when Collin had asked how she was holding up. But then
she'd pulled herself together and went back to the firm. In
many senses, knowing how proud her father had been of
her hard work had made it easier to do that—she knew he
would want her to carry on, to keep going with her career
as far as she could. But something had been missing.

Four weeks after the funeral, she was in court when
she figured out what that something was. She'd been waiting to argue an evidentiary motion that once would've
seemed particularly important, but after her father's death
had felt dismayingly insignificant. Then the court reporter
called the case before hers.

United States versus Markovitz. A simple felon-in-
possession of a firearm case. It had been a straightforward
court appearance, nothing flashy, a motion to suppress
evidence filed by the defendant. Procedurally the motion
was very similar to the one Cameron herself was scheduled to argue that day, so she'd paid attention, wanting to
gauge the judge's mood. After a brief oral argument, the
judge ruled in favor of the government, and Cameron saw
the look of satisfaction in the assistant U.S. attorney's
eyes.

Since her father had been killed, she hadn't once felt
that same kind of satisfaction.

But that morning, as she watched the defendant being escorted out of the courtroom wearing his handcuffs and orange jumpsuit, she felt as though something had been accomplished, no matter how small the degree. Justice had been served. The man who had shot and killed her father had been a felon, too. Maybe if more had been done, maybe if that gun hadn't been on the streets, maybe if *he* hadn't been on the streets . . .

She could do something about that, she'd realized.

That very week, she applied for an assistant U.S. attorney position.

One aspect of being a prosecutor Cameron hadn't anticipated, however, was the politics that often came into play with government jobs. While sitting across from Silas that day, discussing his reasons for pulling out of the Martino case, she realized that the U.S. attorney's office was no exception. She could guess Silas's real problem: simply put, he didn't want to stick his neck out and potentially lose a trial that would be covered by every national newspaper, television, and radio station.

She was surprised by his decision. And frustrated. And disgusted by the thought that someone like Roberto Martino would be allowed to go on, unchecked, with business as usual. But unfortunately, unless she planned to hand over her assistant U.S. attorney badge right then and there, her hands were tied. She'd been with the office for only a year—openly challenging her boss on such an issue would not be the smartest move if she wanted to remain an employed crime-fighter. So she kept her thoughts to herself.

"Okay. No charges." She got a pit in her stomach, saying the words out loud.

"I'm glad you understand," Silas said with a nod of approval. "And there's one last thing: I haven't had the chance to speak to anyone at the Bureau about this. Somebody needs to tell Agent Pallas and the others that we're pulling out of the Martino case. I thought, since you seem to have a good rapport with him, that it should be you."

Now *that* was a conversation Cameron wanted no part of. "I think it might be more appropriate if Agent Pallas heard this directly from you, Silas. Especially given everything he went through in this investigation."

"He was doing his job as an FBI agent. That's how these things turn out sometimes."

Sensing from his tone that the matter was no longer open for discussion, Cameron nodded. She wasn't sure she trusted herself to speak at that moment, anyway.

Silas held her eyes. "And just so we're on the same page, the only thing the FBI needs to know is that there aren't going to be any charges brought against Martino and his men. This office has a strict policy that we do not comment on our internal decision-making process."

When Cameron still said nothing, Silas cocked his head. "I need you to be a team-player on this, Cameron. Is that understood?"

Oh, she understood all right. Silas was selling her out—letting her take the fall for his decision to back off of Martino. But that was how the game was played. He was her boss, not to mention an extremely important and well-connected member of the Chicago legal community. Which meant there was only one thing she could say.

"Consider it done."

JACK WATCHED AS Wilkins checked his rearview mirror. The passenger in the backseat had been silent for a while.

"Is she asleep?" he asked.

Wilkins nodded. "Been a long night."

"True. Let's pick up another round of coffee before

heading back. The stuff they have in the office tastes like shit."

"I meant that it's been a long night for her."

Jack knew exactly what Wilkins had meant. But he was trying to avoid thinking about *her* as much as possible.

"Kind of strange, the two of you meeting again under these circumstances."

Wilkins apparently had not received his let's-just-drop-the-issue memo.

Jack glanced in his mirror to double-check that Cameron was sleeping. "It would've been strange no matter what circumstances we'd met under," he said, keeping his voice low.

Wilkins looked away from the road. "You have any regrets?"

"About what I said?"

"Yeah."

"Only that they had a camera there."

Wilkins shook his head. "Remind me to never get on your bad side."

"Don't ever get on my bad side."

"Thanks."

Jack liked working with Wilkins. He'd hesitated at first when his boss had decided to partner him with a guy who'd just graduated from the Academy. He'd hesitated even more when he'd gotten a look at the expensive suit Wilkins had been wearing the first day they met. But underneath the grins and jokes, Wilkins was a lot savvier than Jack had first given him credit for, and he respected that—even if the two of them couldn't have been more different in their approach to most things. Besides that, Jack welcomed having a partner who actually talked for a change, considering his last partner in Nebraska had spoken an average of about six-point-three words a day and had the personality of a doorknob. Stakeouts with the guy had been a real hoot. Not that stakeouts in Nebraska were all that interesting to start with. He'd been bored out of his mind the last three years—which, of course, had been the whole point of the disciplinary action the Department of Justice had taken against him.

Jack glanced again in his mirror to check out Cameron sleeping in the backseat.

He wasn't being entirely truthful, telling Wilkins that he had no regrets about what had happened three years ago. Of course he did—what he said had been uncalled for. He knew that all of about two seconds after the words had flown out of his mouth.

When he'd found out that he was being transferred back to Chicago, he'd vowed to put everything behind him. Unfortunately, he hadn't counted on running into Cameron Lynde within his first week of being back. Being around her brought back a lot of old memories.

For starters, he still couldn't forget the way she had refused to look at him the day she told him about the Martino case.

Late that Friday afternoon, three years ago, Cameron had called to say she was coming to his office to speak with him and his partner at the time, Joe Dobbs. When he had heard the knock and seen her standing in his doorway, he'd smiled. Jack distinctly remembered that, probably because of how rare it was that he smiled back in those days—there hadn't been a lot to be chipper about during the two years he'd worked for Martino. He was still, to put it bluntly, pretty fucked-up from being undercover for so long and having trouble getting back into the routine of normal life. He also wasn't sleeping at night, and that certainly didn't help matters.

But as much as he had been finding it difficult to transition back to an office job, there was one part of it he didn't mind: working with Cameron Lynde. He'd begun to worry, in fact, that he was starting to not mind it a little too much. They'd only ever talked business—the Martino case—yet the couple of times they'd been alone together, he felt some sort of undercurrent between them. He didn't know how to describe it, except to say that whatever the undercurrent was, it was enough to make him wish he wasn't still so screwed up.

"Come on in," Jack had told her.

When Cameron stepped into his office that Friday afternoon, for once she didn't return his smile.

"Will Agent Dobbs be joining us?" she asked.

"He's on his way. Why don't you have a seat while you wait?" Jack gestured to the chairs in front of his desk.

Cameron shook her head. "I'm fine, thanks."

Over the course of the last month, Jack had gotten to know her well enough to know that she was not fine right then. Something was wrong—she had skipped over the tough-as-nails-but-not-really sarcastic/semi-flirtatious pleasantries he had come to expect and enjoy as part of their usual discourse. Not to mention, she seemed skittish.

He had a bad feeling about this.

"You said you wanted to talk about Martino—is there a problem with the case?" He watched as she hesitated.

Bingo.

Cameron's eyes shifted to the door. "I think we should wait until Agent Dobbs gets here." She bit her bottom lip worriedly, and Jack couldn't decide what was more troubling—her sudden display of vulnerability or the fact that he now couldn't take his eyes off her lips.

He got up from his desk, walked over, and shut his office door. He stood before her. "Something's got you upset."

"Agent Pallas, I think—"

He cut her off. "It's *Jack*, okay? I think it's probably time for us to be on a first-name basis." When her gaze darted again to his office door, he did something that surprised them both—he reached out and touched her chin gently.

He turned her face to his. "Talk to me, Cameron. Tell me what's wrong."

When her incredible aquamarine eyes met his, he felt it—something akin to the jolts of electricity Martino's men had hit him with during his two days of captivity. Only infinitely more enjoyable.

"Jack," she whispered. "I'm so sor—"

A knock at the door interrupted them.

Jack and Cameron sprang away from each other as the door to his office opened. Joe walked in, surprised to find them both standing there.

"Oh, hey—sorry I'm late." He took a seat in one of the chairs in front of Jack's desk—they had been partners for four years and were comfortable in each other's offices. He crossed his leg and looked up at Cameron. "Jack said you wanted to talk to us about Martino?"

"I do," Cameron said. She sounded stiff and nervous again, and oddly focused her attention on Joe. "I wanted to let you know that we've made a decision. We won't be filing charges against Roberto Martino. Or anyone else in his organization, for that matter."

There was a silence in the room.

Jack broke it. "You can't be serious."

Cameron still didn't look at him. "I realize this isn't the result either of you expected."

"What do you mean, you're not going to file any charges?" Joe asked. He had been the liaison between Jack and the Bureau during the two years Jack had been undercover and knew all the dirt they'd dug up on Martino.

"Our office has decided there isn't enough evidence to take the case to trial," Cameron said.

Jack was struggling—hard—to keep his anger in check. "Bullshit. Who made this decision? Was it Briggs?"

Joe stood up from his chair and paced. "That fucking guy. All he cares about is his own reputation," he said disgustedly.

"I want to talk to him," Jack demanded.

Cameron finally turned to face him. "There's no need for that. This . . . is my case. It was my call."

"Screw that—I don't believe you."

Joe glanced over, a cautionary note in his voice. "Jack."

Cameron remained cool. "I realize how frustrating this—"

Jack took a step toward her. "Frustrating? Frustration doesn't begin to cover what I'm feeling right now. You've read the files—at least I assumed you had until about a minute ago—now I'm not so sure what you or anyone else in the U.S. attorney's office has been doing. You know who Martino is and the things he's done. What the hell are you guys thinking?"

"I'm sorry," she said woodenly. "I know how much you put into this investigation. Unfortunately, there's nothing more I can tell you."

"Sure there is. You can tell me who the hell Martino paid off in the U.S. attorney's office to make this miracle happen. If Briggs didn't make this decision, then . . ." Jack paused to give Cameron a scrutinizing once-over. "What do you think, Joe, should we do a little digging into Ms. Lynde's accounts? See if she's had any unusually large deposits lately?"

Cameron walked over and stared him dead in the eyes. "You are way out of line with that, Agent Pallas."

Joe moved between them. "Okay, I think we all need to take a step back for a moment and cool down."

Jack ignored him. "I want an explanation," he said again to Cameron.

She stood her ground, holding his gaze angrily. "Fine. You blew your cover too early. I hope that explanation satisfies you, because it's the only one I can give you."

A wave of fury washed over him. And guilt. Her words struck a nerve—although he'd had no choice, he still blamed himself every day for the fact that his cover had been blown.

Jack's voice was ice-cold. "Get out of my office."

"I was just leaving," Cameron said. "But one last thing— if you ever have any concerns about where my loyalties lie, or regarding my dedication to my job, you can just ask me yourself, Agent Pallas. But if you poke around in my bank accounts, you better have either a court order or one hell of a defense attorney." She nodded at Joe in good-bye. "Agent Dobbs." Then she turned and left without further word.

Joe watched her go. "I know you're angry, Jack, and I'm mad as hell, too, but be careful. Cameron Lynde might be new to the office, but she's still an assistant U.S. attorney. Probably not such a good idea to accuse her of corruption."

Barely listening, Jack said nothing. All he could think about was one thing.

Two years of his life down the fucking drain.

Joe sprang into action. "All right—I'm going to talk to Davis," he said, referring to their boss, the special agent in charge. "I'll see if I can find out what's really going on." He walked over and put his hand on Jack's shoulder. "In the meantime, you need to calm the hell down. Go home, go get drunk, whatever—just get out of this office before you say anything else you'll regret."

Jack nodded.

Two years.

In the elevator on his way out, he stared numbly at the

doors, wondering if Cameron Lynde had any clue what he'd gone through to get all that evidence that she had just rendered meaningless. Yes, his cover had been blown, but only because—in a move that was two parts plain stupid and one part a piss-fight over jurisdiction—the DEA had sent in their own undercover agent to make contact with Martino. Jack had figured out who the guy was in all of about five seconds. It took Martino ten.

He'd ordered Jack to kill him.

Now Jack had done a lot of not-so-nice things in order to maintain his cover while working for Martino, but up to that point he'd always managed to avoid actually *killing* anyone. But this time Martino wanted the agent's body brought back to him—he planned to send a message to the DEA—and no amount of craftiness could get Jack out of having to produce an actual corpse. So he stalled. He was on his way to meet the DEA agent, warn him, and get them both the hell out of Dodge, when Martino's men grabbed them.

They killed the DEA agent immediately. Martino stuck to his plan and had his men dump the body on the Chicago DEA office's doorstep that night.

With Jack, he was less forgiving.

Enough said.

On the second day of Jack's captivity, however, Martino's men made a fatal mistake.

Actually, it was one man in particular who made the mistake: Vincent, one of Martino's interrogators, wanted to take his questioning up a notch and decided to untie Jack's hands. Sure, he immediately re-disabled one of those hands by ramming a nine-inch carving knife all the way through Jack's forearm, pinning it to the chair. But he momentarily left his other hand free.

For such stupidity, Martino surely would've killed Vincent himself. That is, if Jack hadn't choked the guy with his free hand, slid the knife back out of his forearm, and beaten him to it.

Luckily for Jack, Vincent had been carrying a gun along with his knife. Also lucky for Jack was the fact that he had been trained in Special Forces to skillfully handle a gun with either hand.

These things, however, were not as fortuitous for Martino's men. True, one of them was lucky enough to shoot Jack in the middle of the gunfight that ensued, but he certainly didn't live long enough to brag about it.

But unlike his men, Martino himself seemed to have all the luck in the world. Not only was he not among the eight dead bodies FBI backup collected when they finally showed up at the warehouse, but apparently, Lady Luck was smiling down on him a second time when she steered his case into the inexperienced hands of Assistant U.S. Attorney Cameron Lynde.

Two years of his life down the drain.

Jack didn't want to believe it. But she said that the decision not to prosecute was hers. And if that was true, then . . . the hell with her.

The elevator hit the ground floor and the doors sprang open. Jack stepped out and was immediately accosted by a throng of reporters. Unfortunately, this was not an unusual occurrence; he unwittingly had become the focus of media attention after the shoot-out at the warehouse—eight dead gangsters tended to pique people's interests—and ever since, reporters had come calling whenever Martino's name popped up in the news.

"Agent Pallas! Agent Pallas!" The reporters shouted over each other, trying to get to him.

Jack ignored them and headed toward the front door. The female reporter from the local NBC affiliate, whose interest in him lately seemed to go beyond a mere profes-

sional level, fell into stride alongside him with her cam-
eraman in tow.

"Agent Pallas—we just got word about the Martino
case. As the FBI agent in charge of the investigation, what
do you think about the fact that Roberto Martino will continue to walk the streets of Chicago as a free man?" She
shoved her microphone in Jack's face.

Maybe it was due to extreme sleep-deprivation. Or
maybe it was because of the fact that (according to the
psychologist he had been ordered to see every week) he
had some lingering "rage" issues related to his undercover
work and capture. Or maybe, possibly, it had something to
do with the fact that he'd been *tortured for two days* by
the guy. But before he realized what he was doing, Jack
fired back a reply to the reporter's question.

"I think the assistant U.S. attorney has her head up her
ass, that's what I think. They should've assigned the case
to somebody with some fucking balls."

Every television station in Chicago led off their six
o'clock evening news with his tirade.

And then they re-aired it again, on the ten o'clock news.

Of course by that point, word had spread to the national
correspondents that a Chicago FBI special agent had ver-
bally bitch-slapped an assistant U.S. attorney on live camera, and then his comments were everywhere: CNN,
MSNBC, the *Today* show, *Nightline*, *Larry King Live*, and
everything in between. Not to mention that the footage
earned the dubious distinction of being the most down-
loaded video on YouTube for the entire week.

Needless to say, Jack's boss was not pleased.

"Are you out of your fucking mind?" Davis demanded
to know when he hauled Jack into his office the following
morning. "You're the one with your head up your goddamn ass, Pallas, making a comment like that on national
television!"

Things pretty much went downhill from there. Some feminist group began making noise in the media, claiming that Jack's comment about assigning the case to somebody with "balls" was—taken literally—a sexist statement that only a male prosecutor could've handled such a tough case.

Which is when the Department of Justice stepped in.

Despite his initial outburst over the situation, Davis worked for two days to appease the DOJ. He emphasized that Jack was Chicago's most talented and dedicated agent and suggested, in terms of a disciplinary action, that Jack issue a formal apology to Ms. Lynde and the U.S. attorney's office and be put on six months' probation. The lawyers at the DOJ said they would take Davis's recommendation under advisement.

That Monday morning, Jack got into the office early to start working on his apology. He knew he'd been out of line, both with the comments he'd made to the reporter and the things he'd said to Cameron before that. Admittedly, he'd handled the situation poorly. Very poorly. On top of the shock and frustration he'd felt when hearing her news, the fact that he'd come to trust her had only increased his anger. But at this point, he hoped that they could somehow figure out a way to get past the situation and move on.

He had left the door to his office open while he worked, and after a few minutes of staring at a blank computer screen—apologies didn't exactly come easy to him—he was surprised to hear voices coming from Davis's office. He'd thought he was the only person in that early.

Davis sounded angry. From across the hall, Jack couldn't pick up much of the conversation, other than to hear his boss say the words "bullshit" and "overreacting." Since Jack didn't hear anyone else speak, he wondered if Davis was on the phone. But regardless of whomever Davis was talking to, Jack had a pretty good idea who he was talking about. He got up from his desk and headed to his door when—

Davis's office door flew open and Cameron Lynde stepped out.

Catching sight of Jack, she stopped in her tracks. A look crossed her face, one that Jack knew well. Over the years, he'd seen that expression many times when someone saw him approaching.

Caught.

Cameron covered the look quickly, and coolly met his gaze across the hallway. She turned and left, saying nothing.

When Davis stepped out of his office next, he also saw Jack. He shook his head somberly.

That afternoon, the Department of Justice issued an order that Special Agent Jack Pallas be transferred out of Chicago immediately.

Jack had a feeling he knew just who he could thank for that.

"WHATEVER YOU'RE THINKING about, you'd probably be better off leaving it in the past."

Jack glanced over and saw Wilkins staring at him. "I wasn't thinking about anything."

"Really? 'Cause the car stopped three minutes ago and we've just been sitting here in front of this house."

Jack looked around to get his bearings—shit, they were just sitting there. Nice to see his exceptionally fine-tuned special agent powers of observation were intact. He blamed their witness in the backseat for this. She distracted him. It was time to put an end to that.

He called over his shoulder. "You're free to go, Ms. Lynde."

No response.

He turned around.

"She's out like a light," Wilkins told him.

"So do something about it."

Wilkins peered into the rearview mirror. "Yoo-hoo, Cameron—"

"Yoo-hoo? That's really FBI-ish."

"Hey, I'm the good cop. I make it work." Wilkins turned back to the task at hand. "Cameron—we're here." He glanced over at Jack, whispering. "Do you think she'd mind if I call her Cameron?"

"Right now I think you could call her anything and get away with it." He even had a few suggestions on that front.

"Okay, time for plan B," Wilkins decided. "Someone needs to go back there and wake her up."

"Sounds good. Hope that works out for you."

"I meant you." When Wilkins saw Jack's expression, he gestured innocently. "Sorry. I have to stay here and man the wheel."

Grumbling under his breath, Jack opened the car door and stepped out, catching his first good glimpse at Cameron Lynde's home. Or at least, the place that was supposedly her home.

He stuck his head back into the car. "Are you sure this is the right place?"

"She said 3309 North Henderson. This is 3309 North Henderson," Wilkins said.

"Yeah, but this is . . ." Jack turned around and tried to decide how best to describe the sight before him.

"One hell of a nice house," Wilkins said approvingly.

That pretty much covered it. As Jack stood there on the street, the elegant house rose grandly before him, three stories above the ground. There was an arched portico framed by columns that flanked the entranceway. Sprawling ivy adorned much of the house, and a garden wrapped around the right side and stretched all the way back to the garage. He guessed the place had to be sitting on at least a city lot and a half.

The first question that popped into his head was how a government-salaried prosecutor could ever afford a house like that.

Wilkins appeared to be of a similar mindset. He leaned over the seat and peered through the passenger-side window. "What do you think? Rich husband?"

Jack considered this. There was a rich somebody, because she certainly couldn't afford that kind of house on her own. Either that, or he hadn't been that far out of line when he'd made the crack three years ago about her being on Martino's payroll.

Wilkins read his mind. "Don't even go there. That's exactly the kind of crap that got you in trouble last time."

Jack pointed to Cameron, still conked out in the backseat. "The only place I'm 'going' is back to the office, as soon as we fix this situation here." He grabbed the handle and opened her door. "Let's go, Ms. Lynde," he said in a commanding tone.

No response.

"She's still alive, right?" Wilkins asked, turning around to look.

Jack leaned into the backseat. He lowered his face toward Cameron's and listened for sounds of breathing. "She's alive." He nudged her shoulder. "Come on. Wake up."

Still no response.

"Maybe you should kiss her." Seeing Jack's glare, Wilkins grinned slyly. "Hey—it worked for that one dude."

Jack turned back to Cameron and considered his options. He could poke her a few times. Tempting. Douse her with ice-cold water. Extremely tempting. But then knowing her, she'd slap him with a battery charge and he'd be back in Nebraska by sundown. Which left him with only one option.

He reached past Cameron and tossed her purse over the seat. "See if you can find her keys," he told Wilkins.

"Are you kidding? What if she wakes up and sees me rummaging around in there? You don't touch the purse. The purse is sacrosanct."

"Either find the keys or get back here and carry her yourself."

Wilkins eyed the purse for a moment, then reached in. "It's worth it. I gotta see you try this. Ten bucks says she wakes up and clocks you before you hit the front steps."

Jack gave that about seventy/thirty odds as well. He told Wilkins to pop the trunk, then grabbed her suitcase and ran it up to the front door. When he got back to the car, he took the purse and set it on Cameron's lap. He got the keys from Wilkins and put them in his own pocket. Without further ado, he scooped her up into his arms and eased her out of the car.

She settled against him, still sleeping, and her head fell against his shoulder. He carried her to the house, thinking that out of all the possible scenarios he had envisioned if he ever again ran into Cameron Lynde, this definitely had not been among them. He wondered what her neighbors must be thinking at the sight of him carrying her up the front steps in broad daylight—if any of them had the friggin' telescope they'd need to see across her little urban estate, that is.

Jack glanced down. She looked so peaceful right then, and for a split second, he found himself sympathizing over the long night she must have had. She'd held up amazingly well, all things considered.

With one hand, he opened the wrought iron gate and carried her up the stairs to the front door. Because of the size of the house, he thought it was a pretty safe bet that she lived with someone, and he wondered if that someone was about to come rushing out, all concerned, and scoop her away from him.

It didn't happen.

Jack reached into his pocket, pulled out her keys and opened the front door. Still no half-crazed-with-worry boyfriend/husband/lover. He looked down at Cameron, snuggled up against his chest. Not that he cared, but whoever the guy was, he was kind of an asshole for not noticing that she'd been out of contact for the last ten hours.

"Cameron, wake up." His voice sounded oddly soft. He cleared his throat. "You're home."

She stirred this time, and Jack set her down on the stoop, quick to put space between them. She stood there for a moment, groggy and uncertain, and peered up as if seeing him for the first time.

"You."

"Me."

She blinked, then threw an arm into the air, slurring her words tiredly. "Go. Pish off."

Now Jack was more than happy to pish off, but first he needed to make sure she was safe. She was his key witness, after all. He tossed her the purse, which she barely caught, and set her suitcase inside the front door.

"Your keys are in the lock—don't forget them. Are you alone here?" He asked this last question solely out of professional responsibility. "You've had a strange night—you might not want to be by yourself."

He watched as she pulled her keys out of the lock and put them back in, then pushed on the door and stared in confusion when she found it already open.

"Yeah . . . now I'm thinking you really shouldn't be here by yourself," Jack said.

Despite being out of it, she had no problem managing to throw a dirty look his way. "I'll call Collin," she mumbled. Then she stepped inside her house and slammed the door in his face.

So.

There was a Collin.

Jack did a quick check to make sure the house looked secure. Then he headed back to the car and climbed in.

Wilkins held out his hands. "Well?"

"We're good to go," Jack said.

"You sure we should just leave her here alone?"

"She's going to call Collin."

"Oh, that's a relief. Who's Collin?"

Jack shrugged. "No clue. All I know is that she's his problem now, not mine."

"Ouch. That's a little harsh."

"Actually, I was going for a lot harsh, but I might be off my game," Jack said. "Been a long night. Don't forget the coffee on the way back into the office."

Wilkins grinned as he threw the car into drive. "You know, I think I'm gonna learn a lot from you, Jack."

Jack wasn't exactly sure where that was coming from. But of course it was very true. "Thank you."

"You're a man who speaks his mind—I respect that. And I bet you respect that in others, too."

Ah. . . . now he saw where this was going. "Just spit it out if there's something you want to say, Wilkins."

Wilkins stopped the car at a four-way intersection. "Your problems with her are your business. I just need to hear you say that those problems aren't going to affect the way we handle this case."

"They won't."

"Good. And for my own personal edification—do you plan to be grumpy and taciturn every time her name comes up?"

Jack studied his partner silently.

Wilkins smiled. "I pushed it with that one, didn't I?"

"Common rookie mistake. The one question too many."

"I'll work on that."

"See that you do." Jack turned back and looked out the window, enjoying the familiar view of all the sights he hadn't seen since leaving Chicago three years ago. After a few moments, he broke the silence. "And another thing: you're not supposed to actually tell witnesses about the glowering thing. It ruins the effect."

"So you do that intentionally?"

"Oh, I've been working on my glowering skills for years."

Wilkins looked away from the road in surprise. "Was that actually a joke there?"

"No. And keep your eyes on the road, rookie. Because I'll be really pissed if you crash this car before I get my coffee."

Five

"I STILL CAN'T believe you didn't call either of us from the hotel."

Cameron could tell from the tone in Collin's voice that he was vacillating between being concerned about her in light of the events of the night before, and pissed that this was the first he'd heard about them.

In her defense, after Jack and Wilkins had dropped her off at home, her first plan had been to call both Collin and Amy. The three of them had been friends since college, and normally she told them everything. But then she'd remembered that it was Saturday, which meant that Collin would be working and Amy would be knee-deep in wedding-related tasks, especially since her big day was only two weeks away. So instead, Cameron had shot each of them a text message asking if they wanted to meet for dinner at Frasca that night. Then she'd crawled into bed and passed out for the next six hours.

At the restaurant, as soon as the hostess had seated

them, Cameron began to tell Collin and Amy about the
occurrences of the night before—omitting any mention of
Senator Hodges's involvement, since the FBI was keeping
that under wraps. From across the table, she'd watched as
Collin grew more and more agitated as her story pro-
gressed. And a few minutes ago, he'd run his hand through
his sandy brown hair and folded his arms across his chest—
his usual gesture when working through something that
bothered him.

To Cameron's left was Amy, who looked as sophisticated
as always in her tailored brown shirt-dress and shoulder-
length blonde hair cut in an angled bob. She was more
diplomatic in her response than Collin. "It sounds like you
had a pretty intense night, Cameron. You shouldn't have
had to go through all that alone."

"I *would* have called"—Cameron said pointedly to
Collin—"if the FBI hadn't restricted my calls." She turned
to her left. "And yes, it was an extremely intense night.
Thank you for your concern, Amy." She started to go for
her wineglass, but Collin reached across the table and
grabbed her hand.

"Stop—you know I'm concerned, too."

Cameron glared at him but didn't pull her hand away.
"Then stop complaining about the fact that I didn't call
you."

He gave her one of his trademark but-I'm-so-innocent
smiles. She'd seen that smile many times over the last
twelve years, and yet it still worked on her. Usually.

"I apologize," Collin said. "I freaked out hearing your
story and inappropriately expressed my emotions through
anger. It's a guy thing." He squeezed her hand. "I don't
like that you were one room away from a murder, Cam.
Strange noises, watching a mysterious, hooded man through
a peephole—this whole thing is far too Hitchcockian for
me."

"And I haven't even told you the twist," Cameron said. "Jack Pallas is one of the agents handling the case for the FBI."

It took Amy a moment to place the name. "Wait—Agent Hottie?"

"Agent *Asshole*," Cameron corrected her. "Agent Hottie" had been her former nickname for Jack, one long since dropped. Ever since he accused her of taking bribes from Roberto Martino.

"That is a twist. How is Agent Asshole these days?" Collin asked dryly. As Cameron's best friend, he was de facto required to exhibit animosity toward Jack Pallas as well.

"More important, how was it seeing him after all this time?" Amy asked.

"We traded sarcastic barbs and insults the whole time. It was nice, catching up like that."

"But is he still just as hot?" Amy exchanged a look with Collin. "Well, one of us had to ask."

"That's kind of irrelevant, don't you think?" Cameron managed a coolly disdainful look as she took a sip of her wine. Then she swallowed too fast, nearly choked, and coughed while gasping for air.

Amy smiled. "I'll take that as a yes."

Cameron dabbed her watering eyes with a napkin and turned to Collin for help.

"Don't look at me—I'm staying out of this one," he said.

"I would like to remind both of you that the jerk embarrassed me on national television."

"No, the jerk embarrassed himself on national television," Amy said.

Cameron sniffed, partially mollified by this. "And I'd also like to point out that because of him, virtually every FBI agent in the Chicago area has carried a grudge against me for the past three years. Which has made things tons of fun, considering I work with the FBI on a near-daily basis."

"You don't have to see him again, do you?" Collin asked.

"If there is a god, no." Cameron thought about this more seriously. "I don't know, maybe if there are some follow-up questions they need to ask. But I'll tell you this: if I do see Jack Pallas again, it will be on *my* terms. He may have caught me off guard last night, but next time I'll be prepared. And at least I'll be dressed appropriately for the occasion."

"What was wrong with the way you were dressed?" Amy asked.

"I was wearing yoga pants and *gym shoes*." Cameron scoffed. "I might as well have been naked."

"Certainly would've made for a more interesting interrogation."

Collin sat back in his chair, all haughty manlike. "You and your high heels. You're lucky you weren't still in your underwear. Between that and being interrogated in your gym shoes, which would you prefer?"

Cameron thought about this. "Do I still get to wear high heels in the underwear scenario?"

"That was supposed to be a rhetorical question. You have a problem," Collin said.

Cameron smiled. "So I like to vertically enhance . . . I'm a five-foot-three-inch trial lawyer. Cut me some slack."

AMY LEFT APOLOGETICALLY as soon as dinner was over, saying that she needed to get up early the following morning to meet with her florist. Cameron and Collin stayed at the restaurant for another round of drinks, then walked the five blocks to her house.

It was a crisp October evening. Cameron pulled her jacket closed, belting it at her waist. "I'm not sure Amy's going to make it to the wedding without having a nervous breakdown. I keep telling her to let me help out more."

"You know how she is—she's been planning this since she was five," Collin said. "Speaking of planning, how's the bachelorette party coming along?"

"Her cousins think we need a stripper," Cameron said, referring to the other two bridesmaids. "But Amy practically made me swear an oath in blood: no strippers, no tacky wedding veil, and absolutely no penis paraphernalia. So I'm doing a wine tasting and desserts at my house, and then we'll go to a bar afterward. I hope she likes it. If she fires me as maid of honor, you have to take on the job, you know."

Collin threw his arm around her shoulders. "Not in a million years, babe."

Cameron smiled and leaned against him, taking comfort in the firm solidness of his chest. In turn, Collin pulled her tighter, turning serious. "You know we were just kidding around at the restaurant, don't you?"

"I know."

"Because we're very both worried about you."

"I know that, too."

They came to a stop in front of her house. Collin faced her, and she could see the worry in his hazel eyes. "Seriously, Cam—you were an eyewitness, earwitness, whatever you want to call it, to a *murder*. And you saw the killer leave. I hate to go down this road but . . . is there any chance he knew you were watching?"

Cameron had asked herself this very question several times over the course of the last twelve hours. "I was behind the door the whole time. And even if he heard me or somehow otherwise suspected I was watching, there's no way he'd know my identity. The FBI and CPD have kept my name confidential."

"Not exactly a good night for you, was it?"

"That's putting it mildly."

Collin cocked his head in the direction of her house. "So, then . . . would you like some company tonight?"

Cameron thought about it. After the bizarre occurrences of the night before, the idea of spending the night alone in that big house was not particularly appealing. But she knew that if Collin stayed, there would be problems. "Thanks for offering. But Richard already thinks you spend too much time with me. I'll be okay by myself."

There was a flicker of emotion in Collin's eyes. "Actually, Richard and I decided to take a break."

Cameron was shocked. She knew they'd been having problems—personally she blamed Richard; he'd always been a little arrogant and strangely unappreciative of Collin, whom half the male population in Chicago practically worshipped—but the two of them had been together for three years and she just assumed they'd work things out.

"When did this happen?" she asked.

"Last night. He said he changed his mind about going to Amy's wedding. He used the old 'But-I'll-be-uncomfortable' excuse, but really he just didn't want to sacrifice a whole weekend in *Michigan*." Collin emphasized this last part in mock horror. "I told him that the wedding is at a nice hotel, but you know him—if it's not a Four Seasons, he thinks he's roughing it. Anyway, we argued about that, and then we argued about a lot of things, and now . . . well, here we are."

"Do you think there's any chance it'll all blow over in a few days?" Cameron asked gently.

Collin shook his head. "If he can't do this for me, then no. He knows what this wedding means to me, and I think that's the problem. It's all part of his stupid competition with you and Amy. So he's moving his stuff out of the condo tonight. Probably right at this very moment."

"I'm sorry, sweetie." Cameron hugged him. "So I guess the real question is: do you want some company tonight?"

"Yes." Collin held open the gate for her. "But you have to promise to get me very drunk."

Cameron walked up the steps. "As long as you promise to still make breakfast in the morning."

"Babe, I always make breakfast. You can't even warm an Eggo."

"That was *one* time." Their senior year, and Collin had never let her live it down. "The stupid box said one to two cycles—I did two cycles. How the toaster caught on fire is just as big a mystery to me."

SITTING IN THEIR unmarked car across the street, Officers Phelps and Kamin watched as the couple headed up the front steps of the house.

"And that will be the last anybody sees of them tonight," Officer Kamin said, satisfied. He folded up his *Sun-Times* as Phelps started the car. "For a minute there, I wasn't sure our boy was gonna get the go-ahead signal. Looks like he's home free now."

Phelps squinted, trying to get a better look at the pair as they stepped inside the house. "Are you sure Slonsky said to check out the girl?"

"Yep."

"'Cuz the guy looks really familiar to me. Can't place him, though."

Kamin shrugged. "Can't help you there. Slonsky said to drive by the girl's house, make sure everything looks secure. That's all I know."

"Maybe we should sit here for a moment, just to be certain we're all clear."

Not exactly in a hurry to seek out more dangerous assignments, Kamin liked the reasoning behind that. "Works for me."

They passed the next twenty minutes in silence, the only noise being the occasional crinkling of newspaper from Kamin. He was reading the sports section when he stopped.

"Well, look at that." He held the paper out so Phelps could see. "That's the guy we just saw, isn't it?"

Phelps leaned over, then sat back in the driver's seat, satisfied.

"I told you he looked familiar."

ACROSS TOWN, JACK was in his office, once again listening to the muffled sounds of Davis's yelling. At least this time, he was pretty sure the ruckus had nothing to do with him. Not directly, anyway.

He and Wilkins were the only other two agents in the office, given that it was nearly eleven o'clock on a Saturday night. Sitting in one of the chairs in front of his desk, Wilkins gestured in the direction of their boss's office. "Is he always like this?"

"You get used to it," Jack said. Actually, he didn't mind Davis's occasional flare-ups; back in the army he'd served under several commanders who'd had their fair share of those. Like his former commanders, Davis was pretty much a straight shooter—and loyal as hell to the agents in his office. He'd fought hard to get Jack transferred back to the Chicago office as soon as the position opened up.

A few minutes later the commotion died down and Davis's door flew open. He stuck his head out and looked over. "Pallas, Wilkins—you're up."

They took their seats in Davis's office, which Jack had always found odd in not being much bigger than those the rest of the Chicago agents had been assigned. He figured the Bureau could at least get the guy a view of something more interesting than the building's parking lot for all the crap he had to deal with as special agent in charge. Then again, knowing Davis, he'd probably specifically requested that office in order to keep track of everyone else's comings and goings. There certainly wasn't much that slipped past him.

"I just got off the phone with one of Senator Hodges's attorneys," Davis began. "He 'requested' that they be kept apprised of any and all updates related to our investigation."

"What you'd tell him?" Wilkins asked.

"That I'm an old man. I tend to forget things. And that if anyone from Senator Hodges's camp called me again tonight, I might just so happen to forget the promise I'd made to keep this investigation confidential. There was a good deal of swearing after that, but so far . . ." Davis gestured to the silent phone on his desk. "Now—let's figure out how we're gonna handle this mess." He looked to Jack. "What's happening with CPD's investigation?"

"Our contact is Detective Ted Slonsky, twenty years on the job, the last ten in homicide. According to him, the only prints they found in the hotel room belong to the victim and Senator Hodges. They found traces of semen in the bed and on top of the desk and bathroom vanity, and there were several used condoms in the bathroom garbage. All of it from the same man."

"At least we know Senator Hodges practices safe sex when cheating on his wife," Davis said. "Anything else?"

"There were bruises on both of the victim's wrists, presumably inflicted by the killer as he pinned her hands down while suffocating her."

"Any blood at the scene? Hair? Clothing fibers?"

"No traces of blood. We're waiting to hear back from the lab on everything else," Jack told him. "And we didn't get much luckier with hotel security. They don't have cameras in the floor hallways or the stairwells—and although they do have them in the lobby, the garage, and other public areas of the hotel, there's no sign of our guy in any of the footage. Which means that so far, Ms. Lynde's statement is our only evidence that this mysterious second man exists."

Jack saw Davis raise an eyebrow at the mention of Cameron's name, but his boss refrained from commenting. At least for the time being.

"All right, here's where we stand," Davis said. "Officially, the Bureau only has jurisdiction over the suspected blackmail aspects of this investigation. Unofficially, however, we've got a U.S. senator having sex on tape with a call girl who, just moments later, gets smothered to death in that very hotel room—there's no way we're sitting on the sidelines. Do you think this Detective Slonsky is going to be a problem?"

"Not likely. He seemed relieved to have our assistance in light of the senator's involvement," Jack said.

Davis nodded. "Good. Theories?"

Jack paused, letting Wilkins take the lead.

Wilkins sat up in his chair. "We're currently working on two theories, both based on the assumption that the victim, Mandy Robards, was involved in a plan to blackmail the senator."

"Do we have a basis for that assumption?" Davis asked.

"The videotape was found in her purse. On the tape, she's the one who shut off the camera after the senator left. So unless she was making the tape for him as an early Christmas present, I think it's safe to say she had nefarious motives."

Davis looked over at Jack with a bemused grin. "Nefarious. This is what we get when we hire a Yale boy."

"You missed sacrosanct earlier. And taciturn and glowering," Jack said.

"What's glowering?"

"Me, apparently."

Wilkins pointed. "Now *that* has to be a joke." He turned to Davis. "You heard that, right?"

Davis didn't answer him, having spun his chair around to type something at his computer. "Let's see what Google says . . . Ah—here it is. 'Glowering: dark; showing a brooding ill humor.'"

Davis spun back around, with a nod at Wilkins. "You know, I think Merriam-Webster here is right, Jack—you do have a glowering way about you." Then he turned to Wilkins. "And yes, that was a joke. It normally takes about a year to accurately detect Agent Pallas's small forays into humor, but you'll get there."

About this time, Jack was trying to remember why the hell he'd been so eager to get back to Chicago. At least in Nebraska a man could brood in peace. "Perhaps we should get back to our theories," he grumbled.

"Right. So our first theory is that the girl set up the blackmail scheme—maybe working with someone else, maybe not—and someone connected to the senator found out and killed her to keep the affair from becoming public," Wilkins said.

"But they left the videotape behind," Davis noted.

"Maybe they didn't know the tape was actually in the room. Or maybe they panicked after killing the girl, or maybe something scared them off, like hearing Ms. Lynde calling security in the next room."

David toyed with his pen, considering this. "And the second theory?"

"Our second theory is that the whole thing was a set up

and someone killed the girl to frame the senator for murder. What they didn't count on was Ms. Lynde seeing the real killer leaving the hotel room."

"Going with those two theories for the moment, who does that put on our list of suspects?" Davis asked.

"Pretty much anyone who either likes or hates Senator Hodges," Wilkins said.

"Glad to hear we're narrowing it down." Davis leaned back in his chair, musing aloud. "What do we make of the fact that Hodges was recently named chairman of the Banking Committee?"

"It's an angle we're looking into," Jack said. "What bothers me are the contradictions: the crime scene is clean—no physical evidence was left behind. That would suggest a professional, somebody who knew what they were doing or at least thought about it in advance. But the murder itself feels amateurish. Angry. Suffocation is a lot more personal than a bullet to the head. Something doesn't add up. I think our first step is to talk to Hodges's people and find out who knew he was having an affair."

"I'm not sure Senator Hodges is going to like that idea. Or his attorneys," Davis said.

"Perhaps when we make it clear that the senator's continued cooperation is the only thing keeping him from being arrested for murdering a call girl, he'll warm up to it," Jack said.

"All right—let me know if you need me to run interference with Hodges's lawyers. Last thing—what's happening with our witness? Sounds like the senator caught a break having Ms. Lynde in the room next to him."

"For starters, very few people outside this room know there is a witness," Wilkins said. "We're keeping that quiet for now. As a courtesy, Detective Slonsky sent a squad to drive by her house tonight, although the officers haven't been given any specifics about the case. They called in just a few minutes ago and reported that Ms. Lynde returned to the house with a male companion and that everything looked secure."

"Do we have a reason to believe Ms. Lynde is in danger?" Davis asked.

"Not as long as her identity is kept confidential," Wilkins said.

Davis saw Jack hesitate. "You have a different opinion, Jack?"

"I don't like the idea of our key witness's security being dependent on our belief that everyone will keep her identity confidential. Seems like an unnecessary risk."

Davis nodded. "I agree. And given Ms. Lynde's position, I'd like to err on the side of caution here. Politically, it would be a nightmare if something happened to an assistant U.S. attorney as part of an FBI investigation."

"We'll set up a protective surveillance," Jack said. "We can coordinate with CPD on that."

"Good." Davis pointed. "I also want twice-daily reports from you two. And I have a call scheduled for Monday morning to update the director on the investigation—I expect you both to be present for that. Now, Wilkins, if you don't mind, I'd like to speak to Agent Pallas alone."

Jack was not surprised by this. He'd had a funny feeling there was a lecture looming on the horizon ever since Cameron's name had come up.

Davis waited until Wilkins shut the door behind him. "Should I be worried, Jack?"

"No."

Davis watched Jack with sharp gray eyes. "My understanding is that Ms. Lynde has been very cooperative in this investigation."

"She has."

"I expect us to reciprocate."

"Of course."

There was a moment of silence, and Jack knew Davis was taking in the taut set of his jaw and the tension that rolled off his body in waves.

"I'm not trying to be a hard-ass here," Davis said, not unkindly. "If it's going to be a problem for you to work with her—"

"There won't be any problem." Jack stared his boss straight in the eyes. Cameron Lynde may have been a problem for him once, but that was not a mistake he'd repeat. "This is just another case, and I'll handle it like any other."

"Ms. Lynde should be made aware of the protective surveillance. I'd like her to feel comfortable with this. It's going to be somewhat of an intrusion."

"Not a problem. I'll talk to her about it first thing tomorrow."

After studying Jack for a moment, Davis appeared satisfied. "Good. Done." He pointed in the direction of Wilkins's office.

"Now—tell me how the kid is doing."

Six

AS COLLIN UNPACKED the groceries, he heard Cameron start the shower in the master bathroom upstairs. From past experience, he knew this meant he had approximately twenty-two minutes before she made an appearance. Plenty of time to whip something up for breakfast.

It never ceased to amuse him, as it had earlier that morning when he'd first checked the fridge, how little her culinary skills—or lack thereof—had changed since college. Actually, what amused him most was just how predictable she was. After twelve years' experience, he'd known exactly what he would find when he opened the refrigerator doors: one solitary unopened Egg Beater carton that had expired four weeks earlier; a bag of bagels and three tubs of different-flavored cream cheeses, all one schmear away from empty; and two dozen Lean Cuisine entrees in the freezer, neatly organized according to the four major food ethnicities: Italian, Asian, Mexican, and macaroni and cheese.

Which was why a trip to Whole Foods had been in short order that morning, if Collin had any intention of keeping his promise to make breakfast. Luckily the grocery store was only two blocks away. Even more convenient, it happened to be right across the street from an independent coffee shop, The Fixx, whose six-shot specialty latte, the "Smith and Wesson," packed enough punch to knock the hangover out of even the sorriest of late-night drinkers. In truth, Collin knew he'd only get through about five sips of the stuff before throwing the rest out in disgust. But what could he say—he got a kick out of ordering a drink named after a gun. Another guy thing, perhaps.

He located a twelve-inch skillet in the cabinet above the stove—actually it wasn't at all hard to find; it was in exactly the same spot he'd left it the last time he'd slept over. He coated the pan with some oil and added zucchini and mushrooms to sauté while he fired up the broiler. He'd decided to make frittatas instead of the omelet Cameron had requested as they'd parted ways at the top of the stairs last night. With frittatas, he figured, she could always reheat the leftovers and might actually have two whole meals in one day that didn't come out of a box.

Collin was feeling very protective of Cameron, more so than usual. For her sake, he was trying not to show it, but he still felt uneasy about her near brush with a killer two nights ago. Of course she'd played the role of the nerves-of-steel prosecutor to the hilt—part of the wall she had put up after her father's death—but he suspected she was more freaked out than she let on. And it certainly didn't help that the FBI had assigned Jack Pallas to the investigation. Given their history, his involvement in the case undoubtedly had sent Cameron's insecurities about showing "weakness" into maximum overdrive.

The sudden reappearance of Jack Pallas in Chicago was indeed an interesting development. Collin remembered how furious Cameron had been, rightfully so, over the infamous "head up her ass" comment. But he also remembered, despite her anger—and he was only one of a handful of people who knew this juicy tidbit—how hard she had tried to dissuade the DOJ from transferring Pallas out of Chicago.

He had always found that particular contradiction quite curious.

Collin was sprinkling cheese on top of the frittatas when the doorbell rang. Considering that it wasn't his house, and also considering that Cameron hadn't mentioned that she was expecting anybody, he ignored it. Just as he was putting the skillet under the broiler, the doorbell rang again. Twice.

Collin shut the oven. "All right, all right," he grumbled. He cut through the dining and living rooms and headed to the front door. It was when he reached to unlock the deadbolt that he realized he was still wearing the oven mitts. He took one off and opened the door. He found two guys on the doorstep, staring at him in surprise.

Collin's eyes passed over the man in the tailored suit and rested on the taller guy, the one wearing jeans and a blazer.

Well, well, well . . . if it wasn't Special Agent Jack Pallas in the flesh.

Collin straightened up. It may have been three years, but no introduction was necessary. He knew exactly who the guy was from all the media coverage surrounding the Martino investigation and the subsequent fallout with Cameron. Not to mention, Jack Pallas was not a man who was easily forgotten. Definitely not his type—meaning straight—but that didn't mean he couldn't recognize that he was looking at one damn good-looking individual. With a lean, muscular build and a face that was just barely saved from being almost too handsome by that five o'clock shadow that probably started somewhere around 9:00 A.M., Jack Pallas was one of those men that made other men wish they weren't standing on a doorstep wearing red-checkered oven mitts.

But just as he was starting to feel a bit territorial and defensive, Collin noticed that Pallas was similarly study-ing *him*. And maybe the scrutinizing once-over was sim-ply the instinctive reaction of the FBI agent, but a man could usually sense when he was being sized up.

Feeling good about having the upper hand, Collin smiled. "Gentlemen. Can I help you?"

Jack's eyes lingered on the oven mitts. What he made of them was tough to say.

He pulled a badge out of his jacket. "I'm Special Agent Jack Pallas with the FBI, this is Agent Wilkins. We'd like to speak with Cameron Lynde."

"She's in the shower. Been in there for a while, so I don't think it'll be much longer." Collin gestured inside the house. "I've got something in the oven. You guys want to come in?"

Leaving the door open, Collin turned and headed back to the kitchen to check on the frittata. As he took the skil-let out of the oven and set it on the counter, he watched out of the corner of his eye as the two agents stepped into the living room and shut the front door behind them. He could see Jack doing a quick survey of the house, taking in the relative lack of furniture in the front two rooms. Due to budgetary constraints, Collin knew, Cameron was furnishing the house in a piecemeal fashion. The living and dining rooms were low on her totem pole given, as she had once said, that she didn't do a lot of formal enter-taining.

Being there as often as he was, Collin had gotten used to the sparseness of the decor, the simple leather armchair and reading lamp opposite the fireplace that were the sole furnishings in the living room, and the modest four-person table and chairs that looked practically Lilliputian in the spacious tray-ceiling dining room. He'd hazard a guess that Jack, however, was speculating right then about the circumstances under which a person would own such a big house and leave half of it sitting empty.

Collin pulled the oven mitts off. "You guys are making me nervous by hovering there. Why don't you come in—I'll go check on Cam and let her know you're here."

He felt Jack's eyes on him as he made his way up the wide, open staircase that led to the upper floors. On the second floor, he entered the first room on the right, the master suite. The shower was still running, so he knocked and opened the door a crack.

"You've got visitors, babe," Collin said, trying not to let his voice carry. "FBI wants to talk to you." He shut the door and went back downstairs, where he found the two agents waiting in the kitchen. "It shouldn't be much longer. Can I get either of you something to drink?"

"I'm fine, thank you, Mr. . . ." Jack cocked his head. "I'm sorry, I didn't catch your name."

"Collin."

He saw that this registered with Jack. A look of recognition crossed Wilkins's face.

"That's it! You're Collin McCann," Wilkins said.

Collin grinned. Ah . . . fans. He never got tired of meeting them. "Guilty as charged."

Wilkins rocked back on his heels excitedly. "I thought you looked familiar when you opened the door, but it took me a moment. Something's different from the picture they've got in the paper."

"It's the goatee. An unfortunate choice in my late twenties. I've been trying to get them to change the photo, but apparently it tests well with the eighteen to thirty-four demographic."

Jack's eyes darted between them. "I'm missing something here."

"He's *Collin McCann*," Wilkins emphasized. "You know, the sportswriter."

Jack shook his head. No clue. Collin tried to decide how offended he was by this.

Wilkins explained. "He does a weekly column for the *Sun-Times* where he writes directly to the teams—you know, 'Dear Manager,' 'Dear Coach So-And-So'—and he makes recommendations on trades, what players to start, how to improve the team, those kinds of things." He turned back to Collin. "That was one hell of a letter you addressed to Piniella last week."

Collin chuckled. He'd pissed off a lot of Cubs fans with that one. "Needed to be said. When people stop dropping thousands of dollars in season tickets for a team that hasn't won a World Series since 1908, maybe the owners and management will finally be motivated to put together a ball club that's worthy of its fans."

Wilkins glanced over, embarrassed for his partner. "Seriously, Jack, I think you might be the only guy in this city who hasn't read his stuff. Collin McCann is like the Carrie Bradshaw of Chicago men."

"You mean Terry Bradshaw," Jack corrected.

"No, Carrie," Wilkins repeated. "You know, Sarah Jessica Parker. *Sex and the City*."

A silence fell over the room as Collin and Jack stared at Wilkins, seriously fearing for the fate of men.

Wilkins shifted nervously. "My ex-girlfriend made me watch the show while we were dating."

"Sure, you keep sticking with that story." Jack turned to Collin. "Sorry I didn't recognize the name. I've been out of touch for a while."

"Oh? The *Sun-Times* doesn't deliver to Nebraska?" Collin quipped without thinking.

Oops.

He saw the flicker in Jack's eyes and could read the agent's thoughts as clearly as if there was a cartoon bubble above his head. *So . . . he knows where I've been the last three years. She's talked about me to this joker, then. Who is he, and how much does he know? Except on the issue of sports, a subject on which he clearly is all-knowing.*

"Actually, I meant that I'd been working undercover the last time I lived in this city and didn't have much time to read the paper." Jack eased back against the counter and took in the kitchen, a room much higher on Cameron's totem pole that recently had been remodeled. His gaze fell to the hardwood at his feet. "The floors turned out great. You have a very nice place here."

"I'll be sure to pass your compliments along to Cameron," Collin said.

"Oh, I assumed you lived here as well."

"Nope, just visiting."

A smoky, feminine voice interrupted them. "And apparently letting unexpected visitors into my house."

The three men turned and found Cameron standing in the doorway. She wore jeans and a gray T-shirt that hugged tight to her chest, and she had her long hair pulled up into some sort of ponytail/bun-type thing. She looked adorable in a fresh-faced, kicking-back-on-the-weekend kind of way.

Collin stood farther from the doorway, where he had a view of Jack. And although it was subtle, he was pretty sure he saw the agent run his eyes over Cameron before resuming his guarded expression.

Interesting.

Cameron folded her arms across her chest. "Agent Pallas . . . this is a surprise. I wasn't aware we had an appointment this morning." She peered around him and her expression turned warmer. "Hello, Agent Wilkins. Nice to see you again. Sorry if I kept you waiting."

"No problem—we were just catching up with your boy Collin here," Wilkins said.

Cameron turned her attention next to Collin. "Can I speak with you for a moment?"

"Of course, dear." Collin followed Cameron into the living room. When they were safely out of earshot, she poked him in the chest.

"What is *he* doing in my house?" she whispered.

"There was a badge. And some mildly intimidating gazes. I felt it was best to cooperate."

She poked him again. "I don't want him in my house."

"I'm sorry, I didn't realize you'd get this flustered over Jack Pallas."

Cameron scoffed at this. "I'm not flustered. I just prefer to handle him on my terms. As in, at my office, at a time when I'm more prepared for a business meeting."

Collin's gaze fell to her bare feet. He recalled her vow to be more suitably dressed the next time she encountered Jack Pallas. "You're losing clothing every time you see him. At this rate, you'll be naked in front of him before you know it."

Then the strangest thing happened.

Cameron blushed.

"I'm perfectly capable of keeping my clothes on around him, thank you," she said, her cheeks tinged rosy pink.

Collin was intrigued. He couldn't recall the last time he'd seen Cameron blush because of a guy.

The plot thickened.

"He's even better looking in person," Collin said, seizing the opportunity to probe deeper. "No wonder you nicknamed him Agent Hottie."

Cameron threw him the evil-eye. "He's in the next room. We are so not going to have this conversation right now."

Collin looked her over. "You seem pretty tense. Are you getting any sex these days?"

"My God, Collin . . . time and place."

He grinned. "Fine. We'll continue this conversation later. I should get going anyway—leave you and the boys to discuss whatever it is you need to talk about."

Cameron frowned. "But you made breakfast—you should at least stay to eat. It smells fantastic."

Collin leaned in and kissed her forehead affectionately. "There'll be more for you this way. You need a home-cooked meal a hell of a lot more than I do."

She chucked him under the chin. "You were poking around in my freezer again, weren't you?"

"It's pathetic, babe. Truly pathetic."

AS CAMERON HEADED back into the kitchen with Collin, the first thing she noticed was that Jack looked uncomfortable. Probably not particularly thrilled to be spending his Sunday morning with her.

"I apologize if we're interrupting," he said.

"Actually, it's fine—I was just leaving," Collin said. "Got some work to catch up on."

Wilkins's face lit up. "Next week's column? Can you give me a hint? I'm a huge fan," he explained to Cameron.

Because Wilkins was such a nice person, she resisted the urge to roll her eyes. Guys geeked out over Collin all the time and, frankly, his healthy ego was a testament to that. "He's a very talented writer," she agreed diplomatically.

Collin snorted. "Like you would know. When's the last time you read one of my columns?"

She pooh-poohed this with a wave. "I read your column all the time."

"Oh? What was last week's about?" he asked.

"Sports stuff."

Collin turned to Wilkins and Jack. "This is why I stick to men."

Cameron watched as Jack and Wilkins processed the meaning of Collin's remark. Wilkins blinked. "Holy shit, I didn't realize you were . . ." he trailed off uncomfortably.

"A Sox fan? I get that a lot," Collin said teasingly. He gave Cameron a quick peck on her cheek. "Thanks for the hospitality, Cam. If you can handle a second drowning of the sorrows, I'll call you later and let you know how it went with Richard. Hopefully when he moved his things out of the apartment, he at least took his CDs. I mean, we might be gay, but . . . Enya? Really?" With a nod in farewell, he addressed each of the two men. "Wilkins—it was a pleasure; it's always nice to meet a fan. I hope the other agents don't make fun of you too much when your partner here tells them about the Carrie Bradshaw comment. And as for you Agent Pallas—man-to-man, if you ever insult my girl on national television again, I'll . . ." he stopped.

Everyone in the room waited, hanging. Jack raised an eyebrow. "Yes?"

Collin turned to Cameron with a look of astonishment. "I've got nothing. I had this whole exit speech going and I was gonna end with some big macho threat but when I got there, it was like—*bleh*—nothing. That's a pisser." He appeared disgusted with himself, then shrugged it off. "Oh well. Catch you guys later."

He strode out without a second glance.

Seven

AFTER COLLIN SHUT the front door behind him, Cameron shrugged at the two FBI agents.

"He gets a little protective sometimes." She said this not as an apology, more an explanation. Although in truth, it would take a lot more time than any of them had that morning to fully explain the wonder that was Collin.

"How long have you two been friends?" Wilkins asked.

"Since college. We lived together our senior year, along with our friend Amy." Cameron eyed the frittata and realized she was starving. She glanced over at Jack, who stood against the counter looking as though he didn't plan to leave anytime soon. She sighed. Apparently she'd be having a side of scowling FBI agent with her eggs that morning.

"I assume this has something to do with the Hodges investigation?" She walked over to the overhead cabinet to the left of the sink and pulled out three plates. She handed one to Wilkins and gestured to the frittata. "Help yourself. If it's half as good as Collin's omelets, you won't want to pass this up."

She offered a plate to Jack, catching his look of surprise. Sure, she had her share of flaws, but being rude to guests in her home wasn't one of them. Correction: being *obnoxiously* rude to guests in her home wasn't one of them. When said guest had declared on national television that she had no balls, she still considered vague aspersions and semitransparent snubs to be within bounds.

"No, thanks," he said awkwardly. "I . . . ate earlier."

Cameron grabbed forks and napkins for her and Wilkins, feeling Jack's eyes on her. She ignored this and paused for a moment at the utensil drawer, debating over what one might use to slice a frittata. A pizza slicer? A pie cutter?

"How about a spatula?"

Cameron saw Jack watching her with amusement.

"It's that flat metal thing with the handle by your left hand," he said.

"I know what a spatula is," she assured him. And she actually knew how to use one, too—for flipping grilled cheese sandwiches. One of the few things she could make without burning. Fifty percent of the time. Maybe forty.

She served herself a hearty slice of the frittata and took a position against the counter on the opposite side from Jack. It felt odd standing close to him in the confines of her kitchen. Too intimate.

"Do you have a lead in the investigation?" Cameron asked between bites.

"Not yet," Jack said. "We're waiting on the lab reports, and we're going to interview Senator Hodges's staff over the next few days. The purpose of this visit is to discuss some security issues related to you."

Cameron stopped eating and set her plate down on the counter, not liking the sound of that. "What kind of security issues?"

"We'd like to place you under protective surveillance."

She felt her stomach tighten into a hard knot. "You think that's necessary?"

"Consider it a precautionary measure."

"Why? Do you have a reason to believe that I'm in danger?"

"I would put anyone who witnessed this high-profile of a murder under surveillance," Jack said vaguely.

"That's not an answer." Cameron turned to his partner. "Come on, Wilkins—you're the good cop. Level with me."

Wilkins smiled. "Surprisingly, I don't think Jack's trying to be the bad cop this time. He's the one who suggested that you be protected."

"If that's the case, then I must really be toast."

Shockingly, Cameron could've sworn she saw Jack's lips twitch at the corners.

"You're not toast," he said. "If it makes you feel better, there are politics in play here. Davis isn't going to let anything happen to a federal prosecutor who's assisting an FBI investigation."

"You're still skirting around the issue. Why is it even theoretically possible that I'd be in danger? The killer never saw me."

"We have a couple of theories about what went on in that hotel room," Jack said. "My instinct is that someone was trying to frame Senator Hodges for murder. If that's the case, when that someone realizes that the FBI hasn't arrested Hodges, he's going to start wondering why. And although your involvement in this case is being kept confidential, we'd be foolish to ignore the risk of a leak. I'd like to be prepared for that possibility."

"But I barely got a look at the guy," Cameron said. "He could walk right up to me on the street and I wouldn't recognize him."

"That's exactly why you're under protective custody."

Cameron fell silent. Sure, she'd always known the situation was serious—a woman had been smothered to death, after all—but in the hours that had passed since Friday night, she'd been hoping, perhaps naively, that her involvement in the mystery surrounding Mandy Robards's death and the blackmailing of Senator Hodges was primarily over.

She reached up and pinched between her eyes, feeling a headache coming on. "I could've stayed at any other hotel that night, but no—it had to be the Peninsula."

"We'll keep you safe, Cameron."

She peered up at the unexpected words of reassurance. Jack seemed about to say something else, then his expression turn impassive once again. "You're our key witness, after all," he added.

"So will it be just you two watching me, or will there be other federal agents involved?" Cameron asked.

"Actually, since the Bureau has primary investigative responsibility, CPD will handle the protective custody," Wilkins said.

So it wouldn't be Jack guarding her. "Oh. Good." The idea of being in continual contact with him unnerved her. Not because she couldn't handle him, but because she didn't need him glaring at her all day long. Those dark, watchful eyes were enough to put anyone on edge.

"How will this protective surveillance work?" As a prosecutor she'd had cases where she'd placed a witness in protective custody—usually, as Jack had said, merely as a precautionary gesture—but she'd never been on this end of things.

"There'll be a car posted in front of your house whenever you're here, and the officers will follow you to and from work. When you get to your office, you'll be protected there by building security," Jack said.

Cameron nodded. The U.S. attorney's offices were located in the Dirksen Federal Building, along with the U.S. District Court for the Northern District of Illinois and the Seventh Circuit Court of Appeals. Everyone entering the building had to pass through metal detectors, and anyone wanting to access her floor needed proper identification. "What about when I go places other than work or home?"

"Such as?"

"I don't know, all the places people usually go. To the grocery store. To the gym. Or to meet my friends for lunch." She deliberately didn't mention that she also had a date on Wednesday evening, thinking that particular information was nobody's business but her own. Well, Collin and Amy knew, but they didn't count. They knew everything.

"I guess you'll just have to get used to having a police car outside the grocery store, the gym, and wherever it is you go for lunch with your friends," Jack lectured. "And this goes without saying: you need to be careful. The police surveillance is a precautionary measure, but they can't be everywhere. You should stick to familiar surroundings, and be vigilant and alert at all times."

"I got it. No walking through dark alleys while talking on my cell phone, no running at night with my iPod, no checking out suspicious noises in the basement."

"I seriously hope you're not doing any of those things anyway."

"Of course not."

Jack pinned her with his gaze.

She shifted against the counter. "Okay, maybe, sometimes, I've been known to listen to a Black Eyed Peas song or two while running at night. They get me moving after a long day at work."

Jack seemed wholly unimpressed with this excuse. "Well, you and the Peas better get used to running indoors on a treadmill."

Conscious of Wilkins's presence, and the fact that he was watching her and Jack with what appeared to be amusement, Cameron bit back her retort.

Thirty thousand hotel rooms in the city of Chicago and she picked the one that would lead her back to *him*.

Eight

"ARFN'T YOU THE least bit curious to know what the hell the FBI's doing?"

Despite the fact that the light was dim—they had deliberately chosen a table in a dark corner of the bar—Grant Lombard could tell that Alex Driscoll, Senator Hodges's chief of staff, was one very nervous man. From both the edge in Driscoll's voice and the way his eyes kept darting around the bar, Grant knew he was looking at a man who was struggling to keep his shit together.

"Of course I'm curious," Grant told him. "But pushing the FBI isn't going to get us any answers. And it might land Hodges in jail."

Driscoll leaned in, lowering his voice to a hiss. "I don't like it—they're hiding something. I want to know why he hasn't been arrested."

"What do the lawyers say? For the money you guys are paying them, somebody should be able to tell you something."

"The little pricks are telling us to lay low."

"Then maybe that's what you should do." Grant took a sip of his beer—not normally his drink of choice, but anything stronger could impair his perception and ability to read Driscoll.

"I would think, as the senator's personal security guard, that you might want to muster up some interest in this," Driscoll spat out. He grabbed one of the cocktail napkins the waitress had brought with their drinks and dabbed his forehead with it.

The gesture did not go unnoticed by Grant. Frankly, he was surprised Driscoll had survived without having some sort of fit or breakdown when the FBI questioned all of them.

"All I'm saying is that we need to be very cautious in how we handle this. Did Hodges ask you to come talk to me?" Grant asked, even though he already knew the answer to that. Hodges didn't do anything he didn't know about.

"Of course not. He's so grateful the FBI hasn't arrested him, he doesn't take a piss nowadays without first clearing it with Jack Pallas." Driscoll took a heavy swig of his whiskey rocks, which seemed to help calm him. Either that, or he was changing tactics and a better actor than Grant thought.

"Look, Grant, we've worked together for a while now. So you've been around long enough to know that a scandal like this can't be contained forever. Eventually somebody's going to leak something to the press. As the senator's top advisor, I need to flush out those leaks. Maybe even catch them before they're sprung."

Grant feigned hesitation. Just as he hoped, Driscoll took it up another notch.

"For chrissakes, Grant, it's not like you're a fucking boy scout. You've been covering up Hodges's affair with that whore for over a year now."

Grant stared Driscoll in the eyes. "What is it you want me to do?"

"Find out what the FBI knows."

"If your twenty-five lawyers can't accomplish that, what makes you think I can?"

"You have other ways," Driscoll said. "You've always come through for us in the past."

"My ways require incentives."

"Use whatever incentives you want—as long as I get my answers. I want to know what the FBI's hiding, and I want to know fast." Driscoll stood up and pulled out his wallet. He threw a few bills on the table. "And remember, you report directly to me. Hodges doesn't know and will never know anything about this."

"The senator is lucky he has you to clean up his messes," Grant said.

Driscoll picked up his glass and stared at the amber liquid. "If he only knew the half of it." He finished his drink in one swallow, set the glass down, and walked off.

Grant took another swig of his beer, thinking about how convenient it was that Driscoll was such a paranoid asshole.

With the chief of staff's orders as a cover, he was now free and clear to go about using his ways to find out what the FBI knew, and more important, how concerned he needed to be about their investigation. They were holding something back, even an idiot like Driscoll could tell that. And given what Grant personally knew about the crime scene—which of course, was pretty much everything— the only explanation for the fact that the FBI had *not* yet arrested Senator Hodges for Mandy's murder was that they found something that Grant had overlooked. And as calm as he might've seemed on the outside, that possibility was starting to make him pretty fucking nervous. Probably because the possibility that he had overlooked something was not entirely far-fetched.

He had, after all, been in a bit of a hurry after killing the bitch.

Mandy Robards.

If his ass wasn't on the line, Grant would've gotten a good chuckle out of the irony of the situation. Even dead, she was still screwing people. Took one hell of a talented prostitute to do that.

And talented she had been, if at least half the stories Hodges had told about her were true.

He'd been working for Hodges for nearly three years now. Because Hodges was both a U.S. senator and an extremely wealthy man (CNN's most recent list had estimated his net worth at nearly $80 million), he had employed a private security guard for years. When his prior bodyguard had left three years ago to work for the Secret Service, a friend of a friend had recommended Grant as a replacement.

Generally, Grant liked working for Hodges. It certainly was an interesting job. In a nutshell, he handled all actual and potential threats, both direct and implied, against the senator and his political career. This meant that he acted as Hodges's personal bodyguard, traveled with the senator wherever he went, and was the liaison between Hodges and the various outside security and investigative agencies they worked with—everyone from the state and federal officials who handled the death threats the senator occasionally received, to the security staffs at both the Capitol and Senate Office Building.

Over the last three years, Grant had become one of the senator's most trusted confidants. In fact, he knew things even Driscoll didn't know.

Like how it had all started with that damn Viagra.

According to Hodges, he'd started down the little-blue-pill-popping path "to help things out with the wife," and Grant believed that was true. The senator was essentially

a good-hearted man, better than most politicians Grant
had met (and in his line of work he'd met quite a few), but
like most politicians, he was susceptible to flattery and had
a misguided sense of invincibility. So when those little blue
pills kicked in, and Hodges got a bit more vim in his
verve, he began to avail himself, so to speak, of female
companionship—of the paid variety.

Within a few months a pattern developed: when business required the senator to be in the city late at night,
he would spend the night at a hotel instead of making the
fifty minute drive back to his North Shore estate. On those
nights, Grant would arrange for one of the girls to stay in
the same hotel. Hodges was either smarter than most cheating men, more paranoid, or both—he would never allow
the girls to come to his room. Nor would he buy a condo
in the city to use as home base for his extramarital affairs,
out of fear that reporters would watch his place and keep
track of the comings and goings of any visitors.

Mandy Robards was not the first girl the escort service
sent, but after only one night, she became Hodges's favorite. Unbeknownst to the senator, Grant had taken upon
himself the task of waiting in his car outside the hotel in
order to make sure that the women "exited safely from the
premises" (aka got the hell out of the hotel in the dead of
night when no one was watching). In the beginning, his reasons for watching the girls had been somewhat altruistic—
it was his job to protect the senator after all—but quickly
he began to see the value in having as much information
as possible about Hodges's dirty secret.

From the car, he had observed the handful of women
the senator rotated through as they went in and out of the
hotel. Mandy wasn't the prettiest of the bunch—in fact,
except for her flaming red hair, her looks were generally
unstriking—but Grant suspected that was part of her ap-
peal. Perhaps the fact that she wasn't drop-dead gorgeous

made it easier for the senator to buy into the four-hour fantasy that she was there because she genuinely *liked* him, not for the two thousand dollars in cash he handed her on the way out the door.

What Grant had seen in Mandy, on the other hand, was an opportunist.

It was after her third visit with the senator, probably about the time she felt safe in assuming that she'd become one of his regulars, that she'd started things in motion. Although it would be months before Grant realized it.

She had exited the hotel—the Four Seasons that time— nearly four hours to the minute after she'd arrived and surprised him by ignoring the open cabs that drove by. Normally, the girls made a fast getaway from the hotel, probably to shower. Instead she lingered for a moment, then turned and strode toward his car in her high-heeled black leather boots. She knocked on his window and cocked her head at an angle when he unrolled it.

"Want to join me for a drink at the bar?" she asked in her pack-a-day voice.

While normally such a suggestion from a woman would have certain connotations, Grant had sensed this was more than a casual invitation. True, he was a good-looking guy and worked out everyday to maintain the muscular build he'd acquired in his Marine Corps days, but seeing how she'd just had sex with another man—his boss, no less— the idea of her hitting on him right then was just gross.

Thus assuming there was more to it, Grant had agreed. Truthfully, he was intrigued. And he was more intrigued, an hour later, when he left the hotel bar having gotten nothing from Mandy other than the distinct impression that she'd been chatting him up over drinks. She'd seemed eager to learn about him and his background, yet all she'd revealed about herself was one minor (and frankly, not exactly jaw-dropping) detail.

"It's not like I want to be an escort forever, you know," she said with a sigh.

No shit, really? And here he'd thought prostitutes had such good 401(k) plans.

But Grant kept his mouth shut. And after her next visit with the senator, Mandy asked him to join her for another drink, and then the visit after that, too. It became an arrangement between them, and it wasn't long before their talk became less casual. Nevertheless, out of an abundance of caution on both their parts, it took about five months of circular conversations, the loops of which gradually grew smaller and smaller, before they finally got down to the point.

Blackmail.

What made it work, in essence, was that they were both gamblers. Grant's game was poker, and some unfortunate losses at high stakes tables had put a real stress on his credit. Mandy's game was sex, and she'd been waiting for the escort service to throw her the perfect score. When the married senior senator from Illinois showed up on her hotel room doorstep, she knew she'd found him.

The plan they devised had three parts: they would catch Hodges on video performing those acts of service generally considered outside the traditional senator/constituent relationship. Mandy would then present Hodges with a copy of the video and her demand. When Hodges balked at the blackmail and turned to his personal security guard and most trusted confidant for advice, Grant would make a big show of exploring all the options. He would then use his influence to steer the senator away from going to the authorities, and would ultimately and most reluctantly inform him that he had no choice but to pay.

They were careful in their planning, only meeting in person. No exchanges by phone or email. No records that could link them together. They decided it would be a one-time deal, after which they would go their separate ways. Mandy would quit the escort service and get out of town, and Grant would continue on with business as usual, with the senator none the wiser to his involvement in the scheme.

They agreed to ask for five hundred thousand dollars.

Then they agreed it wasn't enough and bumped it up to a cool million.

Not an exorbitant sum to Hodges, whose family had founded one of the largest grocery store chains in the country and owned an NFL football team, and certainly an amount he could pay without much doing. But it was enough to get Grant back on his feet after the gambling losses and more than enough to get Mandy off her back. The profits would be split fifty-fifty, they agreed.

Or so Grant had thought.

The time to strike came when the senator was invited to a thousand-dollar-per-plate charity fund-raiser for a children's hospital that would keep him in the city late into the evening. Hodges asked him to make the "necessary arrangements" and Grant set about doing exactly that. They would be staying at the Peninsula, where Hodges was a frequent visitor, and Grant knew the layout of the hotel well. He'd been given a tour by hotel security earlier in the year when the senator's son, daughter-in-law, and two grandchildren had stayed there that had pretty much told him everything he needed to know, including that which was most important: where the hotel kept their cameras.

Mandy requested room 1308, a room she'd stayed in before. Given its location, it suited their needs perfectly. It was in a corner and right across the hall from a stairwell, providing Grant a low-visibility means to sneak in and out of the room. And, personally, he got a kick out of the sinister connotations that came with the number thirteen. Another man in his position might have felt guilty, planning to screw his boss out of a million dollars, especially when that boss had been fair and respectful to him. But Grant was not that man.

Senator Hodges was weak. Sure, Grant had vices, everyone did, but the senator had put himself in a position to be preyed upon by others, and that made him a fool. Plus the guy had more money than sin and Grant didn't see anything wrong with redistributing some of that wealth in his direction. Given what he knew about the senator's private affairs, he'd earned that money just for keeping his mouth shut.

When the night finally arrived, everything started out smoothly enough. After Hodges headed to the hotel after the fund raiser to—how thoughtful—call his wife to say good night, Grant drove his car into a dark alley a few blocks away and quickly shed the trademark suit and tie he always wore when working with the senator. He threw on a nondescript black blazer, hooded T-shirt, and jeans, an outfit that would make him less identifiable on the off chance anyone spotted him around room 1308. A few minutes later, he parked the car and entered the hotel through its back entrance, located the stairwell that would lead him to Mandy's room, and hurried up the thirteen flights of stairs. Having timed things nearly to the minute, Mandy had just arrived herself and was waiting in the room. She had a small video camera she had purchased, per his instructions, from a spy shop on Wells Street.

Grant set up the camera, gave Mandy a thirty-second tutorial, and hid it behind the television that was conveniently located in front of the king-sized bed.

"What's with the gloves?" Mandy asked, taking in his black leather-clad hands while he worked.

In hindsight, Grant probably should've given the answer to this question a little more consideration, as it was the first sign of trouble.

"Just being careful," he'd said matter-of-factly while opening the armoire doors another quarter inch and checking to make sure the camera wasn't visible.

"Just being careful how?" Mandy asked.

When Grant turned around, he saw she had her arms folded across her chest.

Her eyes narrowed suspiciously. "You mean, just being careful, as in, if Hodges doesn't go for this, and he turns me in to the cops, there's no proof you were ever involved? Is that the kind of being careful you're talking about?"

She might not have been the prettiest call girl Grant had ever seen, but she wasn't the dumbest, either. Unfortunately, he didn't have a lot of time to finesse the situation.

"We're blackmailing a United States senator, Mandy. Yes, I'm being careful. And so should you. But it's not exactly going to be a secret to Hodges that you're involved in this. You're the one screwing him, remember? Not to mention, the one who's making the deal with him for the money."

"Funny how, when you say it like that, it sounds like I'm the one who's doing all the work," she said. "*Not to mention*"—she mimicked him—"the one taking all the risks."

Fucking women. He should've known she'd start bitching about something last minute.

Grant took her by the shoulders, tempted to give her a good shake. "This was your plan, Mandy. And it's a good one. Just keep cool, and let's do this."

It took a moment before Mandy nodded. "You're right." She exhaled. "I'm sorry, Grant. I think I'm getting nervous about all this."

"Don't be nervous," he told her. "All you need to do is turn the camera on when you hear Hodges knock—make sure you put the armoire doors back in the exact spot

they're in now, then turn the camera off when he leaves.
The rest of it is no different than any other job. I'll be
watching in my car from the street below. Turn the lamp
by the window on and off three times so I'll know when
you're done. I'll come up, check the tape to make sure
everything's okay, and then you'll leave just like you would
any other night."

"Thanks, boss. Anything else?" she asked sarcastically.

"Yes. Make it look good."

And did she ever.

As planned, Grant re-entered the hotel as soon as he
saw the signal in the window and hurried back up to her
room. When Mandy let him in, he pulled the camera out
from behind the television and checked the tape. He
started at the beginning, then played the tape back on fast-
forward. He stopped intermittently to watch, being sure to
keep the volume down. Soon, Senator Hodges would very
likely come to regret his ever having met Ms. Mandy Robards, but for that night at least, he was quite vocal in
expressing his pleasure with their acquaintance.

"See anything you like?" Mandy drawled as she reclined on the bed in one of the hotel bathrobes.

"Just making sure the tape's clean all the way through,"
Grant told her. The beauty in blackmail videography was
in the details. Those doggie-style spanks were probably
worth five hundred grand alone.

Grant continued to watch the replay on fast-forward,
the senator pumping, Mandy bouncing, and the bed all
a-shaking at comical speeds, until he got to the end. He
slowed to watch approvingly as Mandy very cleverly ma-
neuvered herself and Hodges in front of the camera as he
paid her in cash before leaving. The last shot on the tape
was Mandy turning off the camera.

When it was finished, Grant pulled out the tape and
handed it over to Mandy. As they'd agreed, she would

make a copy before showing it to Hodges. "Nice work," he said.

Mandy smiled as she slid off the bed. "Thanks." She grabbed her purse off the desk and put the tape inside. She leaned against the desk, taking him in.

"Sorry I was a bitch earlier." She nodded at his hands. "The gloves, they threw me off for a second. But you were right, this is serious business and we need to be careful. I understand why you need to take your precautionary measures, and I know you're going to understand why I need to take mine."

There was a sudden gleam in her eyes that Grant didn't trust. "Understand what, exactly?"

In answer, Mandy reached into one of the deep pockets of her bathrobe and instinctively Grant went for the gun in the shoulder harness he always wore. But she beat him to the punch as she pulled her hand out of the robe and Grant saw the flash of silver—

Of a small tape recorder.

He let out a deep breath in frustrated relief. "Jesus Christ, Mandy. What the hell is that?"

"I told you—my precautionary measures." She hit play on the tape recorder, keeping the volume low, but high enough so Grant could hear well and clear.

"I'm sorry, Grant. I think I'm getting nervous about all this."

"Don't be nervous. All you need to do is turn the camera on when you hear Hodges knock—make sure you put the armoire doors back in the exact spot they're in now, then turn the camera off when he leaves. The rest of it is no different than any other job. I'll be watching in my car from the street below. Turn the lamp by the window on and off three times so I'll know when you're done. I'll come up, check the tape to make sure everything's okay, and then you'll leave just like you would any other night."

"Thanks, boss. Anything else?"

"Yes. Make it look good."

Mandy shut off the tape with a smug grin. "That spy shop on Wells Street you sent me to was quite a find." She held up the recorder. "It's amazing how small they can make these things nowadays. The whole time you were here earlier, you never noticed I had it in my pocket."

"I'll have to remember to frisk you next time," Grant said sarcastically. "What's with the tape, Mandy?"

"I want to renegotiate the terms of our arrangement."

"You think you should get more than half?"

"I think I should get it all."

"Why the hell would I ever agree to that?"

"Because if you don't, I'm going to Hodges with this tape and telling him this whole thing was your idea," she said.

"As if he'd ever believe that."

"Men believe a lot of things they shouldn't when they're thinking with their dicks." Mandy gave the tape a little shake for his benefit. "Besides, he doesn't have to believe me. I have it all right here. I love how this little clip makes it sound like it's your idea—like you had to talk me into the whole scheme. And that, of course, will be exactly what I tell Hodges. And the police."

Grant knew he should've been nervous. Panicking, even. But instead, he felt a cold blue flame of anger beginning to burn inside him. And he felt strangely calm.

"I'm not giving up my half," he said.

Mandy laughed scornfully. "Half. As if you even deserve one-tenth of this money. I set this up. I did all the work. The only thing I've ever needed you for is to make sure Hodges doesn't go to the cops. And that you will still do, unless you want to do twenty years in jail for blackmailing a federal official. Because if I go down in this, trust me—you will, too." She flashed him a smile. "Sorry,

Grant. But like we said, this is a one-shot deal. I have to make the most of it."

She was so proud of herself right then. So smug and confident.

Too confident.

As Grant stood there, pointing his gun at her, he had one thought on his mind.

He would not be out-smarted by a fucking whore.

Mandy slipped the tape recorder back inside the pocket of her robe and eyed his hands unconcernedly. "You can put the gun away, Grant. We both know you're not going to shoot me." She turned her back on him and began heading toward the bathroom.

Grant reached under his blazer and tucked the gun back inside his shoulder harness. "You're right. I'm not going to shoot you." Without warning, he lunged for her—pleased she never saw it coming—and grabbed her by the throat and threw her onto the bed. She hit it with enough force to bang the bed loudly against the wall. Before she could scream, Grant was on top of her, and the bed slammed against the wall a second time as he pinned her. He slapped his hand over her mouth.

"You don't know who you're messing with. You need to understand who's in control here, bitch," he hissed.

Mandy's eyes widened—his sudden burst of rage finally put some fear and respect into her—and she began to fight back. Grant grabbed one of the pillows next to her head and brought it down over her face. Her arms flailed, her hands clawed for his face, and she kicked out with her legs, trying to buck him off. Probably not the way she was used to being ridden in bed, Grant thought, using his elbows and chest to hold the pillow down while he grabbed for her wrists and pinned them under his knees.

She fought really hard at that.

Grant let it go on for a nice long moment, finding her

panic and the power he held over her to be strangely thrill-
ing. Intoxicating. He was about to pull the pillow away,
ready to see the submission in her eyes, when it hit him
that she was such a dumb-ass scheming bitch that she
would never really submit, and he knew then that he never
should've trusted her in the first place and in that moment,
he hated himself for being so naive. He knew that, no matter what she might say, no matter what she might promise
right then, he'd never be able to believe anything that
came out of her lying mouth. For all their plotting, he
wasn't going to get a fucking dime because of her, and
worse, now she had *him*. Sure, he could take the tape
away from her, but he could never, ever trust her to keep
her mouth shut, she'd always have this thing she could
hold over him, that he'd planned to blackmail the senator.
And even if he could convince her to walk away, he'd
always be wondering when the day would come when
she'd be back, wanting something.

He knew this for certain: he did not want to spend the
rest of his life looking over his shoulder. He didn't want
her to have that kind of power over him. They were supposed to be partners, but now it seemed to be every man
and woman for him or herself. And he didn't see any other
option.

So he kept the pillow right where it was.

It took longer than he expected. Her struggles grew
weaker, feeble, but still she persisted, and it wasn't until a
good two minutes or so had gone by without any movement
that Grant dared to lift the pillow with his gloved hands.

Her eyes were open and empty. Staring down at her
lifeless body, Grant's first thought was that he was surprised he didn't feel more. No remorse, just . . . nothing.
Though he'd been in the Marines, he'd never actually
killed anyone and he'd always assumed it would be kind
of a big deal.

Hmm. Apparently not.

Grant sat up and smoothed back a lock of hair that had fallen into his eyes. He climbed off Mandy's body, thinking he'd better get out of that hotel room. Fast. His mind raced, the adrenaline kicked in, and it took him a second or two to clear his thoughts. He needed a plan and was impressed by how quickly one came to him.

The senator.

Hodges's fingerprints were all over the room. The escort service would have a record that he was the one who'd been with Mandy that night. And if he left behind the videotape of the senator and Mandy having sex, that would give the authorities enough of a potential motive. A crime of passion, they'd guess. She'd tried to blackmail the senator and when he found out, he'd panicked and killed her.

It would be enough, Grant told himself. It had to be. It wasn't like he had a lot of options. There were only so many scenarios one could explore when unexpectedly finding oneself in a hotel room with a dead hooker. Plan A: get the fuck out. Bonus plan B: pin it on someone else.

Grant reached into the pocket of Mandy's robe and found the tape recorder. He slipped it into the back pocket of his jeans, making sure it was hidden by his blazer. He put the videotape and recorder back behind the television, then hurried to the door. He flipped up the hood on his T-shirt.

After all, one never knew who might be watching.

AND NOW HE needed to finish what he'd started.

Grant set his empty beer bottle off to the side and took out his wallet to add a few bucks to the cash Driscoll had thrown down earlier. As he left the bar and stepped outside, he flipped up the collar of his coat to guard against the crisp fall wind that came rolling in off the lake. An L train roared by on unseen tracks somewhere in the near distance.

Grant thought back to Driscoll's orders.

Find out what the FBI knows.

He had every intention of doing just that.

It wasn't going to be easy getting the information, he knew, but his mind was already working. Jack Pallas could potentially be a problem—if the stories going around about him were even partially true—but Pallas had made enemies with some people that no one should make enemies with, and Grant had a feeling he could use that to his advantage.

The FBI obviously had something. Although not enough to point them in his direction—yet—he didn't like having any loose ends lying around. And as soon as he found out what the loose end was, he planned to take care of it. For nearly fifteen years he'd been covering up other people's secrets and lies. He would handle this with the same objective precision. No more being played the fool. No more mistakes. From now on, he was in control.

And he would do whatever it took to keep it that way.

Nine

BY WEDNESDAY AFTERNOON, as Cameron headed off to court for a preliminary hearing, she could almost convince herself that her life was getting back to normal. Almost.

Fortunately, the police surveillance had turned out to be less intrusive than she'd feared. She barely saw the officers assigned to the day shift—they started duty outside her house at 6:00 A.M. while she was sleeping, nodded to her as she pulled her car out of the alley on her way to work, followed her downtown to her office, then had virtually nothing to do until they ceded all responsibility to the night shift at 6:00 P.M. She'd had several court appearances that week, but because the courtrooms for both the Northern District of Illinois and the Seventh Circuit Court of Appeals were located in the same building as the U.S. attorney's offices, there'd been no need for the officers to accompany her. Not a bad gig for them, Cameron supposed, to be assigned to protect someone who worked in one of the most secure, heavily guarded buildings in the city. Maybe tomorrow she'd get crazy and make a run to Starbucks just so they could see a little action.

The guys on the night shift were a different story. They'd taken the time to introduce themselves the first night of their surveillance, and Cameron found herself warming quickly to Officers Kamin and Phelps despite the oddity of the situation. They'd established something of a routine over the course of the last three nights: they followed her home from work, checked inside her house to make sure all was secure, waited outside in their unmarked car while she changed into her workout clothes, then walked her back and forth the three blocks to the gym. Sure, it was a little strange, looking up from the treadmill and seeing two police officers watching her from the juice bar, but then she recalled that the alternative was getting herself *murdered*, and that pretty much got her past the awkwardness of the situation.

Countless times in her head she had replayed that moment when she saw the killer through the peephole as he left room 1308. And the more she thought about it, the more she was convinced there was no way he could possibly know she had been watching. He didn't look once in the direction of the door, and nothing about his actions suggested he suspected she was there.

That being said, this certainly wasn't a point on which she had any desire to be proven wrong. Generally speaking, when it came to any possible connection between her and a killer who smothered women with pillows, she firmly believed that an overabundance of caution was best. And until they caught the guy, she was more than happy to have the FBI and CPD watching out for her.

As expected, the preliminary hearing Cameron had

scheduled that afternoon went smoothly. It was her first court appearance since her trial victory the prior week. It felt good to be back in court, although not necessarily for this particular case. The defendant was a cop from the Cook County Sheriff's Office who had been charged with "freelancing" his security services in twelve purported drug transactions staged by the FBI.

It gave Cameron absolutely no pleasure to have to prosecute a police officer. Yet she'd insisted on taking the case nevertheless—if there was anything that offended her more than a regular criminal thug, it was a criminal thug who wore a uniform. The defendant was a dishonor to her father's profession, and because of that Cameron had absolutely no sympathy for him. The case certainly wasn't going to make her popular with the Sheriff's Office, but she would have to live with that. If she took cases just to be popular, well, then she'd be no better than Silas.

"Any redirect, Counselor?"

Cameron stood up to address the judge. "Yes, your honor—just a few questions." She walked over to the witness stand where Agent Trask waited. He was her final witness that afternoon and she sensed the judge was eager to wrap things up for the day.

"Agent Trask, during cross-examination, the defendant's attorney asked you several questions about the arrangement you had with the defendant while you were working undercover. In your conversations with the defendant, did you have specific discussions that he would be providing you with security for drug deals?"

The FBI agent nodded. "Our arrangement was crystal clear. I paid the defendant five thousand dollars. In exchange, he agreed to serve as a lookout and to be ready to intervene in the event other police officers attempted to interfere with the drug transfer."

"Is there any possibility the defendant was not aware that you were purportedly transferring narcotics?" Cameron asked.

Agent Trask shook his head. "None. Before each transaction, I confirmed that the defendant was carrying his firearm, then I would discuss with him the specific amount of cocaine or heroin involved. My partner would then arrive at the scene pretending to be the buyer, and the defendant would assist me in carrying the duffel bags of narcotics to the car. One time, he even joked with me and my partner that we were stupid to be doing the exchanges in fast food parking lots in the middle of the night—he said that would be the first place he and his fellow police officers would look for trouble. He informed us that if we wanted to deal drugs, the better location to do that was the train station."

The defense attorney rose from his chair. "Objection, hearsay. Move to strike."

Cameron turned to the judge. "It's a preliminary hearing, your honor."

"Overruled."

Cameron wrapped up her redirect and took her seat at the prosecutor's table. Because her office was swamped and understaffed, and because it was a preliminary hearing for what she considered to be a virtually open-and-shut case, she sat alone.

The judge glanced over at the defense attorney. "Any recross?"

"No, your honor."

Agent Trask stepped down from the witness stand. Then, as he passed by Cameron's table, the strangest thing happened.

He gave her a polite nod.

Cameron blinked twice, not sure she'd seen that correctly. Maybe he had some sort of tic she'd never noticed.

Because for the last three years, the Chicago FBI agents she'd worked with hadn't given her the time of day once they stepped off the witness stand, let alone the courtesy of a head bob. Apparently now that Jack was back, they'd decided to "forgive" her supposed crimes.

"Counselor?" the judge asked her.

She stood. "I have no further witnesses, your honor."

The judge issued his ruling. "In light of the testimony I've heard today, along with the detailed FBI affidavit the government submitted with its complaint, I find there is probable cause to bind this matter over for trial. Trial is set for December fifteenth at ten A.M."

They wrapped up the few remaining housekeeping items, then everyone rose as the judge exited the courtroom. The defense attorney whispered something to the defendant before making his way over to Cameron's table.

"We'd like to talk about a plea bargain," the attorney said.

Cameron was not surprised, but also not interested. "Sorry, Dan. It's not going to happen."

"There were several other Cook County Sheriff's officers doing the exact same thing. My client can give you names."

"I've already got names from Alvarez," she said, referring to another man the FBI had arrested, a civilian, who had provided additional backup "security" for several of the fake drug deals.

"But Alvarez wasn't at the meeting on June fourth," Dan argued.

Cameron packed up her briefcase. "If I cared that much about the meeting on June fourth, I would've come to you with the deal instead of Alvarez's lawyers."

Dan lowered his voice. "Come on, Cameron—give me something I can tell my client. Anything."

"Okay. Tell him I don't make deals with dirty cops."

Dan called her a bitch and walked off, taking his client with him.

Cameron shrugged and watched him leave.

Ah . . . it was great being back in court.

WHEN SHE GOT back to her office later that afternoon, Cameron spent a couple hours returning phone calls and kidding herself that she'd somehow squeeze in the time to work on an appellate brief she had due the following week. At six thirty, she gave in and wrapped things up. Never enough hours in the day, particularly not this one.

After clearing it with Officers Phelps and Kamin, she was set that night for her date with Max-the-investment-banker-I-met-on-the-Bloomingdale's-escalator. They'd seemed to get a kick out of the story—a few weeks ago she'd been doing some shoe shopping on her lunch break and was on her way back to the office, on the down escalator, when her phone vibrated, indicating she had a new message. She saw it was a notification from the court on a ruling she'd been waiting for, so she'd gotten off at the landing to read the decision. When she'd finished, she forgot where she was and stepped right into the path of a man getting off the escalator. They'd collided, and her purse and shopping bag went flying.

"Oh my gosh, I am so sorry," Cameron said as she stumbled, then righted herself. "I wasn't looking."

She caught sight of the tall drink of water standing before her. Not just tall, but also blond, bronzed, and gorgeous. She was looking now, all right.

She smiled demurely. "Oh. Hello."

He spoke. "I think you dropped some things."

He bent down to scoop up her purse and shopping bag and Cameron practically felt the breeze coming off her eyelashes as they fluttered. *Such a gentleman.* And he looked great in his navy suit—an expensive one, judging from the cut.

The shoe box had spilled open and one of her new four-inch silver strappy Miu Miu heels peeked out.

"Nice shoes," the bronzed god said approvingly, handing over the bag and her purse. He raised an eyebrow. "For a special occasion?"

"My best friend's wedding," Cameron said. "I'm the maid of honor. She said we could wear any silver shoes we want, but now I'm not so sure. I hope she approves."

The bronzed god grinned. "Well, I don't know about the bride, but I think your date will definitely approve of them."

"My date, right . . . I'm still working on that part," Cameron said.

The bronzed god stuck out his hand. "In that case, my name's Max."

Five minutes later, he walked away with her cell phone number.

"And what would his name have been if you'd already had a date to the wedding?" Collin teased when she called him later that evening.

She hung up and called Amy.

"Four-inch heels? Are you sure you're going to be able to walk down the aisle in those?" she wanted to know.

"You guys are missing the point of this story," Cameron told her.

"Are you bringing him to the wedding?"

"You know, in the all of six minutes we spoke, I somehow forgot to ask."

"Right, of course." There was a pause on Amy's end of the line. "But hypothetically speaking, in case you do bring him to the wedding, do you think he looked like a steak or a salmon kind of guy? Because I'm kind of supposed to give the caterer a count by Friday."

As if Cameron already hadn't been feeling enough pressure to find a date, now her single-hood threatened to throw the finely tuned inner workings of The Most Perfect Wedding Ever into utter chaos.

"Can I get back to you on that, Ame?" she'd asked.

But nearly three weeks later, she still hadn't given Amy an answer. And not just on the steak vs. salmon issue. Despite the fact that they'd been on a few dates, she hadn't even made a decision on whether she wanted to ask Max to go with her to the wedding. If it had been in Chicago it would be a no-brainer. But she was on the fence about whether she wanted to spend the entire weekend with him in Michigan, sharing a hotel room. Sure, he would look oh-so-fine on her arm at the wedding—a factor not to be entirely discounted—but personality-wise, he was turning out to be not what she had expected from their initial meeting.

At first she'd thought Max had gotten her phone number so quickly because he was confident. Now she realized he moved that fast because he had to. The man was a workaholic—he ate, slept, and breathed his job. Cameron understood being committed to one's career—she'd put herself in that same category—but in the three weeks they'd been seeing each other, Max had already needed to reschedule two of their dates. He'd apologized, but still, it was a warning sign.

So tonight she would decide. She was a single woman in her thirties, she didn't have time to play around with these things. Max was either in or out.

Calling it a day, Cameron powered down her computer and packed up her briefcase. She had just gathered her coat and was on her way out when her phone rang. She saw it was Silas calling and momentarily thought about not answering. But seeing how he had the corner office down the hall, he undoubtedly knew she was in.

Cameron grabbed the phone. "Hi, Silas—another minute and you would've missed me. I was just heading out."

"Great. Stop by on your way." He hung up.

Cameron looked at the receiver. She and Silas always did have the nicest chats.

Some of that could be her fault, she supposed. She'd never gotten past the fact that Silas sold her out on the Martino case. And from what she'd seen with the other assistant U.S. attorneys, that wasn't the first time he'd pulled a stunt like that, or the last. Over the last three years, she'd watched several times as Silas let his assistant prosecutors take the heat for any criticism directed at their office but stole the limelight from them whenever there was a significant victory.

Many of the other AUSAs accepted this as part of office politics, and to some extent, Cameron understood why. Several of her coworkers, like her, had been associates at large law firms prior to coming to the U.S. attorney's office and understood that this was simply how things often worked: the lawyers at the top of the food chain got all the glory, while the grunts at the bottom did all the work, waiting for the day when they would rise to the top and inevitably do the very same thing to the grunts working for them. The lawyer circle of life.

Additionally, there wasn't much they could do about Silas, anyway. Aligning himself with powerful people was the thing Silas did best (since he certainly didn't try cases anymore); it was how he'd risen to his position in the first place. And because U.S. attorneys were appointed by the president himself, barring some unforeseen circumstance, Cameron and everyone else in the Northern District of Illinois was stuck with Silas at a minimum until the next election.

That wasn't to say that Cameron simply took all his crap—far from it. A lot had changed in their relationship over the last three years. She wasn't a junior prosecutor anymore; in fact, she had the highest caseload in her office and managed nearly seventy-five cases at any given time, some charged, some in the investigation stage. She also had the best trial record among the nearly 130 prosecutors in the criminal division of the Northern District of Illinois—a fact that made her pretty darn indispensable and gave her a lot more leverage. Because of that, a sort of unspoken agreement existed between her and Silas: as long as her courtroom victories continued to reflect well upon and bring praise to his office, he basically stayed out of her way. In this, they'd developed at least a tolerable work relationship.

But it was a tricky relationship, no doubt. Silas demanded loyalty—or at least the appearance of it—from his assistant U.S. attorneys, and Cameron continually felt as though she had to keep her guard up around him. Although she'd taken the fall for the Martino case, Silas knew she hadn't liked it and had watched her closely ever since.

Which was why she could never let him find out how she'd stepped in to help Jack three years ago.

Silas had raised holy hell with the Department of Justice, demanding that Jack be fired for inappropriate conduct because of his comments. Cameron suspected this had less to do with Silas being offended on her behalf, and more to do with keeping everyone's focus on something other than the real issue: his decision to not file charges against Roberto Martino.

What Silas hadn't known was that Cameron had a contact at the DOJ—an old friend from law school—and that she had worked behind the scenes, trying to get him to agree to transfer Jack instead of an outright dismissal. To help strengthen her case, she'd gone to Davis's office early one morning a few days after Jack's comments. It was a risk, she'd known, but she'd also known that Davis had been fighting for Jack and her instincts had told her she could trust him. She explained the situation, that Silas was angling for Jack's dismissal, and passed along the name of her contact at the DOJ. Two people working behind the scenes were better than one, she'd told Davis, then asked that he never discuss with anyone the purpose of her visit.

"Why are you doing this?" Davis had asked as he walked her to his office door. "After what Jack said about you, I would've thought you'd be happy to see him dismissed."

Cameron had asked herself this very question. The answer, simply, came down to her principles. No matter how angry she was with Jack for his comments, when it came to her job, she put personal differences aside. Even in this case.

She'd read the files. Silas hadn't read them, and the higher-ups in the DOJ hadn't, either, but she doubted anyone could know the things she knew about those two days Jack spent in the hands of Martino's men and not have complete, utter respect for his dedication to his job. He may have had a lot of room for improvement in the personality department, but he was an incredible FBI agent.

"Do you want to see Jack get fired?" she'd asked Davis in response to his question.

"Of course not. He's probably the best damn agent in the Bureau."

"I agree." With that being said, Cameron had opened the door and walked out of his office—

And spotted Jack standing across the hall, staring at her.

She'd had a moment of panic—no one was supposed to know she was there. But she kept her expression flat and emotionless, and walked out without a word.

She knew what Jack thought, the assumptions he'd made that day. He thought she'd been the one to get him transferred—probably assumed that she'd gone to Davis that morning to complain about him. Unfortunately, there wasn't much she could do about that. She'd gone over Silas's head to defend Jack, and in his book that was a major breach of loyalty. She had no doubt that Silas would fire her on the spot if he ever found out. So she'd bitten the bullet and let Jack go on believing the worst about her.

After all, he'd already despised her because of the Martino case. Adding another log to the fire wasn't going to make much difference.

WHEN CAMERON GOT to Silas's office she knocked on the door. He gestured for her to come in.

"Cameron—have a seat."

She stepped into the office—a large one, by government standards, and richly decorated, too—and took a seat in one of the chairs in front of Silas's desk. "Sorry that I'm going to have to keep this short. I have to be somewhere in less than an hour and I need to stop at home first."

"I won't keep you long," Silas said. "I just wanted to make sure you're doing okay. You know, with everything you went through last weekend." Although his words were polite, there was a hint of annoyance in his eyes. Perhaps anger, even.

Cameron answered cautiously, unsure how much he knew. "I'm doing fine. Thanks for asking."

"You can knock off the vague routine, Cameron—I know all about the Robards investigation. The FBI director called me from D.C. this afternoon to say how much he appreciated our office's cooperation in the matter. Of course I had no idea what he was talking about. I guess he just assumed that I would be in the loop when one of my AUSAs is an eyewitness to a crime that involves a U.S. senator and is placed under protective surveillance. I guess I would've assumed that, too."

Since the cat was out of the bag, Cameron tried to smooth things over. She could imagine how much Silas had disliked being caught unaware with the head of the FBI. "I'm sorry if you were caught in an awkward position with Godfrey," she said. "The FBI agents in charge of the investigation said I wasn't supposed to discuss the specifics of what happened with anyone."

"I understand it's a confidential matter, but I need to be aware when threats have been made against one of my attorneys."

"And if I receive any actual threats, I'll let you know. But so far this is just a precautionary measure." Cameron couldn't tell if he was appeased or not. She thought it might be best to distract him, get him off topic. "I don't know if the director mentioned this, but Jack Pallas is running the case."

Silas's eyes widened with surprise. "Pallas is back? When did that happen?"

Cameron shrugged. "I think just recently."

The point, in her mind anyway, was that he was back and—at least temporarily—tangled up in her life once again.

"SO WHAT ARE you thinking?"

Jack rubbed his hand over his face and looked across his desk at Wilkins. "I'm thinking that if I never see another lawyer again for the rest of my life, it'll be too soon."

As expected, the footage from the hotel's video cameras hadn't produced any leads, and they'd now turned their attention to questioning Senator Hodges and his staff. Of course, his team of attorneys had made things as difficult as possible. But at least they'd learned a few things: several members of Hodges's team had admitted knowing about his various affairs with call girls, and a handful even acknowledged knowing about Mandy Robards specifically.

The first two people they had interviewed were Alex Driscoll, the senator's chief of staff, and Grant Lombard, his personal security guard. When questioned, both Driscoll and Lombard claimed to have been at home sleeping at the time of Mandy Robards's murder. For both men, there appeared to be no evidence to either contradict or confirm this. They both acknowledged that they were aware of Hodges's affair with Mandy Robards; in fact both admitted knowing that Hodges planned to see her the night of her murder. Lombard had made the arrangements with the escort agency (which Hodges admitted was something he asked Lombard to do "from time to time"), and Driscoll had attended the charity dinner with the senator and claimed to have learned then of Hodges's plans to see Robards later in the evening.

Neither Lombard nor Driscoll had been particularly forthcoming about Hodges's affairs, but as the senator's bodyguard and chief of staff, they weren't expected to be. And though neither had an alibi, seeing how both men claimed to be home at the time of the murder, sleeping alone (Driscoll was divorced and Lombard had never married), this again was not unusual. However, both did fit the rough physical description Cameron had given of the man she had seen leaving room 1308.

It wasn't a lot, Jack knew, but it was enough to look into both men further.

"Let's get Driscoll and Lombard's phone records and cross reference them with the numbers we have for Mandy

Robards," Jack told Wilkins. "And we should pull their credit card statements for the past two years—see if anything unusual turns up. In the meantime, we need to get started on that list Hodges gave us of people he believes might have a grudge against him."

Wilkins nodded in agreement just as the phone rang. Jack saw the call was coming from the lobby security desk.

"Pallas," he answered.

"Officers Kamin and Phelps from the Chicago Police Department are here to see you. They say they have something for you from a Detective Slonsky," said the evening security guard.

"Thanks—send them up."

Jack hung up the phone and looked at Wilkins. "Kamin and Phelps are on their way up." He frowned. "Aren't those the guys Slonsky put on Cameron's surveillance?"

Wilkins glanced at his watch. "They're the evening shift, I thought."

"So what are they doing here?"

"You'll have to ask them that." Wilkins seemed to sense the dark cloud of displeasure that was quickly moving in. "Let's try to play nice here, Jack—remember that we're working *with* these guys."

When Kamin and Phelps arrived at his office, Wilkins rose from his chair and greeted them with a cordial smile. "Hello, officers. What brings you by this evening?"

The older cop introduced himself and his younger partner. "I'm Bob Kamin, this is my partner, Danny Phelps." He held out a large sealed envelope. "Detective Slonsky asked us to bring this to you. He says it's the lab report you've been waiting for."

Jack got up from his desk and took the envelope from Kamin. "Thanks." He caught Wilkins's sideways glance and shot him a look to let him know that everything was cool. "So . . . for some reason we thought you were the guys assigned to Ms. Lynde's surveillance. Guess we were mistaken?"

"Nope, you got it right," Kamin said. "We do the night shift. Nice girl. We talk a lot on the way to the gym."

"Oh. Then I guess Agent Wilkins and I are just curious why you two are here instead of with her."

Kamin waved this off. "It's cool. We did a switcheroo with another cop, see?"

"A switcheroo . . . right. Remind me again how that works?" Jack asked.

"It's because she's got this big date tonight," Kamin explained.

Jack cocked his head. "A date?"

Phelps chimed in. "Yeah, you know—with Max-the-investment-banker-she-met-on-the-Bloomingdales-escalator."

"I must've missed that one."

"Oh, it's a great story," Kamin assured him. "She crashed into him coming off the escalator and when her shopping bag spilled open, he told her he liked her shoes."

"Ah . . . the Meet Cute," Wilkins said with a grin.

Jack threw him a sharp look. "What did you just say?"

"You know, the Meet Cute." Wilkins explained. "In romantic comedies, that's what they call the moment when the man and woman first meet." He rubbed his chin, thinking this over. "I don't know, Jack . . . if she's had her Meet Cute with another man that does not bode well for you."

Jack nearly did a double take as he tried to figure out what the hell *that* was supposed to mean.

Phelps shook his head. "Nah, I wouldn't go that far. She's still on the fence about this guy. He's got problems keeping his job from intruding on his personal life. But she's feeling a lot of pressure with Amy's wedding—she's only got about ten days left to get a date."

"She's the maid of honor, see?" Kamin said.

Jack stared at all three of them. Their lips were moving and sound was coming out, but it was like they were speaking a different language.

Kamin turned to Phelps. "Frankly, I think she should just go with Collin, since he and Richard broke up."

"Yeah, but you heard what she said. She and Collin need to stop using each other as a crutch. It's starting to interfere with their other relationships."

Unbelievable. Jack ran a hand through his hair, tempted to tear it out. But then he'd have a bald spot to thank Cameron Lynde for, and that would piss him off even more. "Can we get back to the switcheroo part?"

"Right, sorry. It was Slonsky's suggestion. Turns out her date tonight is at Spiaggia. You know it?" Phelps asked.

Jack nodded. He'd never been, but he knew of it. A five-star restaurant—one of the top in the city—it was located at the northernmost point of the Magnificent Mile and known for its romantic views of Lake Michigan.

"Well, Slonsky knows a cop who does security there in the evenings—says he figured he'd put that guy on Ms. Lynde's detail while she's at the restaurant, since he already knows the layout of the place and everything," Kamin said.

Phelps nudged him. "Tell him about the other part."

Kamin folded his arms across his chest in a huff. "Slonsky also said this guy will *blend* better than we would at the restaurant. Whatever that's supposed to mean."

Jack's eyes were drawn to the cuffs of Kamin's faded-blue denim shirt, both of them stained with some sort of mystery red sauce. He'd put his marker on a chili dog as the likely culprit.

"So we dropped her off at the restaurant and made sure she got in okay, and we'll go back when she's ready to leave. She's gonna call us," Phelps said.

Jack did not like the sound of this plan—he wasn't exactly thrilled about Slonsky sending in some new guy to watch over Cameron. Although after spending three minutes with Phelps and Kamin, he wasn't sure he felt much better about them watching her, either. Still, he supposed he didn't have anything specific he could complain about— Slonsky was in charge of this side of the investigation and they seemed to have thought things through—but the whole idea of this date just generally put him in a foul mood.

Instead of saying anything that would give this away, however, he thanked Phelps and Kamin for bringing by the lab report and sent them on their merry way. Before they started babbling on again about Cameron and Max-the-guy-he-couldn't-give-a-crap-about and their Meet Cute or whatever. So he told her that he liked her shoes—so what? The whole thing sounded more like a Meet Lame to him.

"I'm proud of you, Jack," Wilkins said after Kamin and Phelps left. "Not a single glowering look."

"We're still on the glowering thing?"

Before Wilkins could answer, Jack's phone rang again. He picked it up. "Pallas."

On the other end, the operator who answered the office's main phone number informed him that she had Collin McCann on the line for him.

Jack frowned. "Put him through."

"I'm sorry to bother you," Collin started right in as soon as the connection went through, "but it's about Cameron and I didn't know who else to call. I know this thing she's involved in is confidential."

"Is something wrong?" Jack asked. Hearing this, Wilkins looked over.

"It's probably nothing," Collin said. "She's on a date tonight. Maybe she's just . . . preoccupied."

Jack gritted his teeth. *If one more person mentions this damn date . . .* "But?"

"She's not answering her cell phone. I've called her several times and I keep getting her voicemail."

"She probably turned it off," Jack said. Wouldn't want anything to interrupt her night with Max-who-apparently-has-a-fetish-with-women's-shoes, after all.

"That would certainly be a first," Collin said. "She's never once turned that thing off as far as I know. She keeps it on for work."

Jack paused at this. "Okay—we'll look into it."

He hung up and turned to Wilkins. "That was McCann. He says Cameron's not answering her cell phone. Probably just a dropped signal, but we should check it out." He picked up his phone and called Slonsky. When the detective didn't answer, Jack paged him and left a message to call back.

Jack frowned. "Did either Phelps or Kamin mention the name of the new guy they've got watching Cameron?"

Wilkins shook his head. "No."

Jack quickly looked up the number for Spiaggia restaurant and dialed. Twenty seconds later, he hung up the phone, his frustration level having risen about ten notches. "I got a recording that says I should try again in a few minutes if I'm calling during normal business hours. Very helpful," he said to Wilkins. "Do we have numbers for either Phelps or Kamin?"

"No."

Great. Clearly, that would have to change ASAP. "Let's call the station and have them paged, too. How nice it would be if we could find somebody who knows something."

"The restaurant is only two miles away," Wilkins said. "Why don't I stay here and keep trying them, CPD, and Cameron, while you head over and check things out? With your ride, you'll be there and back in fifteen minutes."

Jack nodded—he'd been thinking along those same lines. There were plenty of perfectly innocuous reasons

Cameron might not have been answering her phone. But the thought of that one not-so-innocuous reason got him moving. Fast. He grabbed his keys and shoved them in the back pocket of his jeans. "Phelps and Kamin said they saw her go into the restaurant, so at least we know that much. If you get through to the restaurant, confirm that everything's okay with this cop Slonsky's got watching her, whoever the hell he is, then call me. Most likely, this is all a lot of nothing."

"And if it isn't nothing?" Wilkins asked.

Jack yanked open the top right drawer of his desk and pulled out his backup gun, a subcompact Glock 27. He strapped it into a harness around his ankle. "Then I'll make it nothing, as soon as I get there."

Because no one messed with his witnesses.

Not even this one.

SIX MINUTES LATER, having raced through the city at vastly illegal speeds only a skilled driver and badge-carrying FBI agent could pull off without fear of death or being arrested, Jack pulled up at the One Magnificent Mile building. He left his Triumph parked out front and flashed his badge to the lobby security guard in order to avoid being towed. After a quick sprint up the escalator, he entered the marble foyer of Spiaggia restaurant.

The maître d' came around the corner, looking harried. "Sorry—I hope you haven't been waiting long. A busier crowd tonight than we had anticipated. Can I help you?" While he caught his breath, he took notice of Jack's jeans and eyed them skeptically.

Jack still had his badge in his hand. "Jack Pallas, FBI. I'm looking for one of your guests, Cameron Lynde. Dark-haired woman, early thirties, about five-three."

The maître d' studied his badge. "Andy told me I'm

not supposed to give that kind of information out. And he specifically said I'm supposed to call him if anyone asks for it tonight."

At least CPD got that right. "I'll tell you what—you call him, and while you're doing that, I'm going to have a look around." Without further delay, Jack entered the main dining room and quickly surveyed his surroundings. The restaurant spanned two levels: the primary dining area, and a lower level where tables were flanked by impressive floor-to-ceiling windows. Despite the ornate chandeliers above, the lighting in the restaurant was low—presumably to enhance the views of the city and Lake Michigan—and it took him a few moments to scan through the guests on the first level. Not seeing Cameron, he headed to the balcony railing and looked for her at one of the tables below. He spotted her at the second table from the left, sitting next to the window. Alone.

For a moment, he had to pause and just . . . look. Because the view he had from the balcony was stunning.

And he wasn't referring to the lake.

The soft candlelight on the table picked up the gold highlights in her long chestnut brown hair. She wore a sleeveless black dress that showed off every curve of what Jack supposed he would have to acknowledge was an incredible body.

She sat at the table, looking out the window next to her. He watched as she took a sip from the wineglass she held. She looked subdued. She checked her watch, then crossed one leg over the other, revealing a slit in the dress at her thigh.

Only one wine menu on the table, Jack noted. It didn't take a special agent to figure out what had happened. Not that he cared or anything, but the infamous Max was kind of a dumbass to leave a girl like that sitting alone in a restaurant.

His cell phone vibrated in the pocket of his blazer. Jack pulled it out and saw it was Wilkins.

"I just talked to the cop at the restaurant. Name's Andy Zuckerman. He's telling me that Cameron is fine," Wilkins said.

"I've got a visual," Jack confirmed. "She seems okay. I'll find out what the problem is with her phone and get back to you."

He hung up and made his way over to her table.

Ten

CAMERON CHECKED HER watch, wondering what the statute of limitations was before a woman—clearly dressed for a date—sitting alone at a table in one of the most romantic restaurants in the city began to look wholly pathetic.

She would finish her glass of wine, she told herself. She'd treated herself to a 2006 Stags' Leap petite syrah, unwilling to let the evening be a total waste.

Max had stood her up.

Technically, she supposed, he hadn't actually stood her up, because he'd texted her—oh yes, a text message, as if he didn't have a moment to spare for a phone call—to let her know that he was stuck in a meeting with a client and wouldn't be able to make it. A lot of help that had been, seeing how she'd already arrived at the restaurant and been seated at the time he sent his message. She'd ordered a drink when the waiter came by her table, hoping to pull off some sort of chic, nonchalant, "Oh no, just one tonight—after a hard day of work, I often unwind alone in five-star restaurants with a richly aromatic Rhone varietal" type vibe. Given the slit in her dress and her knockout high heels (if she did say so herself), she doubted anyone, including the waiter, was fooled.

When she hadn't immediately answered Max's text message, wanting to calm down first, he'd sent her another message asking when they could reschedule their date. Again. In response, she'd sent a message saying that she would check her calendar for the month of Probably Never, Buddy and get back to him. Then, thinking Max might have a thing or two to text in response to that, she'd turned down the ringer on her phone, not wanting to disturb the other restaurant guests with further incoming message beeps. Frankly, at that point, she didn't want Max bothering her, either.

As Cameron finished her wine, she looked out the window, taking in the view of the lake and reflecting upon those things a single woman in her thirties tended to think about when sitting alone in a restaurant. Her best friend was getting married, and she had no one to take to the wedding. No one to share the moment with, other than Collin, but that was different. It wasn't the biggest deal, she knew—particularly with the much more serious issues she'd faced lately—but she certainly wouldn't kick up too much of a fuss if Fate wanted to throw her a bone or two in the man department.

"What happened to Max?"

Surprised to hear the voice, Cameron looked over and saw Jack standing at her table.

Fate was so clearly mocking her.

Cameron frowned. "What are you doing here?" Perfect. Just the man she wanted to run into right then.

"You haven't been answering your phone. Are you having problems with it?" Jack looked displeased. Big surprise there.

"It seems to be working fine." Cameron reached into her purse and pulled it out to check. She realized what she'd done. "Oh . . . I turned the ringer down. I must not have heard the calls over the noise of the restaurant." She peered up at him. "Were you trying to call me? Is something wrong?"

"Collin called. He couldn't reach you, got nervous, and called me. Then we couldn't reach you or get through to the restaurant, so here I am," Jack said.

Cameron ran her hands through her hair, feeling very tired. It had been a long day—she'd gone one round with her opposing counsel in court, another round with Silas, and then had been ditched by her date. From the look on Jack's face, he was gearing up for another sparring match and she wasn't sure she had it in her right then.

"I'm sorry," she said. "I wasn't thinking when I turned down my phone. I apologize that you had to run all the way over here for nothing. Glower at me all you want— you've earned it this time."

Jack took a seat in the chair across from her.

"That being said," Cameron continued, "I would like to point out that Officer Zuckerman has been over there at the bar, watching me all night, so it's not as though I had any reason to believe I was in danger. And I'd also like to state, for the record, that there was never any discussion about me keeping my cell phone on at all times. If that was something you expected as part of this surveillance, you should have stated it clearly up front to avoid exactly this type of scenario."

Okay, so maybe she had just a *tiny* bit left for one last round.

Jack rested his arms on the table. "That has to be the worst apology I've ever heard."

"I've had a chance to think things through. Seeing how I was only about thirty percent at fault here, you get thirty percent of an apology."

"I see."

Cameron waited for him to say something further. "That's it? I expected there to be a lot more. You know, with the growling and scowling."

"I could add a few curse words to that, if you like."

Cameron checked her grin just in time. "Not necessary, but thanks for the offer."

They sat in silence for a moment, each one studying the other warily.

"So you never said what happened to your date," Jack led in.

"He had a last-minute conflict with work. For the third time in three weeks." Cameron had no idea why she'd added that last piece of information.

Jack's dark eyes studied her. "I hope you had better luck picking out shoes that day."

He never ceased to amaze her. "How do you know how I met Max?" Cameron asked.

"Kamin and Phelps are a wealth of information. They seem to be having a blast being assigned to your detail."

"Shockingly, some people actually find me charming."

"I once found you charming, too," Jack said quietly.

It was as though the proverbial record had skipped to a stop, silencing the room.

For the last week, she and Jack had danced around this very issue, never actually discussing the past. But now that he had launched the first salvo, she could either retreat or face him head-on. And she wasn't a retreating kind of girl.

"The feeling was once mutual."

Jack mulled this over for a moment. "Now that we're working together, maybe we should talk about what happened three years ago."

Cameron took a sip of her wine, trying to look casual. She chose her words carefully. "I don't think there's anything that could be said that would do us any good."

Jack surprised her with his response. "I was wrong to say those things to that reporter. I knew it right after I said it. That was . . . a rough time for me. I was going to apologize to you. Of course, I never got the chance."

It was as she'd expected. He blamed her for his transfer, never realizing how close he'd come to being dismissed from the FBI. Part of her was tempted to tell him the truth and just get it all out there. But he was so angry with her about the Martino case—about everything—that she didn't know how he'd react. Logically, there was no good reason why she *should* trust Jack. So she continued dodging the issue. "I appreciate your apology," she said matter-of-factly, hoping that would end the conversation.

His face hardened. "That's it?"

"There's not much more I can say about what happened back then." Without taking a risk that the information would get back to Silas.

"You can tell me why you did it. I know you were pissed off about the things I said, but did the sight of me really offend you so much that you needed to have me thrown out of the entire city?"

Cameron knew it was time to end this conversation. "This isn't a good idea, us talking about this."

Jack leaned forward, his dark eyes glittering in the soft light coming off the candles in the center of the table. "I *saw* you come out of Davis's office that morning, Cameron."

Anger got the better of her. She leaned in, meeting him halfway. "You saw what you wanted to see," she snapped.

Cameron saw surprise register on Jack's face and knew she had said too much. "Dammit, Jack. Just let it go." She stood up from the table and walked away, not daring to utter another word.

Eleven

WHILE WAITING IN the lobby, Cameron slipped on her jacket and tied the belt around her waist. It was a warm night for October in Chicago, but given that it was nevertheless still October in Chicago, the concept of "warm" when wearing a sleeveless dress was relative.

"I can take it from here, officer. Thank you."

At the sound of Jack's voice, both Cameron and the police officer Slonsky had substituted for Kamin and Phelps turned. She watched as Jack strode down the escalator.

"Thank you, Agent Pallas, but there's no need," she replied coolly. "I'll stick with Officer Zuckerman until Kamin and Phelps arrive."

Jack ignored her and showed his badge to Zuckerman. "Jack Pallas. You spoke with my partner on the phone a few minutes ago, so you're aware that the FBI has jurisdiction over the investigation Ms. Lynde is involved in. I'll make sure she gets home safely."

Cameron watched as Officer Zuckerman nodded and

wished her a good night. After he left, she glared at Jack. "Why did you do that?"

"Because we're not finished with our conversation."

"Believe me, we're finished."

He shook his head. "No." He moved toward her, close enough that Cameron had to tilt her head back to look at him.

"What did you mean, when you said that I saw what I wanted to see that morning?" He studied her face, searching for answers. "What else should I have seen?"

Cameron held her ground. "If this is some kind of interrogation technique, it's not working."

"I'm awfully good at this when I need to be, you know."

"How fortunate then that I don't plan for us to do a lot of talking."

"Maybe you'll warm up to the idea on the way home."

It took Cameron a second to catch that. "I'm not going home with you."

Jack nodded. "I already called Kamin and Phelps and told them to meet us at your house."

"Why?"

"I told you, we're not finished with our conversation." He smiled slightly. "What's wrong? Don't trust yourself around me?"

Cameron raised an eyebrow. Hardly. "Fine. Let's get this over with. Where's your car?"

"Parked on the street in front of my apartment." He pointed behind her. "We're taking that."

Cameron turned and saw a motorcycle parked in front of the building. She was no expert on motorcycles—far from it—so later when Collin interrupted her at this point as she recounted the details of the evening to ask her five thousand damn questions about what *kind* of motorcycle Jack drove, the best she could tell him was that, no, it wasn't a Harley, and no, it wasn't one of those crotch-rocket sport bikes either.

It was silver and black, and it was definitely a bad-boy bike, she decided as she looked it over. But bad-boy in a refined, understated sort of way. It suited Jack well.

But still. It was a motorcycle.

"I'm not getting on that," she told him.

"Never been on a bike before?" he guessed.

"Ah, no. Not my thing."

"How do you know they're not your thing if you've never been on one?"

"For starters, they're dangerous."

"Not in the right hands." Jack walked over to the motorcycle and climbed on.

Cameron had a retort ready, but it died on her lips.

Holy shit, he looked ridiculously hot on the bike.

Jack nodded. "Come on—let's go."

She walked over. "How am I supposed to ride that thing in a dress?"

He didn't so much as blink. "That slit at your thigh should do the trick."

So.

He'd noticed the slit of her dress.

Cameron hiked up her dress and climbed on, showing a lot of leg in the process. Oops. She adjusted her jacket to cover up, wondering how much Jack had seen. From the look on his face when she glanced up, he'd seen plenty.

"Oh yeah—the dress works just fine," he said with a warmer gleam in his eyes than she was used to seeing.

Cameron looped her purse around her wrist and settled it into her lap. She searched around the seat for her handles. "What do I hold on to?"

"Me."

How convenient. "Maybe I should just stick with Phelps and Kamin," she said nervously.

"Too late to back out now." Jack reached around her and pulled a helmet off the back of the seat. "You never know, maybe you'll surprise yourself and actually like it." He handed her the helmet. "Put this on."

"What about you?" she asked.

"I'll get by."

At least it would make him drive more carefully. Or so she hoped. She slid the helmet over her head as Jack fired up the engine with a loud roar. Without thinking, she grabbed his waist and slid closer to get a better grip.

Before they took off—since these could very possibly be her last words—she flipped up the helmet visor and leaned forward to speak over the bike's engine. "Don't do anything crazy. I'm the maid of honor in my friend Amy's wedding, and she'll kill me if I have to be wheeled down the aisle in a body cast. Plus I got these new four-inch heels just for the occasion and they will not go well with crutches."

She flipped the visor down.

Jack spun around in his seat and flipped the visor back open. "Don't worry—since it's your first time, I'll be extra gentle." With a wink, he flipped the visor shut.

She flipped the visor back open. "Nice innuendo. Am I supposed to be charmed by—"

Jack reached around and cut her off by flipping the visor shut again. "Sorry, no more talking, it distracts the driver."

From behind the helmet, Cameron clamped her mouth in frustration. If he killed them both on the stupid bike, it was really going to piss her off that she didn't at least get the last word in.

But as they drove away from the building, her fear of motorcycles quickly surpassed her annoyance with Jack. She wrapped her arms tightly around his waist. They drove down Michigan Avenue for less than half a block before pulling to a stop at the light that would take them onto Lake Shore Drive. Through the helmet visor, she watched as the light for the cross street turned yellow, then red, and she closed her eyes as their signal turned green and they took off at a breathtaking speed.

When she opened her eyes, they were shooting through the Oak Street underpass, then suddenly they were up and out in the open air with nothing but the wide expanse of Lake Michigan on their right. The formidable waves of the lake crashed against the breakers and, unable to help herself, Cameron glanced over her shoulder at her favorite view of the city: the Hancock building and the other skyscrapers rising majestically next to the lake along with the twinkling lights of the Ferris wheel at Navy Pier. Every bitterly cold February when she asked herself why she lived in Chicago, this view was the answer.

She turned around and pulled closer to Jack as they raced along the drive past Lincoln Park Zoo and the harbor. The air was brisk, but she had her jacket and he blocked most of the wind. And as much as she hated to admit it, the ride was . . . exhilarating. Her adrenaline was flowing, and several minutes later when they slowed to exit off Lake Shore at Belmont Harbor, she flipped open the visor of the helmet.

"Take the long way," she said breathlessly in Jack's ear.

It was hard to tell over the motorcycle engine, but she was almost certain she heard him chuckle. When they slowed down, she relaxed and loosened her grip around his waist. Without thinking, her right hand just sort of happened to graze along his stomach, and she felt his abdominal muscles tighten in response, firm and hard as a rock.

And that was pretty much the moment she started thinking about sex.

In her defense, to start things out, he was the hottest

man she'd ever laid eyes on—and now her hands, too—
and it certainly didn't help that she was straddling him between her legs. As they drove, nice and slow along the side
streets, Cameron tried to pull her mind out of the gutter.
But then they stopped at an intersection and she noticed
how Jack's hands worked the handlebar/clutch thingy as
he revved the engine—almost like a caress—and she began imagining other things his hands could caress, strong
hands that could lift her up, hold her down, flip her over,
pin her against a wall . . . and she realized then that her
mind was already so far down in the gutter she'd need an
extension ladder to get it out so she might as well just give
in to the whole darn fantasy.

They were just getting to the good part in her head—in
her mind she had revised the scene from the other day
when Jack and Wilkins came by to tell her about the surveillance, only this time it was only her and Jack (no clue
how he actually got inside her house, useless details) and
this time she had just stepped out of the shower (with perfect makeup and hair, of course) and he was waiting in her
bedroom (an act that would be stalker-ish in real life but
was necessary to advance the storyline) and he said some
sly bit about was she going to be a cooperative witness
and she said something equally sly back (she hadn't come
up with the exact line yet but at this point the dialogue
became superfluous) and then she dropped her towel to
the floor and walked over and without saying anything
else they tumbled onto the bed and—

Pulled in front of her house.

The motorcycle came to a stop, and Cameron blinked
as she came back to reality. She sat there, needing a moment to regroup, trying to focus on the fact that the man
she was with was *Jack Pallas*, who had only meant trouble for her in their brief, but bad, history together.

Noticing that she hadn't moved, he turned around and flipped open the visor of her helmet.

"You okay in there?"

Cameron snapped out of it. "Sure—I'm fine." She pulled off the helmet, handed it over to him, and even managed a nonchalant look. Or so she thought.

Jack looked at her closely. "Are you blushing?"

Cameron shrugged. "I don't think so. Maybe there's a little color on my cheeks from the wind."

"You were wearing a helmet."

Right.

Time to go.

She climbed off the bike as quickly as she could in her dress and heels. Jack had parked the motorcycle next to the curb, and the added inches made it easier for her to get down. With an efficient nod, she said her good-bye. "Thanks for the ride. Good night." She turned and headed toward her front gate.

"Hold on—I need to check out your house."

She stopped, having forgotten about that. "Well, let's hurry up, then," she said over her shoulder. She got to the gate and reached for the handle when his hand came down over hers.

"Anxious to get rid of me, are you?" he asked.

Cameron turned around. "Yes."

Jack paused, as if seeing something he hadn't expected. He took a step toward her. "Why are you looking at me like that?"

Uh-oh . . . *trouble.*

She tried to play it off. "Like what?" She opened the gate and backed toward the front steps.

Jack continued to advance on her. "Like that."

Cameron put her hand on the stone ledge and slowly climbed up the stairs. "You're imagining things."

He shook his head slowly. "No."

"I must've gotten worked up from my first motorcycle ride," she lied. And possibly from thinking about riding something else, too.

Shameless.

Jack clenched his jaw. "Christ, Cameron." As he backed her toward the door, his expression was part angry, part . . . wow—something else entirely. "What the hell am I supposed to do when you look at me like that?"

"Ignore it. Stay focused on the fact that you hate me."

"I'm trying. I'm really trying here."

He had her trapped against the door. Cameron wondered if he could hear the pounding of her heart, it was beating so fast.

Jack put his hand on her hip. Such a simple touch, but Cameron's breath caught nevertheless. With her back pressed against the door, the only movement of her body came from her chest, her breathing short and quick in anticipation.

Jack's gaze fell on her parted lips. He slid his other hand to her nape and tilted her head, pinning her with dark eyes so hot she felt the burn in her stomach.

She knew she could push him away if she wanted to.

She didn't want to.

His gaze softened. "Cameron," he said huskily, and she felt as though she melted right there. Knowing what he was about to do, she closed her eyes and felt his lips brush lightly against hers right before he—

Stopped.

Blinking in confusion, Cameron watched as Jack pulled back.

"We've got company," he said in a thick voice.

She looked over his shoulder and saw a familiar unmarked car parked on the street in front of her house. Phelps and Kamin.

"When did they get here?" she asked.

"Just now. I heard the car pull up." Jack gestured to her door. "Do you have your keys?"

She nodded, trying to clear her head. "In my purse." She pulled the keys out and unlocked the door.

Jack moved past her and stepped inside. "Stay in the doorway, where Kamin and Phelps can see you." Then he went to search her house.

Cameron stood there and waited, trying to process what had happened between her and Jack. Her mind was quickly coming to terms with the fact that she'd almost just made a very big mistake, although her body seemed not as willing to accept this as fact.

Get a grip, she told herself as Jack came down the stairs from the second floor.

"All clear," he said as he approached.

Cameron stepped out of the doorway, knowing that physical distance was her best defense against him right then.

Jack noticed her quick retreat. "Don't forget to lock the door behind me," he said tersely.

He walked out the door.

JACK HURRIED DOWN the steps, trying to figure out when, exactly, he had become such an idiot.

He'd almost kissed her. And if Phelps and Kamin hadn't pulled up when they had, he would have.

Clearly, a bad idea. On this, at least, they seemed to agree.

He'd been momentarily caught off guard by that look she'd given him when she'd gotten off the bike—whatever the hell that had been—but now he was focused once again. She was his *witness*. More important, she was Cameron Lynde, and that meant hands off. The last time he'd

gotten too close to her, he'd gotten burned. Big time. Not
something he wanted to go through again.

He liked being back in Chicago. Being a solitary person, he didn't have a ton of friends, but his younger sister
and two-year-old nephew lived close to the city. He planned
to stay in Chicago for good this time, and that meant no
screw ups, particularly in cases where Cameron was involved.

Jack walked the perimeter of the house and confirmed
that all the windows and doors were secure. When he
finished, he closed the front gate and headed over to the
unmarked car parked at the curb. He had no idea how
much Kamin and Phelps had seen, but they weren't smirk-
ing or gawking as he walked up, so he took that as a good
sign.

The window of the passenger side unrolled as he walked
up. Jack knew he was in trouble as soon as he saw the
older cop's expression.

Kamin grinned approvingly. "So that's why you wanted
to drive her home from the restaurant."

Phelps leaned across the seat. "Does this mean she's not
going to the wedding with Max-the-investment-banker?"

So much for hoping they hadn't seen anything.

Twelve

ON THE WEST side of the city, Grant put on his game face as he approached the bar with the red neon side that blinked "Club Rio." He felt naked without his gun and shoulder harness, but only a man with a death wish would attempt to bring a piece into this kind of place.

He opened the door and the loud rhythmic beat of salsa music spilled out. Almost immediately upon stepping inside, a bouncer dressed in black and wearing an ear wire frisked him. He asked the bouncer where he could find Mr. Black—that was all his contact had told him, to ask for a Mr. Black. The bouncer nodded in the direction of the few empty booths in the back of the club.

Grant chose the booth in the corner and took a seat. It was doubtful that anyone would hear him and "Mr. Black" over the music, but given the stakes and the purpose of his visit, he didn't want to risk having any eavesdroppers. A waitress came for his order, and he asked for a whiskey neat. He didn't plan to drink it, but appearance was everything in situations such as these and he didn't want to look overly nervous or suspicious.

After the waitress came back with his drink, he sat back in the booth and feigned interest in watching the dancers out on the floor in the center of the club. In the middle of the second song, a tall, thin man in his forties showed up at his table. He wore an open-neck white cotton shirt that hung loosely over dark jeans and had shortly cropped bleached-blond hair. His arms, exposed by his rolled-up sleeves, were covered with tattoos. Not exactly the image he'd had in mind.

"Are you Mr. Black?" Grant asked.

"Good guess," the man said in a slightly raspy voice. He took a seat across the table. "I hear you're looking for information about an FBI investigation, Mr. Lombard."

Grant decided against asking how he knew his name. "I heard that Roberto Martino might be able to assist me."

Mr. Black lit up a cigarette and exhaled smoke across the table. "Mr. Martino doesn't assist people, Mr. Lombard. People assist him. Tell me something—does Senator Hodges know you're here?"

Grant also decided against asking how they knew who he worked for. "He doesn't need to know. His chief of staff sent me," he said, playing up the charade that he was there only on Driscoll's orders. Not that anyone was likely to find out about this meeting. Club Rio was not a bar that told its secrets.

"Why should I care about Senator Hodges's chief of staff?" Mr. Black asked.

"He has the ear of a very influential man. Having a connection to Senator Hodges could be useful to your boss one day."

Mr. Black considered this as he took another drag of his cigarette. "Maybe. Maybe not."

"Perhaps you'd be more interested to learn that Senator Hodges and Mr. Martino share a common enemy."

"Martino has many enemies. You'll have to be a lot more specific."

"Jack Pallas."

Grant caught the quick flash of recognition in Mr. Black's eyes. "So you know him."

Mr. Black nodded. "Yes . . . I know Jack Pallas. Although he had a different name when I knew him." He appeared far more interested now. "What do you know about Pallas?"

"I know that he got inside your organization," Grant said. "That he betrayed Martino and took out several of your men in the process."

Mr. Black paused for a moment. "What is it you want, Lombard?"

"Pallas is the lead agent in a murder investigation that implicates Hodges. The FBI is hiding something from us. The senator's chief of staff has asked me to find out what that something is. He would, of course, be very grateful for your help with this matter. As the senator's primary advisor, he would hope to be able to return the favor some day." Sure, he'd embellished on Driscoll's orders, but the way Grant figured it, if Roberto Martino ever came to collect on the favor, that would be Driscoll's problem, not his.

As if silently beckoned, a waitress appeared out of nowhere and set an ashtray before Mr. Black. He flicked the ash off his cigarette then rolled it against the ashtray, rounding off the cherry. He took another drag, and Grant could tell he was considering his offer.

"Look at it this way—by helping us out, you get to fuck with Pallas's investigation," Grant added. "Whatever it is he's hiding, it's important enough that he doesn't want anyone to know about it."

Mr. Black eased back in the booth with a humorless grin. "You seem pretty confident that we'll give you this information just for the hell of it. I think you've overestimated Martino's dislike of Pallas."

"Have I?"

Mr. Black said nothing at first. After another drag of his cigarette, he stood up. "Wait here."

Grant slowly exhaled. Assuming he didn't return with a couple of goons and a car with a plastic-lined trunk, it looked like he might be on his way to getting some answers.

Mr. Black returned a few minutes later. He tossed a folded piece of paper onto the table. "This man will help you. Meet him at this address at ten o'clock on Saturday night. You now owe us, Lombard. Not some chief of staff or anyone else—you. So I hope whatever information this man has, it's worth it."

Grant felt the anger rise in him, although he refused to show any reaction. He hoped the information was worth it, too. He was counting on it.

He unfolded the paper and saw a name and an address. He looked up, sure he was being played. "This can't be right."

"It's right." Mr. Black walked away from the booth and disappeared into the crowd.

Grant glanced back down at the paper in his hand. This was a surprising turn of events. He didn't know the man personally, but of course he recognized the name. Anyone connected to U.S. politics and law enforcement, especially in Chicago, would recognize it.

Silas Briggs.

Thirteen

JACK CHECKED HIS watch as he and Wilkins stepped off the plane. The delay in their flight had put them over three hours behind schedule. The joys of air travel.

Granted, he'd already been in a bad mood before the flight delay. Davis had called to check in while he and Wilkins had been waiting to board, wanting an update on the investigation. Jack knew Davis was getting pressure from the director, which meant Davis was pressuring him. And, unfortunately, Jack hadn't had much to report.

They'd spent the last three days interviewing witnesses and not learning much in the process. First, they'd tracked down Mandy Robards's old clients and ex-boyfriends, looking for anyone who might've been jealous over her liaisons with Senator Hodges. They'd gotten zero leads on that front. Although Mandy seemed to be a favorite amongst her clients for her professional skills, none of them—nor any of her ex-boyfriends for that matter—seemed particularly troubled by the fact that she had sex with other men. Few, if any of them, appeared to have any significant emotional connection to her. She did what she needed to do as part of her job—quite fantastically, apparently—but had made very few personal attachments along the way.

In an odd way, Jack related somewhat to the picture painted of Mandy Robards. Some jobs required a certain level of detachment; a turning off of emotions in order to do the things that needed to be done. That was one of the reasons his outburst to the reporter about Cameron had surprised him more than anyone—he rarely lost his cool, even under the most high-pressure of situations. She, however, had the most infuriating ability to get under his skin.

And "infuriating" was apparently the theme of the week. Lately, it seemed like Jack couldn't take two steps without bumping into somebody who clearly had nothing better to do than to seriously piss him off. His trip with Wilkins had been one frustration after the other.

Yesterday they'd flown to New York to follow up on the list of individuals who might hold a grudge against Hodges, a list based primarily on his recent appointment as chairman of the Senate Committee on Banking, Housing, and Urban Affairs. Hodges was a staunch proponent of increased regulation and oversight of financial institutions—most notably Wall Street investment banks and hedge funds. His first initiative as chairman had been to open a series of Senate investigative hearings into improper trading practices and the stock market collapse, an act that had made him extremely unpopular with Wall Street CEOs.

Jack hadn't thought he could possibly find a more difficult team of lawyers to deal with than those representing Hodges. This trip to New York had proven him wrong. While he and Wilkins had eventually been able to meet with most of the hedge fund and investment bank CEOs on their list, getting face-to-face time with them hadn't been easy. Most had eventually caved because of Jack's persistence, others because of Wilkins's charm. A few stubborn ones, however, just flat-out refused to speak to anybody from the FBI. All in all, it had been a long couple of days.

While he and Wilkins were in New York, he'd had one of the investigative specialists at their office pull together a file of photographs of all the people they had interviewed over the last week. The original plan, before their flight had been delayed, had been that he and Wilkins would drop by the office to pick up the file, then swing over to Cameron's place to show her the photographs. Jack hoped she might recognize someone she'd seen earlier in the evening, prior to the murder—perhaps someone she'd noticed in the lobby, the restaurant, or even better, on the thirteenth floor.

"What do you think?" Wilkins asked as they strode through the United terminal, heading toward the overnight parking garage where they'd left his car the morning before. He checked his watch. "It's seven fifteen. Think it's too late to head over to Cameron's? I told her we'd be there hours ago. She said she had plans this evening—she might not even be home anymore."

Jack glanced over. "What kind of plans?"

Wilkins shrugged. "She didn't say. Why?"

"No reason. Just asking." Jack pulled out his cell phone and called Kamin. After the fiasco on Wednesday, he'd gotten both his and Phelps's numbers so that he could reach them at any time.

Kamin answered his phone and confirmed that Cameron was still home. "Should be here for a while—she's got a few girlfriends over and they look to be settling in," he said.

Jack thanked him and hung up, not wanting to give the cop any chances to comment on what he'd nearly seen Wednesday night. The "nearly" part was key in Jack's mind—if he'd actually kissed Cameron, he'd have to acknowledge that fact, even if only to himself. But when it was only nearly a kiss, he could go on pretending that nothing had ever happened. Which was exactly what he planned to do.

"Why don't you just call Cameron and ask if she minds if we stop by?" Wilkins asked.

"Because she'll say no, and I can't do this tomorrow," Jack said. It would be his first day off since he'd gotten back to Chicago and he'd made plans to take his nephew to the Shedd Aquarium. "And Monday she'll be back in her office and I'd prefer not to talk there. No one's supposed to know she's working with us on this case."

"If you want to see her, Jack, it's okay to just admit it."

"Sure, I want to see her—so that she can look at these photographs."

Wilkins patted him on the shoulder. "You keep sticking with that story, buddy."

SOMETIMES, BEING A stubborn SOB really came back to bite him in the ass.

This was one of those times.

Jack stood outside Cameron's house, eyeing the scene. From what he could see through the windows, there had to be at least fifteen or twenty women inside.

"I thought you said she had a *few* girlfriends over," he said to Kamin. The two of them, along with Phelps and Wilkins, stood in a row against the undercover car, watching from the street as another woman in her late twenties/ early thirties, wearing jeans and high heels, and carrying a pink gift bag, walked up the front steps of Cameron's house and rang the doorbell. A slender, stylishly dressed blonde woman answered the door. There was a flurry of loud squealing and hugging, then the door shut and all was quiet again.

Kamin shrugged. "At the time, it was just a few girl-friends."

"You didn't think it was worth mentioning on the phone that she was having a bachelorette party tonight?"

"Didn't realize you were planning on racing over here, Agent Pallas."

Jack shut up, realizing he'd set himself up for that one.

"What do you think the pink bags are for?" Wilkins asked, his voice filled with wonder.

Phelps stood next to him, similarly wide-eyed and awe-struck. "It's a game. Each girl buys a pair of underwear, something she would normally wear herself. The bride has to guess who brought which pair. If the bride guesses wrong, she has to do a shot. If she guesses right, the other girl drinks."

"Cameron was afraid Amy would think the game was tacky, but the cousins insisted, see?" Kamin said.

Jack glanced over. "You guys sure are getting into all this."

Phelps grinned. "When a girl like Cameron talks about underwear, you listen."

"How about you, Jack? Could you do it?" Wilkins asked.

"Do what?"

"Twenty pairs of underwear. Think you could figure out which pair belongs to Cameron?"

Jack had been interrogated at knife-point, gun-point, pretty much at all-points a man could think of, but hell if a question had ever made him squirm as much as that one.

Because now he was thinking about her underwear.

"I don't see why I'd have any particular insight into that," he answered gruffly. "Think you could figure it out?"

"No, but I didn't try to kiss her three nights ago," Wilkins said.

Jack glared at Kamin and Phelps. "You two tell all sorts of tales, don't you?" He nodded to Wilkins. "We should get going."

Wilkins shook his head. "No way. We came to show Cameron those photographs, and that's what we're going to do."

Jack pointed to the house. "You can't seriously be thinking about going in there."

Wilkins's eyes sparkled with excitement. "Oh, I'm going in all right. And you are, too, partner."

"You thought going into a purse was sacrosanct? Infiltrating a bachelorette party is way beyond that."

Wilkins rubbed his hands together eagerly. "I know. And I'll never have an excuse like this again."

"You're an FBI agent, Sam," Jack reminded him.

"I'm also a single man, Jack. And inside that house are twenty gorgeous women who are drinking and showing off their panties. It's a no-brainer." He pushed off the car and headed toward the house.

"Easy for you to say, good cop. I'm the one who's going to catch hell for this," Jack grumbled as he followed.

Wilkins grinned. "I know. That's what makes it so perfect."

CAMERON STOOD IN front of her refrigerator, trying to find a place to put all the leftover trays of cheeses, fruits, and truffles. Amy's cousin, Jolene, sidled up from behind the door.

"So when is the stripper coming?"

Cameron shook her head. "I told you—no stripper." She kept her voice low. If Amy even heard the word "stripper" that evening, there'd be hell to pay. As maid of honor, she had been given a detailed list of acceptable activities and events for the bachelorette party, and naked man-flesh unequivocally had not been on it.

Not surprisingly, Amy's other cousin, Melanie, popped her head around the refrigerator door next. Like book-ends, they came as a pair—if you saw one, the other was sure to be bringing up the rear close by.

"We thought you were just saying that so Amy didn't suspect anything," Melanie said.

Cameron had noticed that the cousins had an odd, passive-aggressive way of using the collective "we" when expressing displeasure with something.

"Yes, we assumed that was all a big charade so that everyone would be surprised," Jolene added.

"If it was an issue of money, we would've been happy to pay for it," Melanie threw in.

Cameron had to bite her tongue. Oh, for the naked man-flesh, they were willing to chip in their time and money. Two things they certainly hadn't been forthcoming with thus far. But in the spirit of bridesmaid camaraderie, she plastered on a smile.

"It's not an issue of money. I promised Amy no strip-pers. Sorry." In exchange, she had extracted a similar no-nudity clause from Amy in the event that she ever got engaged. Something that did not look particularly likely as of late, considering that she had (a) no boyfriend, and (b) no prospects. She was definitely going through some sort of rough patch, first with Max, and then with that bizarre almost-kiss with Jack on her doorstep.

Post-traumatic stress, she had decided. Definitely. She'd ear-witnessed a murder, after all—one could practically be expected to behave in bizarre, erratic ways under such circumstances.

Amy walked into the kitchen. "There's someone at the door, Cameron. A man."

The cousins' eyes lit up as they exchanged greedy looks: *the naked man-flesh has arrived.*

Amy pointed at Cameron accusingly. "You promised. If this is what I think it is, be forewarned: you will pay for it ten-fold when it's your turn."

Cameron smiled as she brushed past Amy to answer the door. "Relax. It's probably the limo driver letting us know he's here." Amy followed her out of the kitchen, then made a sharp left and bolted up the stairs.

"Seriously, Ame—it's not a stripper." Cameron laughed.

"Just touching up my makeup," Amy called down as she high-tailed it out of sight.

Cameron checked the peephole. Surprisingly, it wasn't the limo driver. She opened the door.

"Agent Wilkins." She stepped outside and partially closed the door behind her for privacy. "Is everything all right?"

Wilkins smiled. "Looks like you've got some party going on in there. Is it a special occasion?"

"My friend Amy's bachelorette party."

"A bachelorette party—you don't say? Wow, I wished we'd known."

"We?" Cameron asked.

"Jack's skulking around somewhere. Said something about checking the security of the outside perimeter. That's FBI code for 'stalling.' Anyway, we're here to show you those photographs we talked about." He shifted to the side, trying to peek around the door.

"I thought we were going to do that earlier this afternoon."

"Darn flight delays. It's okay—you're busy, I can see that. We can come back some other time." Wilkins flashed her what undoubtedly was one of the best good-cop grins she'd ever seen.

Cameron nodded approvingly. "Not bad. And this time

you didn't even have to bring me coffee. Can we get this
done in twenty minutes?"

"Fifteen," Wilkins promised.

She gestured for him to come in. "I'll tell everyone
you're here to talk about one of my cases. I obviously
haven't told the other girls about all this." Other than
Amy, who, like Collin, knew she was being watched as a
precautionary measure.

The door behind her flew open. Jolene and Melanie
stood in the doorway.

"Haven't told the other girls about what?" Jolene demanded to know. She spotted Wilkins and smiled. "I knew
it! Cameron, you really had us going there. We knew you
wouldn't let us down." With a careful eye, she sized Wilkins up from head to toe. "Hmm. You look a little skinny.
You better at least do full-frontal."

"Excuse me?"

"They think you're a stripper," Cameron explained.

Wilkins seemed flattered by this. "Oh—sorry, ma'am.
I'm just an FBI agent."

Melanie winked. "Sure you are."

"Shouldn't you have some kind of uniform?" Jolene
asked. "It makes things seem more authentic."

"But I'm a special agent. Only trainees wear uniforms."

Jolene shared a look with Melanie. "That's a new one."

Cameron was just about to suggest that Wilkins show
the cousins his badge, when Jack walked up the steps and
stopped in her doorway.

"Sorry we're late," he said with a curt nod.

The cousins' mouths dropped open as each of them
caught their first glimpse of Jack. He wore jeans and a
dark blazer with an open-necked shirt. Objectively, Cameron knew what they saw: the tall, dark, whatever-ness;
the gorgeous face, blah, blah; the sexy, lean, body that was

tailor-made for all kinds of sin—who cared? Certainly *she* wasn't paying any attention to those things.

Jolene reached out and grabbed Cameron by her sleeve. She pulled her off to the side.

"Holy shit—how much did you have to pay for that one?" she whispered.

Cameron paused. "You know, the agency didn't say. Someone should probably ask him what he charges for full-frontal."

Jolene and Melanie looked at each other. "We're on it."

Cameron smiled to herself as the cousins made their way over to Jack.

Fourteen

"IT'S A NEGOTIABLE rate."

Cameron turned around from the cabinet she'd been reaching into and saw Jack standing in the doorway.

It took her a second, then she smiled. "Sorry about that."

She adjusted her sweater, a thin, deep V-neck black wrap that tied at her waist. When she'd been reaching for the glasses, the neck of the sweater had slipped off her shoulder, exposing the camisole she wore underneath.

Jack said nothing as she pulled the sweater back up. He gestured to the shelf she'd been reaching for. "Need some help?" He walked over and set down the file he'd been carrying on the counter below the cabinet.

"Um . . . sure. We need more glasses. And, apparently, I need to start wearing five-inch heels." She pointed. "The ones on the left. I didn't realize I'd have so many white wine drinkers."

"How many do you want?"

"Two for now."

Jack barely had to lift his arm as he plucked the glasses off the shelf and handed them to her.

Cameron took the glasses, surprised that the two of them momentarily had managed to have a normal conversation. Hoping he wasn't going to say anything about the other night, she turned away and set the glasses onto the center island.

"So, do you and Wilkins often crash bachelorette parties?" she asked as she poured two glasses of wine. If she acted normal, maybe he would, too, and then they could just forget about that odd little encounter on her front stoop.

Jack rested against the counter. "For the record, it was Wilkins's idea to come inside."

"Where is Wilkins, anyway?" Cameron asked.

"In the living room, being accosted by eighteen women who think he's a stripper. I thought it was best to duck in here."

"So much for never leaving a man behind."

"If he starts screaming, I'll lay down a cover fire and go pull him out." Jack held up the file. "Ready to do this? I don't want to keep you from your party."

Cameron nodded and took a seat at the counter. Jack began spreading out photographs on the granite in front of her. He set down the first two photos, then paused, giving her a thorough once-over.

"What?" she asked.

"How much have you had to drink tonight?" he asked suspiciously.

"Not enough to be your concern."

How nice, the scowling was back. Cameron had almost begun to miss it.

"How much?" Jack repeated.

"Just one glass of wine," she said. "I wasn't planning on doing a photo lineup in my kitchen tonight."

"What about the shot?" he asked.

"What shot?"

"You know, for the underwear game." Jack shifted uncomfortably, as if he'd said too much.

Cameron raised an eyebrow. "What do you know about the underwear game, Agent Pallas?" she asked, mock-interrogation style.

Jack scoffed. "More than I want to. Now—the photographs."

He placed three more in front of her before pausing again. "What happens to the underwear after the game?"

"The bride keeps them for her honeymoon."

"Oh." He continued on with the photographs, about fifteen total. "Now take your time, and look at each one carefully. Maybe it's somebody you saw in an elevator. Or someone you passed in the lobby or in the hallway. If we could put any of these guys at the hotel on the night of the murder, that would be a huge break in the case."

"I take it all of these people deny being at the Peninsula on the night in question?"

"At the time of the murder, yes." Jack pointed to two of the photographs. "These two men are members of Hodges's staff: Alex Driscoll, his chief of staff, and Grant Lombard, his bodyguard. They both say they went to the hotel early the following morning. According to their statements, Hodges called them after I finished interrogating him."

Cameron focused first on Driscoll and Lombard's photographs, then went through each of the others, one at a time. When finished, she set the stack back down. "I'm sorry. No one looks familiar to me."

"In the past week, have you remembered anything else about the man you saw that night?"

Cameron thought for a moment—there did seem to

be something there, something right at the edge of her memory . . . but whatever it was, it remained just out of grasp. "I can't think of anything else. It all happened so fast."

Jack ran his hand through his hair and briefly closed his eyes. The gesture suddenly made him seem so . . . normal.

"You look tired," she said.

He opened his eyes, his expression softer than usual. "Just a long couple of days."

"There you are." Amy strolled into the kitchen. "Cameron—what's this about an underwear game? I don't recall that being on the list of approved activities."

"Talk to your cousins—it was their idea."

"As maid of honor, it's your sworn duty to take charge of these kinds of things."

Cameron laughed. "My sworn duty? You do realize how crazy you've become with all this, right?"

"Oh, I'm totally off the deep end at this point." Amy turned her attention to Jack. "Agent Pallas . . . how nice to meet you in person. I recognize you from that time you were on the news, of course. Gee, what was that for? Oh, right—when you told half the world that my best friend had her head up her ass."

Jack turned to Cameron. "Do you just line them up, waiting to yell at me, on the off chance I'll stop by?"

"No, but that's a really good idea for next time." Cameron explained to Amy, "He met Collin last Sunday."

"Ooh—who does a better Angry Friend? Me or Collin?"

"Great starts. Then you both fizzled out at the end."

"Damn."

Out of the corner of her eye, Cameron was pretty sure she saw Jack trying not to smile.

"I should probably go grab Wilkins," he said. "If he hears the underwear game is starting, I'll never get him out of here. Cameron—thanks for your time. I can see myself out."

Amy waited until Jack had left the kitchen. "He could barely keep his eyes off you in that camisole."

Cameron looked down and saw her sweater had fallen off her shoulder again. The stupid thing had lost its shape after she tried hand washing instead of dry cleaning it. She pulled it up. "I didn't see him look at me once."

"He looked when you were talking to me," Amy said. "By the way, Agent Wilkins suggested that he and Jack go with us to the bar instead of those guys out front."

Cameron pointed firmly. "No."

"It's too late. I already said yes."

"Why in the world would you do that?"

"Because I'm curious to see how this all plays out tonight. I was standing on the stairs when Jack first showed up at the door, and I saw the way you looked at him, Cam."

Cameron threw her hands up in frustration. "What is this so-called 'look'?" Whatever it was, she was going to have to start taking extreme measures to guard against it.

Amy grinned. "You know the Tom and Jerry cartoon where Tom hasn't eaten for days and he imagines Jerry looking like a ham? Kind of like that."

"ABSOLUTELY NOT."

Jack stood on Cameron's front stoop, arguing with Wilkins. Partners or not, he had to draw the line somewhere. No more bachelorette party, no more games involving underwear, no more Cameron in that black sweater, gray silky camisole, and pencil-thin skirt that showed off many, many inches of her sleek legs. Any more of that, and he might start getting a little fuzzy on all the reasons why he didn't like her.

"Too late. I already told Phelps and Kamin that we'd cover Cameron for the next couple of hours," Wilkins said.

Jack checked. Their car was still parked on the street. "They haven't left yet. I'll tell them we're going back to the original plan."

"Have you ever been to Manor House, Jack?"

He scoffed at the question. "Our assignment here isn't to get into some hot club."

"I'll take that as a no," Wilkins said. "I've been there. Opened just a couple months ago. It's big—three stories. Originally a mansion built at the turn of the century. You know those old houses. Lots of rooms and hallways. And dark corners, too, especially since the club keeps the lights low for the ambience. Tons of places for someone to hide. The club will be packed, and the music will be loud. It'd be really easy for a person to find herself in trouble in a place like that, if the right people aren't watching out for her." Wilkins expression was serious. "Cameron's my witness, too. Kamin and Phelps are good guys, but this is the kind of assignment I'd rather handle on my own. If you don't mind."

Jack remained silent, needing a few seconds to finish chewing the big piece of humble pie he'd just been served.

"Caught you off guard with that one, didn't I?" Wilkins grinned, back to being Wilkins.

"Let's not make too big a deal out of it. Shockingly, once a decade or so, even I can be wrong."

AT TEN O'CLOCK that evening, Grant waited in his car at the location Mr. Black had given him. The address had turned out to be an abandoned warehouse on the city's west side. It took about five minutes of waiting before it occurred to him that the warehouse was the same one that had been in the news three years ago, the site of the legendary shoot-out between Jack Pallas and Martino's men. Also, if rumor was true, the site where Pallas had been tortured for two days before escaping.

Grant grew uneasy. It was possible he was being set up. Then he discarded the thought, finding it more likely that Mr. Black had chosen the location as a reminder of what happened to those who betrayed Martino. Not that he had any such intentions.

He had killed a woman.

Grant wasn't particularly bothered by this fact, if anything he was more annoyed by the inconvenience of having to clean up the mess he'd left behind. He had turned a corner—in his line of work he'd dealt with many an unsavory character, but doing business with the likes of Roberto Martino's men was an entirely different matter. Unfortunately, it was a necessary evil given the FBI's involvement in the murder investigation. He felt confident that he could've handled the situation had only the Chicago police department been involved. But he worried about Jack Pallas and whatever it was that the FBI agent knew.

He didn't like having to worry about these things.

Grant heard the crunch of gravel and saw a black Mercedes pull up in front of the warehouse. He got out of his car and walked over.

The door of the Mercedes opened, and the driver got out. Grant grinned. Martino really did have friends in high places.

"Mr. U.S. Attorney. How ironic that we should meet under these circumstances."

Silas Briggs glanced around, looking both annoyed and nervous. Martino must've kept him on a very tight leash.

"This isn't how I usually do things, Lombard," he said.

Grant leaned casually against the Mercedes. "It's a first

for me, too. But the senator needs your assistance, and
I've been told by Mr. Black that you could be helpful."

"What is it the senator is looking for?"

"Information. The FBI is hiding something, and we
need to know what that is."

Silas laughed scornfully. "So Hodges really killed that
girl, huh? Hell, I didn't think he had it in him. And you're
stuck with cleanup duty now, is that it?"

"Something like that."

Silas looked Grant over carefully. "Hmm . . . or maybe
it's not the senator at all. Maybe you've got a mess of
your own that needs to be cleaned up."

Grant took a step closer. "Maybe you shouldn't ask so
many questions. Maybe instead you should just tell me
about the Robards murder investigation."

Silas made a big show of trying not to look nervous,
but Grant could see it in his eyes. No balls. Frankly, he
was an embarrassment to his office. He doubted it took
much for Martino to buy him off.

"That investigation is being kept confidential," Silas
said.

"Glad to hear it. Now cut the crap and tell me what
Pallas knows."

Grant saw beads of sweat forming on Silas's forehead.

"I told you, it's confidential. Even I'm not in the loop."

"Why don't I believe you?" Grant asked. "I'd hate to
have to leak it to the press that Chicago's U.S. attorney has
been accepting bribes from one of the country's biggest
crime lords."

More sweat. A rivulet trickled down Silas's hairline.

Grant cocked his head. This was getting interesting.
"What's with the hesitation?"

Silas cleared his throat. "There's a witness."

Grant's self-preservation instincts immediately kicked
in and the cold blue flame of anger was back.

A witness.

He grabbed Silas by the collar and was satisfied when he saw the look of surprise and fear in his eyes.

"What does this witness know?" he nearly spat in his face.

"I don't know. That's the truth," Silas stammered. "Pallas is protecting her. That's all I know. I swear."

Her. So it was a woman. Another fucking woman.

Grant curled his fingers tighter around Silas's collar. "What's her name?"

When Silas continued to stall, Grant gave him another shake for good measure. "Answer me."

Silas swallowed.

"Cameron Lynde."

Fifteen

AS SOON AS they arrived at Manor House, thanks to the reservation Cameron had made several weeks prior (and, possibly, also thanks to a flash of Jack's trusty FBI badge) their entire party was shuffled inside and promptly escorted to the VIP room.

Jack walked by Cameron's side along the candelabra-lit hallway, taking in their surroundings.

"Interesting place," he said.

Indeed it was. Manor House fit true to its name. The club had several rooms on each of its three floors, and every room continued the turn-of-the-century theme in the original style of the mansion. There was a library, a study, and even a billiard room. Kind of like the board game Clue, Cameron had joked to Collin, after dropping by to check the place out for the bachelorette party.

As she knew from the tour she'd been given when she made the reservation, the VIP room—the "master suite"— was upstairs. Their party climbed up the wide oak staircase, with Wilkins in the lead and Jack and Cameron bringing up the rear. When they got to the top and stepped into the VIP room, she saw a glimmer of amusement in Jack's eyes.

"Very interesting." He focused on the ornate wood canopied king-sized bed—yes, a bed—in the corner of the room.

Cameron watched as Amy and the other girls headed over, settled themselves on the bed, and got down to the serious business of drink orders. The cousins started hollering for Buttery Nipple shots.

"I give the place a year before the novelty wears off," she told Jack.

Amy strode over and stuck out her hand. "Look what Jolene just gave me." She held out a beaded necklace with little plastic penises and condom packets taped to it.

"Oh, look—it's just what you always wanted. A penis necklace. Maybe that can be your something new for the wedding," Cameron suggested.

"Get rid of it," Amy said. "And make sure there aren't any others."

"I'll get right on it." Both Cameron and Jack watched as Amy hurried back to the bed and demanded that all the girls open their purses for inspection.

"She seems a little . . . intense about all this," Jack said.

Cameron stuck the penis necklace into her purse. "It's a phase. Thankfully one that will be over in a week, after the wedding. She's actually a very sweet person." Not that she was going to bring this up right then, but after her father had died, Amy had been a godsend. Being the only child of parents who had divorced years ago, all the responsibility for her father's funeral arrangements had fallen on Cameron. In her emotional state, she'd been overwhelmed by the task, to say the least. Without saying a word, Amy had shown up on her doorstep with a suitcase, moved in for two weeks, and had taken care of everything

Cameron couldn't handle on her own. In exchange, Cameron figured she could deal with the bridezilla routine.

Wilkins came over to them, carrying what Cameron guessed was a club soda. "I never made it to the VIP room the last time I was here." He stared at the waitress who passed by with a bottle of vodka lit up with sparklers. "No one told me that they've got waitresses dressed up like turn-of-the-century maids. Ooh—with sparkly things."

Cameron tilted her head in concession at Jack. "Maybe two years before the novelty wears off."

"NOW THIS IS what I call an assignment."

Jack gestured to the bartender for another club soda. "Soak it in while you can," he said to Wilkins. "Because they're not all like this."

"Really, this is better than Nebraska?" Wilkins joked.

Jack caught sight of Cameron, sitting on the bed across the room. She was laughing with Amy and two of the other girls while telling a story. As she gestured, the neck of her belted sweater slipped down, once again exposing her shoulder and the thin strap of her camisole. He watched as she reached forward to put her hand on Amy's arm and her camisole dipped lower, revealing a hint of what appeared to be a lacy black bra. "It's not all bad, I suppose," he found himself murmuring.

He turned back and caught his partner's expression. "Don't say it."

"Say what?" Wilkins asked innocently. "Oh . . . you mean I shouldn't comment on the fact that you haven't taken your eyes off her since we got here? Is that what I'm not supposed to talk about?"

"It's my job—our job—to watch her."

Wilkins nodded. "Of course."

Jack muttered under his breath. At least in Nebraska a

man could glance at a woman once or twice—for professional reasons—in peace.

He stole another look, for security purposes, and watched as the sweater once again slid away from her collarbone, inching down, taunting him, teasing him, dipping lower and lower, revealing creamy ivory skin and that delicate gray silk strap he could rip away with his teeth.

A shoulder. He was going crazy over a fucking *shoulder*.

He swore, turning to Wilkins. "What's the deal with that sweater, anyway? Is there a reason she can't keep herself clothed? Did she buy the wrong size? Seriously, somebody needs to throw a coat over that woman." He shoved away from the bar. "I'm going to walk the room. Make sure everything is still secure."

AMY LEANED OVER and whispered in Cameron's ear. "Okay, now he's pacing back and forth."

"You don't have to give me the play-by-play," Cameron whispered back. "If I want to know what he's doing, I'll just look myself."

Of course, that's exactly what she did. She snuck a quick glance across the room and watched as Jack did a loop around the bar, then looked back. When he saw her watching him, he turned and began crossing the room toward her, like a panther stalking its prey. From the intense look in his eyes—whatever he was about to say—he was a man on a mission.

Sitting next to her, Amy was wide-eyed, mesmerized at the sight of Jack heading over in all his seemingly pissed-off-once-again glory. "I changed my mind, Cam. If this was all a big setup and he's coming over to strip for me, I think I can handle it. I definitely can handle it."

Hearing Amy's words, the other girls stopped talking.

Following her gaze, they turned to watch as Jack approached. He stopped in front of the bed of women who lounged about like a sultan's idle harem and stared down at Cameron.

"I want to talk to you."

"Okay. Talk."

"Alone."

Cameron didn't like being ordered around by Jack, but she didn't want to make a scene in case he needed to discuss some security issue. With a nonchalant look, she slid off the bed—oopsie, another flash of leg, strange how that kept happening around him—and followed Jack out of the VIP room.

He took her by the arm and led her through the hallway into a barely lit corridor.

"You're not going to kill me, are you?" she asked. From the look on his face, she was only partially teasing.

"Not today."

He released his grip and paced the corridor in front of her. Cameron had no idea what he was so worked up about, but she looked him over closely right then and was satisfied to say that he looked nothing like a ham to her.

More like a chocolate molten lava cake. A dessert so sinful, so luscious, so filled with inner heat it made a girl want to lick each and every crumb right off the plate. *That* was Jack Pallas.

Cameron regrouped. "So am I supposed to guess, or do you want to tell me what this is all about?"

"I think you know."

Oh, balls. He was going to bring up The Thing That Never Happened on her doorstep.

"The investigation?" she asked hopefully.

He threw her a dark look that reminded her why Jack Pallas was not a man to be trifled with.

She leaned against the wall, thinking she might as well

make herself comfortable. Jack stopped his pacing. His eyes ran over her.

"We're going to finish that talk of ours from the other night." He crossed the hall and put one of his hands on the wall next to her. "You said that I saw what I wanted to see that morning at Davis's office. Explain."

Cameron stared up at Jack defiantly. Ha—like he could intimidate her into talking. Well, he probably could; he could probably get anyone to talk eventually. But she was decidedly immune to any of his so-called sexual char—*wow*, he smelled fantastic. His shampoo, perhaps? Couldn't be aftershave, with that I-just-rolled-out-of-bed scruff of his.

Decidedly immune.

"We're back to this again?" Cameron asked, feigning disinterest.

Jack put his second hand on the wall to the other side of her, trapping her in.

She eyed her predicament. *Wits don't fail me now.* "I think this constitutes false imprisonment, Agent Pallas."

"Probably. And I'm about to throw in an illegal inter-rogation." He peered down into her eyes. "Let's start at the beginning. Three years ago. Martino. You told me the decision not to file charges was yours."

"You think we're going to have this conversation now? Like this?" Cameron gestured to their closeness.

Slowly, Jack grinned. His voice was warmer now, whisky-rich. "Actually, I think this is perfect." But his gaze remained unwavering. "Start talking, Cameron. I saw you come out of Davis's office that morning. Why were you th—"

They were plunged into darkness as all the lights in the club went out.

Cameron felt Jack's hand grip her arm. She felt his other hand brush against her chest as he reached underneath his blazer for his gun.

Her eyes tried to adjust to the darkness, and she heard squeals of laughter and mixed voices coming from the VIP room. Despite that, the club seemed quiet. It took her a moment to realize the music had stopped.

"The power went out?" she asked Jack.

"Seems that way." There was the sound of approaching footsteps and a creaking floorboard. Jack pulled her away from the wall. "Get behind me," he ordered her. He turned, gun ready.

A shadow stood at the end of the hall.

Jack shifted, using his body as a shield to cover her.

"Jack—it's me," Wilkins said through the dark. "You two all right?"

Jack lowered his gun. He led Cameron out of the corridor, where the moonlight streamed through the windows and allowed her to see better.

"Is the power out in the entire place?" he asked.

"From what I can tell," Wilkins said. His eyes fell on Cameron.

She had never seen Wilkins look so serious. That, more than anything, scared her.

"Do you think this has something to do with me?" she asked.

Neither of the men answered her. "Go check it out," Jack told Wilkins. "I'll stay with her. Call me on my cell when you know something."

Wilkins nodded and took off.

Jack slipped his hand into Cameron's. "Stay close to me."

Her head was spinning with how fast everything had changed. She forced herself to stay calm.

"I'm taking you to a more secure location until we get this sorted out," Jack said.

As he began to lead her away, they nearly ran into Amy, who stood in the doorway of the VIP room. Her eyes fell on Jack's gun. "What's going on? Where are you taking her?"

"We need to move now," Jack said low in Cameron's ear.

"Everything's fine," she told Amy. "Just stay with the other girls."

Before she could say anything else, Jack took her by the arm and led her away.

NAVIGATING HIS WAY through the dark, Jack led Cameron through the maze of people hanging out in the hallway. People who, unlike him, enjoyed the thrill of the power outage.

He needed a confined space, preferably one with a lock on the door.

Having no such luck on the second floor, he found a back staircase and led Cameron upstairs. The first door on the right was shut. He pushed it open and barged in.

The room was small. An office. A man and a scantily clad woman sprang apart at the desk.

"What the hell?" the man asked, half pissed, half startled.

"Who are you?" Jack demanded.

"The manager. Who the fuck are you?"

Jack gestured to the door. "Get out."

"Screw that. This is *my* office."

Jack gestured to the door, this time with his gun. "Get out."

The manager's mouth fell open and he nodded. "We're going." He grabbed the girl and hurried out.

Jack locked the deadbolt on the door behind them. He let go of Cameron's hand so that he could check out the room. A small loveseat along the south wall, a steel file cabinet, and a desk with one rolling chair. No closets or other doors, but there was a large window that led out onto the fire escape. He tested the window and saw it rose easily enough. In case of an emergency, it would do.

Realizing that Cameron had fallen quiet, he headed over. "Are you okay?"

"I'm okay." She paced around the room restlessly.

"Stay away from the door," Jack told her. "And the windows. Stick to the center of the room."

"Right. Sorry." She moved quickly toward the desk, putting it between her and the door. She glanced down at her purse, then set it on the desk, as if wanting her hands free. "This is probably just a coincidence, right?"

"I'll tell you that when I know it."

In the moonlight, Jack saw her bite her lip anxiously. Then she put on a brave face and nodded. "Fair enough."

Jack felt something pull at him.

"But if it makes you feel better, I don't give a fuck what comes through that door. They're not getting to you."

She gazed at him through the dark, surprised. Turning away, he walked over to the door and listened.

Presumably following his lead, Cameron fell silent. The room was eerily quiet until the sound of his vibrating cell phone cut through the tension.

Jack grabbed the phone out of his pocket, saw it was Wilkins, and answered. "Talk to me."

"We're all clear."

"What'd you find out?" he asked, not yet abandoning his post at the door.

"The power is out for the entire block," Wilkins said. "I had our office patch me through to ComEd, who said they've got a power line down. They've got a team working on it as we speak."

Jack strode over to the window, looked outside, and saw that the buildings around them were dark as well. He spoke into the phone in a low voice. "Any chance this is a setup?"

"Not likely. I talked to both the director in charge of the district and the foreman on site. It's an underground power line—an overnight construction crew got sloppy trying to fix the water pipes to that church across the street and dug a little too deep. It's just a coincidence, Jack."

Through the window, Jack could see the construction crew outside the church and several ComEd trucks. He looked over at Cameron. Her eyes stayed with him as she listened to his end of the conversation. "Thanks. We'll meet you back at the VIP room."

"Where are you guys now?" Wilkins asked.

"In an office on the third floor. We should be down in just a few minutes." He hung up the phone and holstered his gun. "We're clear."

Cameron exhaled. "Okay. Good. That was definitely not on the agenda for tonight." She self-consciously smoothed her skirt and picked up her purse. "So we're going to rejoin the others, then?"

"Yes."

She headed toward the door and Jack followed her. She reached for the handle, then paused and looked over her shoulder. The sweater slipped off her shoulder once again.

"Thank you for—" She stopped. "What's wrong?"

Jack stood behind her, staring at that damn gray strap. He caught himself wondering what was softer, the silk or her skin. If he was a smart man, he wouldn't dare to even think about getting the answer to that.

He reached out to her anyway.

He took hold of her sweater and gently pulled it over her shoulder. He stopped when he reached the strap of her camisole. "This thing has been driving me crazy all night," he murmured.

Cameron's voice sounded a little shaky. "I . . . think I ruined it the last time I did laundry."

The air hung thick between them.

"We should go," Jack finally said. He needed to get out of that office before he did something he regretted. Something they both regretted.

She nodded, turned back, and unlocked the deadbolt. She grabbed the doorknob . . . then stopped.

Jack waited for her to open the door. When she didn't, he reached around her, placing his hand over hers. "Cameron, we have to get out of here," he said in a guttural voice.

"I know."

Still, neither of them moved. Jack took his hand off hers and moved it to the deadbolt.

He knew he shouldn't.

But he locked the door anyway.

He heard Cameron inhale unsteadily. Before he could give it a second thought, he brushed her long hair off her shoulder and bent his head to kiss her collarbone.

He got his answer. Silk didn't hold a fucking candle to her skin.

WITH A SOFT moan, Cameron sank against Jack's chest. She briefly wondered what she was doing, and why. Then she felt Jack's lips burn a path along her neck and decided to table those issues for a moment.

His hands moved to her hips and she didn't know if he spun her around or if she turned herself, maybe both, but suddenly she found herself facing him. She caught the hot glint in his eyes and reached for him just as his mouth came down on hers.

She expected Jack's kiss to be hard, angry even, but instead it was just . . . wicked. He took his time, tasting her with his mouth, his lips, and his tongue. When his hand moved to the small of her back and pressed her closer, Cameron dropped her purse to the floor and threaded her fingers through his thick hair.

They slammed against the door.

Jack's hand moved to her chin as his mouth explored hers roughly. Sensing his need for control but not yet willing to give it to him, Cameron cupped his face with her hands and slowed the kiss. Setting the pace, she teased him, biting gently at his bottom lip and sliding her tongue lightly along his. She did it again, playing with him, taking charge.

He growled low in his throat, then grabbed her hands and pinned them against the door.

Too late she recalled that Jack Pallas was not a man to be trifled with.

He wound his tongue around hers in a kiss that was rich and drugging. He settled between her thighs, and Cameron felt his hard, thick erection pressing into her. He could hide nearly every emotion behind that wall of his, but his body betrayed him right then, telling her the only thing she needed to know.

He wanted her.

Heady with that knowledge, Cameron closed her eyes as Jack blazed a trail with his mouth along her throat. The scruff of his jaw scratched against her neck, an erotic sensation that set every nerve of her body on fire.

"Jack," she whispered.

"Tell me," he said in her ear.

This was a new side of Jack. Gone was the guarded, controlled exterior. For once, she was seeing . . . him.

Cameron strained against him, helpless with her hands pinned in his. "Let me touch you." She needed to see—feel—more of him.

He pulled back and let his eyes roam over her, soaking

in every inch. He let go of her hands and watched as she pushed his blazer off. She slid her hands past his shoulder harness, feeling the taut muscles of his chest. She found it intoxicating, having such power and strength literally beneath her fingertips.

"This works both ways, baby," Jack said in a husky voice.

He took her mouth in a kiss so demanding it left her breathless. His hands worked impatiently as he unbuttoned her sweater and pushed it off her shoulders.

"I need to see you," he muttered against her mouth.

He pulled down the front of her camisole and the cup of her bra, and Cameron gasped as the cool air hit her exposed breast. He stroked her nipple between his fingers, toying with it until she trembled. When he cupped her breast and plumped it up for him, Cameron arched into his hand eagerly. Then he lowered his head and took her nipple into his mouth.

Liquid heat coiled between her legs so fast she nearly sank to the floor right there. Jack slowly drew his tongue over the tight peak, first being gentle while he licked, then taking the rosy tip into his mouth hungrily. Meanwhile, his hand slid underneath her shirt and his fingers began to caress her other breast.

Cameron felt exposed yet also incredibly sensual. And while a voice inside her head told her that she needed to stop, another voice, a devilish one, told her to give in for once, to *let go*.

Jack pulled her camisole lower, his mouth on the hunt for her other breast. Cameron moaned, knowing which voice had just gained the upper hand.

Then a loud knock on the other side of the door startled them. Both she and Jack jumped.

They heard Amy's voice. "Cameron? Are you in there?"

Cameron and Jack froze as the door handle turned at her hip.

Amy called through the door again. "Cameron? Are you all right?" She spoke to someone out in the hallway. "You said they were supposed to meet us back at the VIP room, right?"

Wilkins's voice. "That's what Jack said."

"Try him on his cell phone again."

Jack's cell phone began to vibrate from the blazer Cameron had thrown onto the floor. She peered up at him. Something passed between them . . . then slipped away.

They unwound and separated. Jack grabbed his blazer off the ground to answer his phone. As he told Wilkins that they were fine and would be out momentarily, Cameron grabbed her purse off the floor and moved away from the door, pulling up the front of her camisole and adjusting her bra. She walked over to the window, grateful for the darkness that covered the awkwardness of the situation.

She was belting her sweater when Jack spoke from across the room.

"The strap of your shirt is torn," he said softly.

"I know." She tucked the strap inside her shirt, hoping the other one would hold. If not, Amy and Wilkins were going to get quite an eyeful. Her lips felt bruised and swollen, not that there was much she could do about that. She moved to the door.

"You're ready?" Jack asked.

"Sure, I'm fine." Actually, that wasn't true, but with people waiting outside there wasn't time to analyze her emotions. She knew it was the perfect time for a quip or a joke, anything that would get her feeling like herself again and bring her and Jack back to familiar ground. But she couldn't do it right then. "We should get out there."

Jack seemed to hesitate at first. Then he switched over to all-business mode and opened the door. She passed by him to step out into the hallway and for a fleeting second their eyes met—the only recognition of what had happened between them.

Amy waited in the shadowy hallway with Wilkins. They both looked confused at first, then amused.

Cameron tried to play it casual as she walked over. "We were waiting to make sure everything was safe."

Amy pulled her to the side. "I was worried when the two of you didn't show up downstairs."

"I know. I'm sorry."

Amy looked her over. "That's a new way of wearing that shirt."

Cameron glanced down and saw her exposed shoulder. Now missing one gray silk camisole strap.

She was going to burn the stupid sweater as soon as she got home.

Sixteen

CAMERON HEARD THE knock on her door and looked up from her computer. Rob Merrocko, an assistant U.S. attorney with the office next to hers, opened the door and poked his head in.

"How'd the arraignment go today?"

"He pled not guilty, as expected," Cameron said. "That'll change. A jury would convict this guy in all of about two seconds." The defendant, a youth soccer coach from one of the northern suburbs, had been charged with receiving child pornography on his computer. If his lawyer had an ounce of sense in him, he'd never let the case go to trial.

It was an ugly case, and one of the few she found difficult to keep a cool head about. Just being in the same courtroom as the defendant had left her feeling disgusted and emotionally drained.

"Why do you still take these kinds of cases?" Rob asked her. "Pawn it off on one of the new guys."

Not really her style of doing things, but Cameron managed a smile, appreciating the sympathy. "I'll be all right." She ran her hands through her hair tiredly and eased back in her chair. "How are things on your end?"

"I just indicted an alderman for bribery."

"Nice," Cameron said approvingly. "Let's talk about that instead."

For the next few minutes, they swapped caseload horror stories, gossiped about a particularly ill-tempered judge in their district, and discussed which law clerk they should assign the ignominious task of cleaning the trial prep room. They were interrupted by a call from Cameron's secretary.

"Collin's here to see you," she said when Cameron answered. No last name was necessary; in the last four years, her secretary had become familiar with Collin's frequent visits.

"Thanks, send him back." She nodded at Rob, who waved good-bye on his way out. About twenty seconds later, he was replaced by Collin.

"You sounded terrible on the phone," he said from the doorway, referring to the quick conversation they'd had about an hour ago. "I'm here to kidnap you."

"I had a tough day in court." Cameron checked her watch. "It's four o'clock. I can't leave work now. It would be . . . indecent."

Collin laughed. "You're running yourself ragged these days between work, Amy's bachelorette party, and that other business we can't talk about here. You need a break. Come on, counselor—I'll treat you to a flight at 404 Wine Bar."

It was tempting. Cameron eyed him knowingly. "You just finished a column, didn't you?" She could always tell.

"Is it so wrong to want to spend quality time with my best friend when she's had a rough day?" Collin asked innocently. "As for whether I also happened to be particularly insightful and witty while writing today, well, you'll just have to see for yourself in tomorrow's paper. It'll be the big column about sports stuff under my picture."

Cameron threw him a wry grin—very funny. Yet despite the pile of work she had stacked on her desk, and also despite the fact that she sensed that Collin was in another one of his god-among-men insufferable moods, she thought that a drink with her best friend didn't sound like too bad of an idea right then.

So for the first time in her four years as a prosecutor, she shocked everyone in the office, including herself, by leaving early.

OFFICER HARPER ENTERED the kitchen, having finished his check of the second and third floors of Cameron's house.

"We're all clear." He looked at his partner, Officer Regan, who had checked the main level. "You good?"

Regan nodded. "We're good."

Cameron followed them to the door and locked it behind them.

"So what do they do now?" Collin asked. He'd taken a seat at the counter while the cops had done their walk-through.

"They'll follow us to the bar and wait outside until the night shift shows up."

"Why do I get the feeling that things are more interesting when Jack Pallas is around?" Collin teased.

"Things with Jack have gotten a little . . . complicated lately," Cameron said.

"Complicated" was certainly one way to describe it. On Saturday night, after she and Jack had rejoined Wilkins, Amy, and the rest of the bachelorette party, they'd barely said two words to each other—the two words on her part being "thank you" after he and Wilkins made sure the house was secure when they dropped her and Amy off, and the two words on his part being "you're welcome." She hadn't heard from nor seen Jack since.

Which was just fine with her. Really. Over the last five days she'd had time to sort through her emotions. Sure, she and Jack had done Those Things She'd Never Admit in a random office in a nightclub, but she'd decided this was all simply part of that post-traumatic stress she'd been fighting off lately. She'd been on some crazed high after the excitement of the power outage, had gotten riled up, and Jack just happened to be there. With his mouth on her breasts.

Tell me.

Let me touch you.

Cameron felt a little flushed every time she thought back to that evening. Apparently, there was one level on which she and Jack had no problem communicating openly.

She filled Collin in on the events of Saturday night, leaving out the most racy parts. Which was odd, because normally she told Collin everything. But some of the things between her and Jack felt . . . private.

"Sounds like I missed quite a party," Collin said when she'd finished. "So where do you and Jack go from here?"

"Nowhere," Cameron said with emphasis. Hadn't he been paying attention to the post-traumatic stress part? She'd mentioned that point at least six times. "Saturday night was nothing. A fluke."

Collin threw her a skeptical look. "Babe, I hope you're at least fooling yourself with that."

Nope, not really. "All right. So I'm physically attracted to Jack," Cameron conceded. It was a big step for her to admit even that much out loud. "Who wouldn't be? You've seen him."

"Rugged hotness, sex in a shoulder harness—yep, I'm familiar."

"Right. But I can conquer a physical attraction. I mean, he told thirty million people I had my head up my ass. What kind of self-respecting woman would I be if I fell for a guy like that?"

"It would be somewhat ironic," Collin agreed.

"Plus, he doesn't even like me," Cameron added.

Collin cocked his head. "Is that what you're worried about?"

"No, I'm not worried. I just think, given our history, that it would be foolish of me to think that Saturday night was about anything other than a mere physical attraction on Jack's part." Cameron paused. "So it's a good thing he and I are on the same page with that."

Collin seemed to be amused by her assessment of the situation. "I think you need a few drinks to help you sort this out."

Cameron waved this off. "I don't need to do any sorting." She gestured to her outfit. "But I do need to change out of this suit before we head to the bar."

"I'll head up with you," Collin said, sliding off the stool and leaving the kitchen with her. "I want to check the guest bedroom. I'm missing my Sox sweatshirt, and I thought maybe I left it here one of the times I stayed over. Either that, or Richard snagged it when he moved out."

Cameron followed Collin up the stairs. "Have you talked to him since then?"

"Not once. I thought I'd get a phone call, or at the very least an e-mail. But apparently he thin—"

Neither of them saw the attack coming.

A dark figure lunged at them when they reached the second floor, a mere blur that moved blindingly fast. With Collin in front of her, Cameron never saw where the man came from. He struck Collin across the head with something in his hand, and Collin moaned and sank to the floor. Cameron screamed his name.

The man, dressed all in black, whirled around. He wore a ski mask that covered all of his face except for small openings at his eyes and mouth, and she noticed that he wore black gloves.

The object in his hand was a gun.

Pointed straight at her.

Cameron felt as though her legs were stuck in quicksand. She looked over to where Collin lay on the floor. He wasn't moving.

The man with the gun moved toward her.

Cameron took a step back, retreating slowly down the stairs. The man followed her.

"What do you want?" she asked, her voice barely more than a whisper.

As he took the next step, he lifted his gloved hand and pointed.

You.

Seventeen

JACK LEFT THE Triumph in an open spot near the end of the block and walked over to the unmarked police car parked in front of Cameron's house. He'd taken his time on the way over, soaking in the fifteen-minute drive along the lake. In about three weeks he'd have to put the motorcycle into storage for the winter and his cold-weather mode of transport, a Ford LTD Crown Victoria, while practical, didn't pack quite the same punch.

As Jack made his way over, Harper, the senior cop on the day shift, unrolled the driver's side window.

"She just got here a few minutes ago. She's with McCann."

Jack noted this information, not happy about the fact that Cameron wasn't alone. He'd called her office and had been surprised to learn from her secretary that she'd gone home early. At the time that had seemed fortuitous, since he preferred to talk to her in person, anyway, and her house would be more private.

He thanked the cops and headed toward the front gate.

For the past few days, he'd been avoiding this conversation. Mainly because of how surprised he was by his actions on Saturday night. He was not an impulsive man. Impulsive men in his line of work quickly found themselves dead. Or worse. He personally had survived the worst of it at the hand of Martino and knew the only way he had lived to tell was because he'd kept his wits through the pain and waited out those two excruciatingly long days for the right moment to strike.

What had happened with Cameron at Manor House had left him feeling unsettled. Off his game. He didn't often let his guard down around people. That made a man . . . vulnerable.

Somehow, she had gotten behind his defenses. And now, every instinct told him to stay as far away from her as possible, to harden himself against her even more than he had in the past. He would ride out the remainder of the Robards investigation, and then walk away without a second glance.

Except for one thing.

You saw what you wanted to see.

That slip-up of hers had been in the back of his mind, nagging him, ever since she'd first said it. Who knew what she meant by that? But if there was some other explanation for her being in Davis's office that morning—the day he'd been transferred by the DOJ—he wanted to know about it.

He *needed* to know.

So this time, he wasn't leaving until she talked. He would get the answers he wanted. Today.

Jack strode up the steps to her front door. He rang the doorbell and waited.

No response.

He tried again.

Still nothing.

Jack looked back at the undercover car parked on the street behind him.

In the passenger seat, Officer Regan rolled down the window and shrugged. "Maybe they're in back. McCann said something about having a drink while we were checking out the house. They're probably sitting on the deck or something."

Officer Harper stepped out of the car. "You want us to check it out with you?"

She probably was just sitting on the deck, having a drink.

But probably was not good enough.

Jack took the steps two at a time. "One of you guard the front and keep trying the doorbell. The other of you should go around the east side of the house." There was a gate that blocked access to the back of the house from that side, but it was still worth checking.

Drawing his gun, Jack went the opposite direction and cut around the side of the house. All the windows appeared undisturbed, and as he carefully peeked in each one, he saw nothing. Nor did he hear anything.

He moved cautiously around the house and into the backyard. Seeing that Cameron and Collin weren't there, he crept up the steps that led to the deck and pressed his back against the house. On his one side was the door, on the other a window. The door was nearly all glass except for a solid oak border. The window at least had curtains that would provide some cover. Being careful to remain as concealed as possible, he peeked through the window.

Nothing.

The kitchen and great room were empty.

She wouldn't leave without the police escort.

Jack tightened his grip on his gun. His eyes searched the house as he tried to stay out of view.

Then he saw it—something that made his pulse race.

On the other side of the kitchen, a large decorative mirror hung on the wall opposite the stairwell. He could see Cameron in the mirror—she was standing on the stairs.

A man wearing a black mask stood behind her, holding a gun to her head.

The front doorbell rang and the masked man looked in that direction, clearly using the gun to keep Cameron quiet.

From the east side of the house came a sudden clanging sound, and Jack ducked out of the window. The sound had come from the gate, and he silently cursed whichever of the two cops had been careless enough to make so much noise. He peeked back into the window.

Cameron and the masked man were gone.

Knowing they had to have gone up the stairs, Jack ran for the fire escape that led to the upstairs balcony, being careful to move stealthily enough so as to not make a sound. He reached the second floor and headed to the French doors outside the master bedroom. He reached out with one hand and quietly checked the handle of the door. Locked. Staying out of sight as much as possible, he looked through the glass.

He watched as Cameron entered the bedroom, the gunman right behind her. The man gripped her neck with one hand, pushing her, and held the gun to her head with the other.

"I never saw your face," Cameron was saying. "You don't have to do this."

Hearing the fear in her voice, a fury took hold of Jack. He raised his gun to take a shot through the window.

But the man must have seen the flash of movement. He looked over, saw Jack through the glass, and yanked Cameron in front of him, blowing the shot. Refusing to leave Cameron alone with the gunman one second longer,

Jack reared back and fired his gun twice at the glass French doors.

He dove through.

Jack burst into the bedroom, barely aware of the glass shattering all around him. He hit the ground on one knee, slid across the floor, and hurtled himself up with his gun aimed at the masked man—

—who had his arm wrapped around Cameron's neck. His own gun pointed at her head.

"Let her go," Jack growled.

The masked man tightened his grip around Cameron's neck. Using her as a shield, he backed out of the bedroom, into the hallway.

Jack followed, his gun trained on the man and ready to fire the moment he had a clean shot. "There are cops on every side of this house. You're trapped. Put down your weapon and release her." Without shifting his gaze, he did a quick assessment of the guy. Five feet eleven, roughly one hundred and seventy-five pounds. Cameron's physical description had been nearly spot-on. And through the slits of the mask, Jack gained one additional piece of information: the man had brown eyes.

The masked man paused at Jack's warning. Then he pressed the barrel of his gun harder against Cameron's temple, digging into her skin.

Jack got the message, loud and clear.

Back off.

He kept his eyes and gun on his target. "You shoot her and you lose your shield." He stole a glance at Cameron. Her face was white. She blinked, and tears ran down her face.

Jack forced himself not to show any emotion. But for the first time in his life, he felt real fear.

The masked man backed toward the stairs, and out of the corner of his eye, Jack saw Collin laying motionless in the hallway. The man dragged Cameron with him up the stairs, nearly choking her as he forced her to keep up with him. Jack followed, his mind running through the mental floor map he'd made of Cameron's house during his two security checks.

"If you want out of this house, you'll have to let her go," Jack warned. "You can't run with a hostage."

The man showed no reaction. At the third floor, the stairs ended in an open-air balcony with pitched ceilings and a skylight. To Jack's left was an office. To the right was a large, unfurnished room. Although he couldn't see it from his position, he knew there was a door on the north wall that led out onto the rooftop deck.

Without hesitating, the masked man pulled Cameron into the room on Jack's right. Jack followed, realizing that however long the man had been inside the house, waiting, it had been long enough to familiarize himself with the layout.

The man headed to the door that led outside. There was a moment's pause as he shifted his position, then, reaching around Cameron's neck, he pinned her against his body with his elbow and forearm. He pointed the gun upward, bracing the muzzle right underneath her chin. He reached his free hand behind him to unlock the door.

So precarious was Cameron's position at that moment, Jack couldn't contemplate taking a shot—one slip of the intruder's arm and it would all be over.

He needed to say something, anything to reach out to her. "Cameron—look at me."

"Jack," she whispered, her eyes holding his and pleading.

He heard a crash downstairs, the sound of wood splintering—a breaking door—just as the masked man pushed open the door to the deck and pulled Cameron outside. With two hands on his gun, Jack followed them across the rooftop. Behind them, the pitched walls of the house and the room they had exited blocked the view of the street, which meant it was impossible for Jack to see what was happening with the police officers below.

The man moved steadily and quickly to the far wall of the rooftop. He kept Cameron in front of him at all times, never giving Jack any opening. Without saying a word, he backed against the wall that overlooked the backyard. He glanced sideways, and Jack assumed he was searching for the fire escape one story below them.

Then he turned and looked at Jack.

Everything happened in an instant—the man suddenly took his gun off Cameron, pointed it at Jack, and pulled back the trigger.

"No!" Cameron shouted. She grabbed for the gun as it fired and the bullet splintered the wood of the deck mere inches from Jack's feet. Cameron faced the man as they struggled. Jack didn't have a shot with her between them, so he lunged for them instead.

The gun went off again and Cameron stumbled back.

"Cameron!" Jack yelled.

He caught her as she sank to the deck. He saw blood spreading over her blazer. While he held her, the man bolted and dove over the side of the roof, onto the fire escape.

"He's getting away," Cameron muttered with a stunned, pale look. "Just leave me."

Like hell he would.

Harper and Regan burst through the doorway with their guns drawn.

"He ran down the fire escape," Jack shouted as he eased Cameron down to get a better look at the gunshot wound.

The cops moved instantly toward the fire escape, then ducked for cover as shots rang out from below. There was a pause, presumably as the killer ran, and the cops took off in pursuit.

Jack focused on Cameron. He reached into his blazer for his cell phone and called for the paramedics and backup.

"Is Collin okay?" she asked when he hung up the phone.

"An ambulance is on the way. Everything's okay now." Jack pushed her blazer off. "Jesus, Cameron—what were you thinking?"

"I couldn't just let him shoot you."

"Wouldn't have been the first time for me." Jack saw that the blood was coming from her shoulder. Not wasting a moment, he yanked open the top two buttons of her shirt and pushed it aside to get a better look.

Cameron closed her eyes. "Tell me the truth—how bad is it?"

Jack hesitated.

She panicked. "Oh God—that bad?"

He decided it would be best to just lay it on the line. "So on a scale of one to ten of all the gunshot wounds I've seen, this is . . ."

Her eyes widened.

". . . about a point two."

She sat up. "A *point two*? I bled through my blazer. Don't tell me that's a measly point two."

"Admittedly, I've seen a lot of gunshot wounds, so my curve may be steeper than most," Jack said, blotting her shoulder with the blazer. "But the point is, you're going to be fine." His throat tightened—he'd seen a lot of things between the FBI and Army Special Forces, but he doubted he'd ever be able to forget the image of her stumbling back after the gun had gone off.

"Well, point two or not, it hurts. A lot."

"Good. Maybe now you'll think twice about getting yourself nearly killed by attacking a man with a gun."

"Gee, with that kind of thanks, I'm thinking that's the last time I take a bullet for you."

"You're damn right it is," Jack growled.

She managed a slight mischievous smile. "You were worried about me, Agent Pallas."

"From your tone, I'm guessing I don't need to be any longer."

They heard the sound of a siren as an ambulance pulled up at her house.

"You probably should go now—try to catch the guy," Cameron said.

Jack looked down at her, cradled in his arms. "I probably should," he said huskily.

He stayed right where he was.

Eighteen

THE STREET OUTSIDE Cameron's house was pure mayhem. There were squad cars, unmarked police and FBI cars, an ambulance, and cops and agents everywhere. Wilkins had arrived shortly after the paramedics with several FBI teams. Quickly thereafter, Detective Slonsky had shown up at the scene with his own men.

The paramedic who had bandaged Cameron's shoulder led her to the ambulance parked against the curb. The back doors were open and Collin sat inside, facing out toward the street. A second paramedic checked his eyes, looking for signs of a concussion.

The instant he spotted Cameron, Collin pushed the paramedic aside and vaulted out of the ambulance.

"Oh, thank God." He pulled her into his arms and held her tight. "They wouldn't let me see you—they said they were keeping you isolated until they were certain the guy was no longer in the area."

"Slonsky said the cops lost him in the alley."

Collin pulled back. His eyes fell on her bloody shirt. "When I heard you'd been shot, I nearly lost it."

"I'm okay," Cameron reassured him. "The paramedic said I might need a couple of stitches, but I was lucky. The bullet just grazed the top of my shoulder." She reached up and brushed Collin's hair aside, being careful to avoid the ugly bruise on his head. "How about you? How does your head feel?"

Collin touched the bump. "Terrible. But my pride hurts far worse. I'm so sorry, Cam. When I think about what could've happened . . . I should've protected you better."

She took his hands and squeezed them. "It turned out okay."

"Luckily the cavalry came when it did," Collin said.

Cameron doubted she'd ever be able to forget the sight of Jack bursting through the glass doors to rescue her. When they'd been on the rooftop deck, right before the paramedics had arrived, she'd noticed a cut above his cheekbone. And when he'd stood up to let the paramedics take over, she'd seen several more cuts on his hands. Visible reminders of the danger he'd put himself in. For her.

Detective Slonsky stood by one of the cop cars, talking to Officers Harper and Regan. When he saw Cameron standing by the ambulance, he headed over.

"We're finishing our check of the house now," he told her. "My guys will follow you over to the hospital and get your statement there."

"Like hell they will."

At the sound of Jack's voice, Cameron looked over and saw him cut through the front gate, followed by Wilkins. Jack strode over to Regan and Harper. "Which one of you checked her bedroom?"

Harper straightened up, as if bracing himself for the worst. "I did."

"Did you go inside her closet?"

"I took a look in there, yes."

Jack waited, the anger visible on his face.

"But, no . . . I didn't actually go inside the closet," Harper admitted.

Slonsky walked over. "What'd you guys find?" he asked Wilkins and Jack.

"Some of the dresses had been knocked off the rack behind the door," Wilkins answered.

"And there were two shoe imprints in the carpet. About a men's size eleven, I'd guess," Jack said. "Your men are off this case, Slonsky. And don't even think about giving me any crap about jurisdiction."

His eyes dared anyone to challenge him on this.

CAMERON SANK AGAINST the ambulance, needing a moment.

Collin's hand touched hers. "You okay?"

She nodded. "Just thinking." And trying not to throw up.

The killer had been hiding in her bedroom closet.

Oddly, more than anything else that had happened that afternoon, that left her feeling violated. And the thing she kept coming back to was this: she'd left work unexpectedly early that afternoon. She wasn't supposed to have been home at that time.

The cops and FBI had examined the doors and windows of her house and found no visible signs of his entry, which meant the killer knew how to pick a lock without leaving evidence behind. During the entire attack, he'd been terrifyingly cold and in control and had never spoken once. Bottom line: he was not an amateur. He knew what he was doing.

But Cameron would've thought that a professional would break into her house at night. Four in the afternoon was a much riskier time—people walked their dogs, picked up their kids from school, and started to come home from work.

Which meant the killer knew that she was being watched. He was aware that his only opportunity to get inside the house was while she was at work. Once she returned home, she was under constant police surveillance.

Cameron thought back to the moment she'd first seen the man coming down the stairs for her. The creepy black mask and gloves, the gun he'd pressed against her temple and under her chin. The sound of the gun going off. She'd have nightmares for weeks, of that she had no doubt. And now the thought that he had been watching her, that he knew her daily routine . . . well, she liked to think she was a strong woman, but this was almost too much.

Almost, she emphasized to herself. She might have nightmares for weeks, but she would not let this asshole, whoever the hell he was, turn her into a helpless wreck. And if he did, well, she would just have to find a way not to show it.

After finishing what looked like a pretty heated discussion with Slonsky, Jack approached her. "I'm going to ride with you in the ambulance. Wilkins will follow in his car. We'll get statements from you both at the hospital."

"At least mine will be short, seeing how I slept on the floor through the whole thing. How clever and brave of me," Collin said, his voice tinged with disgust. He climbed into the ambulance.

"I spoke to Davis," Jack said to Cameron. "After we're finished at the hospital, he wants to see you, me, and Wilkins in his office." His gaze fell to her shoulder. "I heard you might need stitches."

He looked so serious right then.

"Oh no—not again," Cameron said. "If you keep up this whole nice routine, there's a good chance I'll lose it right here. And personally, I was hoping to postpone all freak-outs over the attack until later, in the privacy of my own home."

Jack studied her for a moment. "You are something else, Cameron Lynde."

He held out his hand to help her into the ambulance.

Nineteen

CAMERON AND WILKINS waited in the chairs outside Davis's office. It was nearly 9:00 P.M., and the FBI agents stared at her curiously as they trickled out of the office after putting in long days.

Davis had asked to speak with Jack first. Alone. Wilkins stood up and paced the room, and Cameron could tell he did not like being left on the sidelines. Frankly, neither did she. With a feigned yawn, she leaned her head back against the glass window of Davis's office. The curtain was drawn, so she couldn't see anything, but if perchance she happened to overhear a word or two . . .

"I already tried that," Wilkins said. "They're speaking too quietly."

"What do you think they're talking about?"

"You."

"Well, I know *me*, but what about me specifically?"

Wilkins glanced at the door. "I don't know."

Cameron picked her head off the glass. "Do you think Jack in is trouble?"

Wilkins answered after a pause. "I should be in there."

The door suddenly flew open and Davis stepped out. He nodded at Wilkins, then gestured to Cameron. "Ms. Lynde, if you would please join us in my office."

She followed Wilkins inside. Jack was perched against a table in the corner of the room. His face was unreadable.

Cameron took a seat in front of Davis's desk, in the chair closer to Jack. Wilkins sat on her other side. Davis folded his hands as he sat down. Like the other time she'd been in his office, three years ago, he wore a serious expression.

"Ms. Lynde, as the special agent in charge of this office, I would like to give you my most sincere apologies. For what it's worth, I've put a call into the CPD superintendent. I plan to see that the officers who had been handling your surveillance this afternoon are disciplined appropriately. I'm furious about what happened. I promise you that it will not happen again."

"Thank you. Luckily Agent Pallas was there. He deserves to be commended for his actions today. I can't imagine what might've happened if he hadn't shown up when he did," Cameron said.

"Jack and I have spoken. I agree with him that the FBI needs to take over your protective surveillance. In light of today's attack, we're going to assign an agent who will be with you at all times. He'll move into your house, follow you to work, go everywhere you go. I've asked Jack, as the lead investigator in this case, to take on this assignment. He has agreed."

Cameron was careful not to show any reaction to this. Out of the corner of her eyes, she could see Jack. His expression remained neutral as well. It was weird, sitting next to him in Davis's office, pretending as though everything was business as usual despite what had happened between them on Saturday night.

"I'm afraid this is going to be a much more intrusive level of protective surveillance," Davis continued, "but unfortunately, we don't have much choice in the matter."

"Trust me—no one wants to make sure we don't have a repeat of today's incident more than I do," Cameron said. "In this case, I'm happy to be inconvenienced."

"With Jack handling the surveillance, we'll need someone else to manage the day-to-day responsibilities of the investigation." Davis turned to Wilkins. "Sam—Jack has recommended that you replace him in this capacity. He assures me that you're ready for the responsibility."

Uncharacteristically speechless, Wilkins paused before addressing his boss. "I appreciate the confidence that Jack—and you—have in me, sir. But Jack and I are partners, and I would like to stick with him on this assignment."

Davis chuckled. "Oh, don't worry—you're not getting rid of him that easily. You'll still be partners, but with different responsibilities. Jack will remain with Ms. Lynde, and you'll lead the team here in our office."

Wilkins grinned. "In that case, I wholeheartedly accept."

"I thought you might," Davis said. "Now—we need to start thinking about what happened today. How the hell did Mandy Robards's killer find out about Cameron? On the FBI side of things, there are the three of us, and the director, who are aware of her involvement in the investigation. Wilkins—I think the first thing you need to do is come up with a list of everyone in the Chicago Police Department who knows. Today's attack tells us one thing: we've got a leak. But we might be able to use that to our advantage. Once we find the leak, we can use him to get to the killer."

"Be careful how you handle CPD on this," Jack warned Wilkins. "These cops are not going to like the implication that one of them may have leaked confidential information either purposefully or inadvertently. So tread lightly."

"Don't worry—finessing is my forte," Wilkins said. "And we need to think beyond CPD. Twenty women at the bachelorette party on Saturday saw that Cameron was under my and Jack's surveillance. Any one of them could've spread that information to the wrong person."

"I can get you their names, but I doubt any of those girls are the leak," Cameron said. "None of them had any clue why you and Jack were watching me."

Jack addressed Cameron. "What about your friends and family? Have you told them anything?"

"Collin and Amy know a little, but nothing specific. And they know to keep quiet. I haven't talked to anyone else about it."

Davis rocked back in his chair. "So we've got CPD to focus on, and, as an outside chance, the women who were with Cameron on Saturday night. By the way, Jack, I don't recall seeing anything in your last report about you and Agent Wilkins attending a bachelorette party over the weekend. Strange how that got left out."

"It was a last-minute determination made based upon the security parameters of the nightclub Ms. Lynde planned to attend."

"Nice answer," Davis said.

"No kidding," Wilkins agreed, looking impressed.

"As long as we're listing everyone who is aware of my involvement in the Robards's investigation, I should mention that Silas knows. He found out through Godfrey," Cameron said, referring to the FBI director. "Apparently, he called Silas last week to thank me for my cooperation in the investigation."

Davis paused at the mention of Silas's name. "Do you think it's possible Silas told someone about your involvement in the case?"

"As the U.S. attorney, he certainly should know better," Cameron said.

"I would hope so," Davis agreed.

The conversation turned to the subject of Jack and Wilkins's recent trip to New York. As Cameron listened while Jack filled in Davis, her eyes couldn't help but be drawn to the cut above his cheek. In the emergency room, after she'd gotten five stitches for her "point two"–level gunshot wound, the doctor had offered to have a nurse take care of the scrapes on Jack's cheek and hands. He'd waved this off, not budging from Cameron's side.

So much had transpired between them over the last few days—first The Thing That Never Happened on her front doorstep, and then Those Things She'd Never Admit on Saturday night. Cameron had no idea what was going on with her and Jack lately, but as she looked at the cut on his face, she did know one thing.

She trusted him.

And since he now would be the one covering her twenty-four/seven, she knew that trust had to go both ways. Which meant she needed to tell him about everything that had happened three years ago.

Tonight.

WHEN GRANT LET himself into his apartment that night, he paused in the doorway, bracing himself to be shoved up against the wall and handcuffed.

It didn't happen.

He exhaled, finding comfort in the fact that, at a minimum, Pallas hadn't yet identified him as the masked man. How long that fact would remain undiscovered, however, was less certain.

To say that the afternoon had not gone as planned would be an understatement.

Grant crept through his apartment with the lights off, checking the view from every window. From his third-story perch, he looked down onto the street below for anything remotely suspicious—strange cars parked out front, a dog walker who just "happened" to be out at that time of night, a homeless person conveniently passed out in the alley behind his building.

He saw nothing.

For the second time in the two weeks since Mandy Robards had tried to blackmail him, he was furious. And now paranoid, too. Not a good combination.

Cameron Lynde wasn't supposed to have come home from work so early. She also wasn't supposed to have brought a friend home with her—not that he'd had any trouble getting *him* out of the picture.

He could've handled the police officers in the car out front. He had not, however, been ready for a standoff with Jack Pallas. The rage he'd seen in the federal agent's eyes as he burst through the glass door was not something he'd expected. Nor had he been expecting the woman—who'd been relatively well-behaved up until that point—to try grabbing the gun out of his hand.

He'd been lucky, he knew, to have escaped when everything had gone so far awry from his plans. Thankfully, however, he didn't need to count on luck in the future.

Satisfied that his apartment wasn't under surveillance, Grant headed back to his bedroom and undressed. As he'd done a hundred times already that evening, he ran through the events of the attack and after, looking for the areas where he was most vulnerable.

No one had seen his face. Nor had anyone heard his voice, since he hadn't so much as coughed during the entire attack. No prints left behind, thanks to the gloves. His getaway had been clean enough—he'd had to outrun those two worthless cops, one of whom had seen leaner days and the other of whom looked barely old enough to drive a squad car. Chicago's finest. He'd lost them in an alley three blocks from the woman's house and then high-tailed it a half mile in the opposite direction to the parking lot where he'd stashed his car. He'd swooped up the backpack he had left in a garbage bin along the way. By the time he got to the parking lot he'd shed the mask, the gloves, and the jacket, and was simply a man wearing black nylon pants and a long sleeve T-shirt while carrying his gym bag after a late-afternoon workout. Once he'd gotten back to his car and driven off, he'd pulled into another alley a couple miles away and changed into the suit he'd left in the car. The backpack, with the remainder of the black clothes and with the addition of a couple heavy bricks, was now sitting on the bottom of the Chicago River.

Grant walked naked into his bathroom and turned on the water to the shower. He studied himself in the mirror as steam filled the air.

There was one weakness.

He had no alibi. He wasn't supposed to have needed one.

Sure, as soon as he'd dumped the backpack in the river he'd driven straight to his evening appointment—he'd met an old friend who worked at the *Tribune* at a bar in River West. Word had gotten out that a high-priced call girl had been murdered in one of the city's most luxurious hotels and the unconfirmed rumor was that Senator Hodges's name had shown up on her client list. The friend, who owed Grant several favors for all the times he'd given him early access to many of the senator's political dealings, called to give him a heads-up and had asked to meet for drinks. Grant had been curious to know whether the senator's name was being tossed around as a potential suspect, and how much his friend knew about the FBI's investigation. As it turned out, his friend knew very little, and Grant got the feeling *he* was the one being pumped for information.

After drinks, he had returned to the senator's offices and attended a series of meetings with the higher-level staff members and two of Hodges's attorneys. The senator originally had planned to be back in D.C. by the following week, but given the FBI's warning that he not leave the state, alternate plans needed to be discussed. First and foremost on everyone's mind was how to explain the changes to the senator's schedule without tipping the press off about his connection to Mandy Robards's murder.

Secretly, Grant got a kick out of these conversations. The hushed tones, the tension-filled rooms, the worried glances over what the press and—gasp—even the *killer* might possibly know about the senator's involvement with Mandy. They had absolutely no idea that the man they were talking about was sitting right at that table.

And he knew everything.

After the meetings finally ended, Grant had driven home, taking a few detours along the way to make sure nobody was following him. All in all, his day would seem like any other to anyone who might ask—except for that one missing hour. He'd have to come up with something to fill the void, just to be ready.

Grant thought back to the moment inside Cameron Lynde's house when she'd first seen him on the stairs— the way she'd taken a step back and whispered, *What do you want?*

He wanted to stop looking over his fucking shoulder when he walked into his apartment, that's what he wanted.

She said she didn't know who he was. Although he liked to think people tended to tell the truth when feeling the cold steel of a gun barrel pressed against their heads, he wasn't sure he trusted her. Fortunately, he didn't have to.

For her sake, he hoped she was telling the truth. Mandy's murder had been near perfect, almost artfully so. The best FBI agent in the city had been assigned the case, and still they had nothing on him. And they wouldn't ever have anything on him as long as Cameron Lynde didn't step out of line.

Of course, he'd taken precautions to know if she did.

They were so stupid. Pallas, the cops, all of them. It was right under their noses, and they didn't even realize it.

If he'd known it was this much fun getting away with murder, he'd have done it years ago.

Twenty

SHE AND JACK would be living together.

The practical realities of the situation struck Cameron during the car ride to Jack's South Loop apartment. He had asked Wilkins to drop them off so he could pick up his car and "a few things." As they pulled away from the FBI building, he leaned over the seat and asked if she had any questions about how the protective custody was going to work.

She nonchalantly answered that there were none she could think of off the top of her head.

This was not true.

She had lots of questions. For starters, where exactly did Jack plan to sleep? Could she still go to work during the day? Did he expect her to cook meals while he stayed at her house? (Certainly the surest way to kill them both.) Would they do normal, everyday things together, like watch television at night? (Which reminded her—she really needed to delete those episodes of *The Bachelor* from her TiVo playlist.) And where, exactly, did he plan to sleep? (This particular question consumed such a vastly greater percentage of her musings, it bore repeating.) Was he allowed to leave her alone at all, like when he took a shower? Or, purely from a safety perspective, would it be better for her to join him in such undertakings . . .

"This will only take a few minutes," Jack said as they rode the elevator to his fourth-floor loft. He looked her over. "Are you okay? You looked like you zoned out for a moment there."

"I'm still processing everything that happened today," Cameron said, hoping she didn't spontaneously combust right there in the elevator at the thought of him naked in her shower.

When they arrived at the fourth floor, Jack led her to the apartment at the end of the hallway. He unlocked and opened the door, inviting her inside.

She didn't know what she expected Casa Pallas to look like, perhaps something stark and Spartan with minimal furnishings and lots of gray, but that was not what she found when she walked through the doorway. The walls were exposed brick and the ceiling was vaulted. In keeping with the loft style, the main level had an open floor plan, with the living room running into the modern kitchen and what appeared to be a powder room and a small office down the hall to her right. There was a second floor; a floating staircase led to a small balcony. Beyond that were open double doors made of frosted glass through which she could see the master bedroom.

To say the least, the place was warmer and far more welcoming than she had expected. But that wasn't what surprised her most. What really caught her attention were all the books.

An entire wall of Jack's living room was filled with books—hundreds of them—organized neatly on dark mahogany shelves. More books rested on the lower shelf of his coffee table.

"Wow," Cameron said, making her way over to the shelves. "You have some collection here." It looked like a mixture of everything, fiction and nonfiction, hardcover and paperback. "You must be quite a reader."

Jack shrugged. "It fills my spare time."

Cameron would have loved to own such a collection of books—one of her plans for her house was to convert part of the third floor into a library. Not that she got a chance to read as much as she would've liked; a lot of her free time was sucked up by Collin and Amy. Which made her wonder whether Jack had a Collin or Amy in his life. Or anyone, for that matter. He seemed awfully . . . solitary.

He pointed upstairs. "I'm going to grab my things. Do you want anything to drink?"

"No, I'm fine. Thank you."

As soon as he went upstairs, Cameron checked out the living room more thoroughly, looking for anything that would give her some insight into the mystery that was Jack Pallas. He had an impressive flat-screen television on the wall opposite the sable couch—of course he had a big TV; he may have been a mystery but he was still a *guy*—and from what she could tell from the books underneath the coffee table, he had an interest in black-and-white photography.

A couple of picture frames on the end table next to the couch caught her eye. Curious, Cameron headed over. One of the photos had been taken several years ago—Jack and three other guys at their graduation from West Point, all formally dressed in their uniforms of gray coats, gloves, white pants, and caps.

Cameron picked up the frame. In the photo, Jack wore a cocky, wide grin and had his arms slung over the shoulders of the guys next to him. It was his smile that struck her—so brash and open. Seemingly so different from the man she knew now.

She turned to the next picture frame. It held a black-and-white photograph of a woman in her late twenties who laughed as she pushed a little boy on a swing. The woman had dark eyes and straight, chin-length hair pulled back with a headband. She bore a striking resemblance to Jack.

"My sister and nephew," came his voice from behind her.

Cameron started and turned around. He stood before her with a duffel bag on the floor near his feet. No clue how long he'd been there.

She tried not to reveal how curious she was as she set the picture frame back down. "Do you see your sister and nephew a lot?"

"Not that much when I was in Nebraska. But hopefully more now." He swung the large duffel bag over his shoulder with one hand. "Ready?"

Cameron couldn't help herself as her eyes drifted over him, remembering the night at Manor House. The strong shoulders and arms that had braced her against the door, the lean hips and muscled thighs that had pressed heatedly against hers, the firm chest and stomach that she'd just begun to explore with her hands. And the intense look of desire in his eyes.

Now he'd be sleeping in the bedroom next to her.

Perhaps she'd be better off taking her chances with the murderer.

WHEN THEY GOT back to Cameron's house, Jack's first order of business was to make sure that the doors had been repaired per his orders—first the front lock, and then the French doors off the master bedroom balcony. As he'd instructed, the agency had sent over a maintenance crew to board the door and clean up the glass.

Cameron eyed their handiwork skeptically. "It definitely adds that certain 'vandalized' quality I was going for with my renovation."

"It's safe. We can worry about style later," Jack said.

The second thing he did was conduct a thorough check of the premises, with Cameron by his side until he was sure they were clear. This was no quick feat, given the size of the house.

"Did you used to be married?" he asked as he opened the closet in one of the guest bedrooms.

"No," she said, seeming surprised by the question.

Rules out the rich ex-husband idea, Jack thought.

Another mystery he would soon get to the bottom of.

Third on his list was to get settled in. He took the room closest to Cameron's—which luckily, unlike the other guest bedrooms, actually had furniture—and unpacked his bag. He shrugged out of his blazer and hung it in the closet. He put his spare gun on the nightstand, then opened one of the drawers of the dresser in the corner.

He discovered a man's sweatshirt inside.

Jack slammed the drawer shut and chose another.

He moved next onto the fourth item on the evening's agenda: taking care of Cameron.

She was doing a pretty good job with the tough criminal prosecutor routine, pretending to be fine with everything that had happened that afternoon. But he had seen the exhaustion that had set into her eyes in the car ride to her house, had heard the nervousness that belied the sarcasm in her voice as she'd commented on the boarded-up French doors, and had noticed the way she'd momentarily hesitated when she'd followed him up the stairs that led to the second floor, undoubtedly thinking back to the masked intruder's earlier attack.

He guessed she hadn't eaten in hours. That seemed as good a place as any to start. Pausing at her bedroom door to make sure everything sounded okay, Jack headed downstairs into the kitchen. He found her junk drawer and a well-worn menu from a Chinese restaurant a couple blocks away and figured that was a safe bet. He had no idea what she'd want to eat, so he ordered a bunch of things—screw it, he'd charge it to the Bureau. Besides, this way they'd have leftovers. From the looks of her refrigerator and freezer, she was an even worse cook than he was. Thank God for delivery, because a six-foot-two-inch man couldn't last more than an hour on those skimpy frozen meals. He'd been stranded in a jungle in Colombia for five nights with four other guys on his Special Forces team and still had seen larger rations than those things.

Next, he checked out the liquor cabinet in her dining room. From the looks of it, she liked wine and she liked it red, so he went with the safe bet and chose a cabernet. Whether she wanted to admit it or not, he knew she would need some help falling asleep that night. While listening to the sound of water running upstairs, he made his way around the kitchen and poured her a glass of wine. The doorbell rang a few minutes later, and, after a brief moment of confusion when Jack frisked the delivery guy, asked him for his I.D., and called the restaurant to confirm his status, they were set to go.

Jack set the bags of food on the counter, grabbed the wineglass, and headed upstairs. Cameron had left her bedroom door partially open, as he'd asked her to. He knocked.

"Come in," she said in quiet voice.

Jack pushed the door the rest of the way open. He found her standing in front of her closet and walked over. "I thought you might want a glass of wine to help you . . ." He trailed off as she turned around, stunned by what he saw.

There were tears in her eyes.

Of course, he realized. The closet where the killer had been hiding, waiting for her.

He set the wineglass on the floor and went to her. "Cameron . . . everything's okay now. You know that, right?"

She blinked, and a tear ran down her cheek.

It killed him.

Jack wrapped his arms around her, pulling her close. He whispered in her ear. "He's not getting near you again, baby, I promise. No one's laying a finger on you ever again."

She turned her cheek against his chest and peeked inside the closet. He could've sworn he heard a sniffle.

"It's such a beautiful dress," she finally said.

Jack took a look. A long, silky, deep-pink dress hung front-out in the closet. No clue why she was crying over it, but he figured it was best to simply nod and be supportive under the circumstances. Maybe the killer had wrinkled it or something.

"It's a very nice dress," he agreed.

Cameron pointed at a pair of silver high-heeled shoes on the closet floor. She'd positioned them directly underneath the dress, as if an invisible woman was wearing them. "And the shoes . . ." She peered up at him, all weepy-eyed. "They would've gone so perfectly with it, don't you think?"

Yeah . . . maybe he should just skip past dinner and put her straight to bed instead. Somebody was clearly a bit out of sorts.

He cleared his throat. Frankly, this was the kind of thing Wilkins was better at. "And now. . . you don't want to wear the shoes again because . . . the killer might have touched them?" Hell, he was a guy, what did he know? Maybe shoes were as sacrosanct as purses and bachelor-ette parties.

Cameron pulled back and gave him the strangest look. "What? Oh, come on, give me a little credit, Jack. It's a *bridesmaid's* dress. I'm upset because I was supposed to wear it to my friend Amy's wedding. It's this weekend, in Michigan. With all the chaos today, I completely forgot about it." She sighed. "You're going to tell me I can't go, aren't you?"

Jack thought this over. "Where in Michigan?"

"At a hotel in Traverse City. Amy used to vacation there with her family when she was a kid. She's planned this wedding for years—it means a lot to her." Cameron forced a smile. "Looks like Collin's going to have to step in as maid of honor after all. He's going to be so pissed."

Jack saw right through the smile. It was impossible not to notice how close she was with her friends.

Traverse City was a good couple hundred miles from their Detroit office, but he could probably get Davis to call in a few favors. Everybody owed Davis favors.

"I can get you to the wedding," he said.

"Really? You think it will be safe?"

"Assuming we can send a few agents over from the Detroit office as backup, yes. Actually, this works out well. This is a big house—a lot of space to be watching over you. I planned to have a security system installed—silent alarm, motion detectors, the works. Now one of our tech teams can put that in over the weekend, and when you and I get back from the wedding we'll be good to go."

She exhaled, seemingly both surprised and relieved. "Great. Okay. That, uh . . . was easier than I thought."

Jack cocked his head. Wait a second . . . He couldn't decide if he was pissed or really impressed. He hooked a finger into the waistband of the workout pants she'd changed into and pulled her closer. "Did you fake me out with those tears, Cameron?"

She peered up at him defiantly, seemingly outraged by

the suggestion. "Are you kidding? What, after the day I've had, I'm not entitled to a few tears? Sheesh."

Jack waited.

"This wedding is very important to me—I can't believe you're even doubting me. Honestly, Jack, the tears were real."

He waited some more. She would talk eventually. They always did.

Cameron shifted under the weight of his stare. "Okay, fine. *Some* of the tears were real." She looked him over, annoyed. "You are really good at that."

He grinned. "I know." He picked the wineglass off the floor and handed it to her. She followed him down the stairs and saw the bags of food on the counter.

"Why don't you take a seat while I set everything up," Jack said. "I wouldn't want you to tire yourself out in your emotionally fragile condition."

She watched as he took the white cartons out of the bags and set them on the counter in front of her. She looked up when he stopped.

"That's . . . pretty much it with the setup," Jack said.

Cameron laughed. "Wow—you sure pull out all the stops for a girl." She grabbed some chopsticks and the carton nearest her, not looking particularly bothered by the lack of presentation.

At first, they discussed the Robards investigation as they ate. Then as they began cleaning up, Cameron steered the conversation toward the three years he'd spent in Nebraska—previously a taboo subject for them. Aware of the potential pitfalls of the conversation, Jack decided to tell her about one of his last assignments there—catching a bank robber the local media had named the "Butt Bandit" because of the perp's fondness for leaving Vaseline imprints of his nether regions on the windows next to the ATMs he robbed at night.

Cameron tried not to laugh as she threw away the empty cartons. She failed miserably. "Sorry. I'm sure it was a very important case. How did you catch the guy?" She started laughing again. "Did you have the suspects drop their pants and do a lineup?"

"Ha, ha," Jack said, reaching around her to throw away the rest of the garbage. "No, we caught the guy because he got Vaseline on his hands while smearing it on his ass during one of the jobs. He left some fingerprints behind and we found a match—he'd been in jail before for robbing a convenience store."

"I wish I could've seen you making that arrest," Cameron said, leaning against the counter and taking a sip of her wine.

"It was the highlight of my career," Jack said dryly, putting the leftovers she'd dished into Tupperware in the refrigerator. He shut the door and saw her watching him with a sudden serious expression.

"What's wrong?" he asked.

"I have something to tell you," she said. "About what happened three years ago. . . . I'm not the one who had you transferred to Nebraska."

Jack ran his hand over his mouth as this sank in.

"Talk."

Twenty-one

JACK PACED THE room while she talked.

Cameron began first with the Martino case, thinking she might as well start at the beginning. She told him about Silas's decision not to prosecute, and his directive that she not speak to the FBI, or anyone, about his decision.

"I was new to the office back then—I didn't want to rock the boat," she said. "Things would be a lot different if he and I had that conversation now."

Then she told him everything else: Silas's attempts to get him fired, her contact at the DOJ, her meeting with Davis to fill him in on the situation, even her response to Davis when he'd asked why she wanted to help out Jack.

"Your transfer to Nebraska wasn't a great result, I realize, but it was better than being dismissed from service entirely," she said. "It was the best I could do under the circumstances."

When she'd finished, Jack said nothing. A moment passed and . . .

He still said nothing.

Then he fixed his gaze on her and stalked across the room.

Cameron braced herself. With that kind of look in his eyes, he was either going to kill her or—

He kissed her. Hot, demanding sweeps of his tongue against hers. When he dragged his mouth away they were both out of breath.

"Why didn't you tell me this three years ago, before I left?" he asked.

"You told thirty million people I had my head up my ass. Funny how that turns a girl off from having any meaningful conversation."

He smiled. "True. So where does that leave us now?"

As if she had a clue. "I guess we should probably talk about the rules of our situation here. You living in this house. With me."

Jack pulled back. "Right. Boundaries. Good idea." He ran his hand through his hair and stood against the counter next to her. He exhaled raggedly and looked over. "I think the first thing we need to talk about is you not running around in tight T-shirts and yoga pants."

"Fine. I'll stop doing that as soon as you shave."

Jack ran his hand along his jaw and grinned. "You like the scruff, huh?"

Did she ever.

His jaw tightened. "I warned you about looking at me like that."

Cameron could see both the heat in his eyes and his internal struggle.

Screw it.

She crossed the space between them and kissed him. As if dispensing with the preliminaries—which was just fine with her—he grabbed her bottom and lifted her up. Not breaking their kiss, she wrapped her legs around his waist as he carried her out of the kitchen and up the stairs.

"This is probably a bad idea," Cameron said as she ran her hands over his muscled arms and shoulders, marveling at the ease with which he carried her.

Jack bit her lower lip daringly. "So stop me. Tell me I shouldn't get involved with you while you're my witness."

Cameron tangled her fingers through his thick dark hair. "That does sound complicated."

At the top of the stairs, he pushed her back against the wall and kissed her neck. "Tell me I should slow down," he murmured against the base of her throat.

Cameron closed her eyes and nearly moaned. "You probably should." She shifted as she straddled him, settling the hard bulge in his jeans right between her thighs.

Jack sucked in his breath and carried her into the bedroom. "Tell me this is just some sort of hero-complex with you, because I saved your life today."

"I suppose that's entirely possible."

He laid her on top of the bed and crawled over her. His voice was husky. "Just tell me you don't want this, Cameron."

She ran a finger over the cut above his cheek. "Sorry. But that I won't say."

Jack kissed her, and something snapped in both of them. Cameron reached for his shoulder harness, having no clue how to get the damn thing off. Jack's hands roamed everywhere. He grabbed the bottom of her T-shirt, ready to yank it over her head.

"Just watch the stitches," Cameron mumbled against his mouth.

"*Fuck*," Jack hissed and suddenly rolled off her.

"No—where are you going?" If it was anywhere other than to grab a condom, they were going to have some serious words. And lots of them were going to be profane.

"You were *shot* today," he said between ragged breaths.

"It's okay," Cameron said, reaching for him. "It's just a point two, remember?"

Jack grabbed her hands and pinned her down on the bed. She looked on approvingly. "Now that's more like it."

"Christ, Cameron. I just found out that I've been a huge asshole for the last three years. Don't make me be the asshole tonight, too. Let's at least get this part right. You're hurt, you're emotional—I don't want to take advantage of that."

She glared up at him. "What a lousy time for you to start being nice again. I thought we talked about that."

"Trust me—this isn't any easier on me." Jack climbed off the bed. "You need to rest tonight, anyway. And if I don't leave now, rest is the last thing you'll be getting." He held out his hand and helped her up.

Cameron got off the bed and followed him to the door. He hung in the doorway for a moment, watching her. His hair was rumpled, and his eyes were a warm chocolate color. Bedroom eyes, except she hadn't gotten the damn bedroom part.

She rested against the doorframe, close to him. "You know, in the morning I'll probably be grateful you were a gentleman tonight."

"But now?"

"Right now my feelings toward you are a lot less pleasant."

Jack smiled. "I'm used to that by now." He turned and headed down the hallway to the guest bedroom. He paused before going in. "By the way, there's a man's sweatshirt in my dresser."

"White Sox?" Cameron asked.

"Yes."

"It's Collin's. He must've left it here one of the times he spent the night."

"Are you sure you two are just friends?" he asked suspiciously.

Cameron laughed at this. "Yes."

"And are you sure he's gay?"

"Definitely."

Jack nodded, seeming satisfied. "Good night, Cameron."

That was the last she saw of him that night.

JACK CHANGED INTO running pants and a T-shirt, leaving the gun strapped to his calf. He paused at his doorway, listening to the sounds coming down the hall of Cameron getting ready for bed. He unhurriedly went through his own routine, then checked his BlackBerry for any emails from the office. When he finished with that, he propped a couple pillows against the headboard and lay down, tucking his hands behind his head. He thought about cracking open the book he'd brought, but wasn't exactly in a relaxed frame of mind.

He waited thirty minutes from the time he heard the noises stop, just to be safe.

He got up and walked down the hall. He entered Cameron's bedroom quietly, pausing just inside the doorway to listen to the soft, steady sounds of her breathing. Satisfied she was sleeping, he moved to the corner of the room and took a seat on the floor next to the boarded-up doors that led out to the balcony and fire escape. He rested his head against the wall.

He sat there in the darkness and watched.

He knew that sleep would eventually overtake him—he'd certainly slept in more uncomfortable places—but it would be a light, dreamless sleep. He would be ready in an instant, if necessary.

God help the man who tried to get past him.

Twenty-two

CAMERON WOKE UP disoriented the next morning. It took her a moment to shake off her bad dreams, to reassure herself that they were, in fact, just dreams.

She sat up, listening for any sounds in the quiet house. She heard nothing, but then again she never heard Jack unless he wanted her to. For a split second she wondered whether she should be worried about him, then realized (a) he was Jack, and (b) if anything had happened to him, she wouldn't be sitting in her bed wondering anything, seeing how she'd be *dead* and all.

Feeling strange still being in bed, knowing he was awake somewhere in her house, Cameron got up and padded into the bathroom. She brushed her teeth and turned on the shower, letting the water warm up as she undressed. Her injured shoulder yelled out tiny screams of protest as she stretched her arm over her head to take off her T-shirt. She peeled back the bandage and checked in the mirror to make sure everything looked okay.

It was hardly a fun task, trying to shower and wash her hair while keeping her stitches as dry as possible. Per the doctor's orders, she was supposed to avoid getting them wet for the first twenty-four hours. She certainly could've used some help in the shower—an arrangement that would've been possible if a certain someone hadn't decided it was time to be all gentlemanly.

Much grumbling about Jack ensued.

After showering, she did a quick job with her makeup before heading downstairs. She left her hair to air-dry, figuring it wasn't worth bothering with since she'd likely just have to do it again before Amy's rehearsal dinner. She walked into the kitchen and found Jack seated at the counter, working.

He glanced at her over his computer. "Good morning."

He looked again. Longer this time. She may have "forgotten" to put a bra on that morning. Another oops.

"Are you kidding me with that?" he asked.

"Deal with it. I had a really fun time getting all the conditioner out of my hair, buddy."

Jack chewed on this for a moment. "Nope. No clue what that means."

Figured. She noticed there was a freshly brewed pot of coffee waiting for her. She sighed. Impossible man—he made it more and more difficult for her to stay cranky with him. She used to be so *good* at that.

She grabbed her Michigan mug out of the cabinet and poured herself a cup. She took a sip of the deliciously hot beverage and slowly began to feel human again. "You look busy."

"Got a full day ahead of us," Jack said.

With his short-sleeve gray T-shirt, jeans, and damp hair, he looked casually gorgeous and far too alert. Cameron figured he must've slept well enough in the guest bed.

Jack frowned at his computer. "You have a weak Internet signal."

Cameron came around the counter and took the seat next to him. "I've never had a problem with it before." As she glanced at his computer, she caught sight of the scar on his forearm—in short sleeves it was hard to miss: jagged, ugly, and several inches long. She knew from reading the files on Jack's capture that there was a scar on the other side of his arm as well, where the knife had come out the other side.

She said nothing about the scar, not wanting to make Jack uncomfortable.

"Not pretty, is it?"

Cameron silently chastised herself for being so unsubtle. Then again, Jack caught everything. "I can't imagine how much that must've hurt." She looked up and saw him watching her.

"A bit more than a point two." He switched the subject. "So we've got about a five-hour drive ahead of us today. That means we'll want to get on the road no later than eleven in order to get you there in time for the rehearsal."

"I need to call Collin," Cameron said, suddenly remembering. "After Richard bailed on him, we decided to drive together."

"I've already talked to Collin—he called earlier this morning to see how you were doing. He's going to take his own car."

"You answered my phone?"

Jack seemed to find the question amusing. "Is that a problem?"

"You just seem to be on a roll, taking charge with everything this morning."

"Perhaps we need to set the record straight, then. No matter what happened last night—"

"Oh, but nothing happened last night, remember?"

"—when it comes to your safety, this works like any other protective surveillance situation. Which means that I'm in charge, this entire weekend and for however long it takes until we catch this guy." Considering that settled, he picked a pink Post-it pad off the counter. "Now—I spoke to your friend Amy about the wedding."

Cameron glanced at the clock on the oven. "You talked to Amy, too? It's only eight thirty."

"I got the number off your cell phone. I needed to ask her to email me the guest list. The FBI team meeting us at the hotel will set up a security checkpoint at the wedding. Only people on the list will be able to get in."

"I bet Amy was thrilled about that."

"Actually she was—she said it would make the wedding seem 'ultra-exclusive.'" He rifled through the Post-it notes. "She had a few messages that she asked me to pass along to you, word-for-word. First, she says not to forget the special maid of honor jewelry she gave you, because you know how much time she put into shopping for it and how important it is that you stand out from the other bridesmaids. Second, she asked that you remove all references to college drinking stories from the rough draft of the wedding toast you sent over last week. Third, she said that you shouldn't interpret her first two messages about the jewelry and the toast as a sign that she wasn't really, really worried about everything that happened to you last night, and how touched she is that you're still coming to the wedding. Finally, she asked if you wouldn't mind pretending that I'm your date for the weekend, because she doesn't want the other wedding guests thinking that the FBI is protecting you because you're some Mafia mistress-turned-snitch."

Jack set the notepad down. "I told her we were okay with that last part."

The part where they pretend to be a couple. "So we're a 'we' now?"

He grinned. "At least this weekend we are, sweetie. Shouldn't be too hard of a cover to pull off, considering we'll be staying in the same hotel room."

Oh boy.

THEIR FIVE-HOUR car ride passed quickly.

Things had changed for Jack, ever since he'd found out the truth about what had happened three years ago. Because of that he asked a lot of questions, wanting to learn more about Cameron. He also asked a lot of questions because he needed to keep his mind off how incredible she looked with her snug-fitting jeans tucked into knee-high brown suede riding boots and ivory V-neck sweater. The outfit was a definite driving hazard—at the first lull in the conversation he'd started thinking about her naked wearing nothing but the boots and riding *him* and had nearly driven the car onto the highway median.

Around the halfway point of the drive, they finally got around to a subject Jack was very curious about. He'd been trying to figure out a way to subtly back into the conversation, when she beat him to it.

"Why did you ask if I used to be married?"

Jack chose his words carefully. "Your house seems big for one person. I thought maybe someone used to live there with you."

She stretched her legs out in front of her, getting more comfortable. Jack kept his eyes on the road and not on the naughty boots. Mostly.

"You're dying to know how I afford it, aren't you?" Cameron asked, amused.

"Given that I accused you of accepting bribes the last time we talked about finances, you've certainly earned the right to tell me it's none of my business. But if you are inclined to share that particular information, I would be happy to listen."

Cameron laughed. "You could be a lawyer, with an answer like that. It's nothing scandalous. I inherited it. My grandmother lived in the house for years—it was the house my dad grew up in, in fact. My dad was an only child, so when my grandmother died, the house would've gone to him. But he died before her, and since my parents had gotten divorced years before that, the house went to me, as my father's only child. I thought about selling it at first, but it didn't feel right. My grandmother's death was somewhat unexpected . . . she just sort of gave up after my father was killed. After losing her and my father back-to-back like that, I couldn't stomach the thought of giving up the house. I think they'd both be happy that I kept it."

Jack glanced over, trying to decide if they were at a point in their relationship where he could ask the next obvious question. Given everything that had happened over the last twenty-four hours, he thought they were. "How did your father die?"

Cameron paused, and at first he thought she wasn't going to answer. "He was a cop here in Chicago. Four years ago he was killed in the line of duty. He and his partner responded to a domestic disturbance call at an apartment building—another tenant had called to complain. No one answered the door, but they could hear a woman yelling inside, so my father and his partner got the landlord and had him unlock the door. Once they got inside, they found drugs everywhere and realized it wasn't a domestic disturbance, but a doped-out woman screaming that the dealers were trying to cheat her. As soon as the dealers—there were two of them sitting at the kitchen table—saw my dad and his partner, they started shooting. My dad's partner was hit in the leg, and the landlord took a bullet in the shoulder. My dad followed one of the perps into the bedroom where a third guy was trying to escape through the window. He panicked and shot my dad in the chest and stomach."

Jack could only imagine how much pain that must've caused her. "Fuck, Cameron . . . I'm sorry." He did the math in his head and quickly put things together. "Four years ago. That's when you joined the U.S. attorney's office."

"I wish I could tell you that the first thing I did as a prosecutor was put away the scumbag who killed my dad. Not that I ever would've been allowed to try that case."

"Did they catch the guy?"

She nodded. "He pled guilty to manslaughter in state court. It was quick, uneventful. Very . . . unsatisfying."

"But now you put other scumbags away for a living."

"That part is more satisfying."

They drove in silence for a moment. "You amaze me, Cameron."

That got a slight smile out of her. "High praise, coming from someone who knows how to kill people with paper clips and everything."

Jack looked over in surprise. "You know about the paper clips?" He stroked his chin. "Hmm. Now *that* was good. Even for me."

Cameron stared at him, stupefied.

He laughed. "I'm just kidding." Mostly. Staples maybe, but never paper clips. "Speaking of your job—and mine—there's something else I wanted to talk to you about, something that came up in the meeting in Davis's office. You mentioned that Silas knows about your connection to the Robards case."

"Davis seemed interested in that, too."

"I keep thinking about how Silas told you to back off the Martino case three years ago. It was one thing when I thought you, the prosecutor who had reviewed all the investigation files, made the decision that there wasn't enough evidence to try the case. But now that I know Silas pressured you into not filing charges, the whole thing leaves a bad taste in my mouth. I don't trust him."

Cameron thought about this. Jack could see she was running through the possibilities in her head.

"We need to be very careful here," she said. "Silas is the U.S. attorney. We can't start making accusations against him merely because of bad feelings. You know better than anyone how vindictive he can be."

"It's just something I want you to think about. You need to be careful around Silas. And the fact that I'll be going to work with you on Monday is perfect—it'll give me a chance to keep an eye on the son of a bitch. If he so much as looks at you the wrong way, I might have to try out that paper clip idea of yours."

Cameron turned her head in his direction. "That was very ominous of you."

"Now that I know he's the one who screwed me over three years ago, my feelings toward him, to use your words, are a lot less pleasant."

"I hope you can control yourself around him, for both our sakes."

Jack took his eyes off the road and looked her over. "In all my years with the army and the FBI, there's only been one person I've ever had any problems controlling myself around."

She smiled at that, but said nothing. She reclined in the seat, crossing one naughty-booted leg over the other, in his direction. Jack fought hard against the images of her straddling him that assaulted his mind.

"You do realize you're driving on the shoulder, don't you?"

"Thanks for pointing that out, Cameron."

Twenty-three

PER JACK'S ORDERS, they entered the Grand Traverse Resort through a back entrance and were immediately escorted to the manager's office. Cameron had never stayed at the resort before but quickly saw why Amy had been so impressed by it: with luxurious décor, over six hundred rooms, gorgeous beach and fairway views, and a full-service spa, the property was indeed grand in every sense of the word. Even Jack, who'd said he would move her to a different hotel if he wasn't one hundred percent comfortable with the security aspects of the resort, seemed to find it acceptable.

"It'll do," he said in response to her silent question as they walked through the white marble and cherrywood hallway.

Jack had spoken to the manager on the phone and had explained the situation in general terms, revealing no details. In the office, he requested a map of the hotel grounds, which he kept, and emphasized one basic point: no one

outside the three of them was to know the location of
Cameron's room. He asked for a private conference room
where he could meet with the hotel's head of security, one
that he and the two agents coming in from Detroit would
also use as a working space throughout the weekend.

Then he asked the manager whether the wedding guests
had been assigned a particular block of rooms.

"Yes, the bride reserved a block in the hotel itself," the
manager said. "The wedding guests will all be staying here."

"Perfect. Delete Cameron's reservation, and book us a
new room under the name David Warner. Put us in the
Tower," Jack said, referring to the seventeen-story building located adjacent to the hotel.

"David Warner?" Cameron asked after the manager left
to get their room keys.

"An old alias of mine," Jack said.

"Ooh . . . an alias. Who does that make me?"

"For this weekend, I suppose it makes you Mrs. David
Warner."

"Hmm. I'm not sure I'm the type to take my husband's
name. I'm on the fence about it."

"For the next two days, you can be the type."

"Boy, Mr. David Warner sure seems a little bossy."

The manager poked his head into the office. "Sorry—
I forgot to mention: the Tower accommodations are all
standard rooms, not suites. I'm guessing you would prefer
two queen beds instead of one king?"

Cameron and Jack looked at each other. Neither spoke.

The manager shifted in the doorway. "I could always
switch you back to the hotel, if you require larger accommodations."

Jack shook his head. "No. I want to be kept apart from
the rest of the wedding guests. And the high-rise is a safer
location. No balconies, no windows accessible from the
outside, only one way into the room."

"We'll take two queen beds," Cameron told the manager, thinking that was the safest thing to say.

He nodded. "Excellent." He took off again.

Twenty minutes later, as they began to get settled in, Cameron realized that the one-versus-two-beds decision really didn't matter. Bottom line: she and Jack were sharing a hotel room. And here she'd thought living together in a five thousand square foot house had seemed intimate.

She watched from the doorway as Jack checked out the closet and bathroom. When finished, he headed over. "So? Which bed will it be?"

"Excuse me?"

He laughed at her expression. "Which one do you want? I'll put your suitcase on it so you can unpack."

"Oh. I'll take the bed farther from the door."

"Good answer."

She watched as Jack lifted her suitcase onto the bed, then threw his duffel bag onto the one closer to the door. She suddenly felt . . . jittery. Up until now, every time she and Jack had gotten physical, it had been under crazy, impulsive circumstances. But staring at those two beds, she now found herself consciously thinking about all those things a single woman in her thirties tended to think about when sharing a hotel room with a man she was really attracted to, and who appeared to be really attracted to her, who she hadn't yet slept with.

Despite all her sass and bravado, she was falling for Jack. Just yesterday—God, was it really only yesterday?— she'd told Collin that all she and Jack had between them was a physical connection. True, she'd been lying to herself. And a *lot* had happened since then. But she'd never found herself wanting to be wrong about something as much as she did right then.

She trusted Jack with her life. The next question, she supposed, was whether she could trust him with her heart.

She watched as Jack threw some rolled-up socks into one of the drawers in his nightstand. He'd taken off his blazer, so his gun harness was exposed and he was looking extra Special Agent Danger–ish right then. But that single act—putting socks in a drawer—made him momentarily seem like any other guy.

"You okay?" he asked, seeing her still standing by the door.

She smiled. "Yeah, sure." She headed over and stood between the two beds, surveying the scene. "Makes me think of the Walls of Jericho."

"From . . . the Bible story?"

Cameron laughed. "No, *It Happened One Night.*"

"Still not following you there. What happened one night?"

"You know, the movie, *It Happened One Night.*" She saw him shake his head. "Really? You should check it out—it's a classic. Clark Gable and Claudette Colbert are on the run and they stop to spend the night at a motel. They're not married, but they have to pretend they are, so for propriety's sake Clark Gable strings a clothesline down the middle of the room and hangs a blanket over it. He calls it the 'Walls of Jericho.'"

Jack stretched out on the bed, tucking his hands behind his head. Of course, being a man, he was already done unpacking and she had barely begun. "So in the movie, after he builds the Walls of Jericho, what happens next?" he asked.

"Things get pret-ty steamy from there. Clark Gable asks Claudette Colbert if she's interested in learning how a man undresses. And then he takes his clothes off in front of her."

"Sounds like a chick-flick. I bet Wilkins has seen it ten times."

"And good for him. I think most men could learn a thing or two from so-called 'chick-flicks.'"

"Like what?"

"Like how women think. What turns them on."

"If I want to know what a woman's thinking, I'll just ask her." The corners of Jack's mouth lifted in a sly grin. "And if I want to know what turns her on, well, I'll just ask her that, too."

"Hmm." Cameron grumbled her way into the bathroom. Impossible man—being all reasonable and everything. She unpacked her toothpaste, toothbrush, shampoo, and conditioner. She set them off to the side on the marble vanity, as if to suggest they were the only four products she would need the entire weekend. Hey—he was a man, he didn't need to know there was a whole routine involved behind the curtain. And about fourteen other bottles in her suitcase.

When she came out of the bathroom, she saw Jack standing by the windows that spanned the length of the room. He gestured. "Come over here for a minute."

She went over. He surprised her by pulling her into his arms, her back against his chest so that she looked out the window with him. Their room overlooked vibrant autumn-colored rolling hills and orchards, and the East Grand Traverse Bay.

"I like this view," he said, his voice husky against her ear.

Cameron leaned her head against his chest—it was rare to have such a quiet moment with Jack in contrast to the chaos that had overshadowed their lives for the last couple of weeks. She pulled his arms tighter around her.

"Me, too."

FOR THE DINNER that followed the rehearsal, Amy had reserved the entire space at Aerie Lounge, which was located on the sixteenth floor of the Tower. A convenient short elevator ride from Cameron and Jack's room. Not so convenient for Cameron, however, was the fact that the cousins had cornered her by the floor-to-ceiling windows overlooking the bay, wanting to play Twenty Questions about Jack. Having recognized him from the bachelorette party, they'd been on her case ever since she'd walked into the rehearsal with him.

Cameron was relieved when she felt a hand at her elbow and heard a familiar voice to the left of her.

"Sorry to interrupt, ladies. I need to borrow Cameron for a few minutes."

"Please make it more than a few," she whispered as Collin led her to the opposite side of the room.

She kissed his cheek in an official hello. Since Amy had asked Collin to be a reader at the wedding, he had been at the rehearsal, too. But she'd been running around with various maid of honor tasks and hadn't gotten the chance to talk to him there.

"I meant to tell you at the rehearsal: you look very dashing tonight. Love the navy sport coat and tie," she said, gently tugging it.

"Richard gave it to me last Christmas," Collin said.

Cameron saw the hurt in his eyes and knew how rare it was for him to show that. "Are you doing okay?"

He nodded. "Just . . . working through some things. Gay man in his thirties, dateless, the fifth wheel at his friend's wedding. That kind of stuff." His eyes held hers. "And aside from all that, I miss him."

"Richard is a fool," Cameron said. "And you're not a fifth wheel. Technically, I only have a fake date to this wedding."

Collin scoffed at this. "Looking like that, that won't be the case for long." He checked out her caramel-colored cocktail dress and heels. Her shoulder had begun bothering her midway through straightening her hair, so she'd pulled it back in a chignon and focused on smoky-eyed makeup instead. "I'm surprised Pallas let you out of the room like that," he said. "At least without being a good hour late to the rehearsal."

"And risk Amy's wrath? No way—that woman scares even me," Jack said from behind them.

As Jack joined them, he momentarily rested his hand on the small of Cameron's back. She faced the party, so no one saw, but her body went warm just at the brief contact.

"I thought you could use a drink." He handed her a glass of red wine.

Cameron smiled—partially because she'd been meaning to make it over to the bar for twenty minutes before being cornered by the cousins, and partially because she couldn't get over how sexy Jack looked in his gray blazer and open-necked black shirt.

"Thank you," she said.

Jack leaned in, and for a second Cameron thought he was going to kiss her. "You didn't tell me this wedding was outside," he said quietly.

"I didn't think about it. From everything Amy's told me about the setup, I barely consider it an outdoor wedding. Will that be a problem?" The last thing she wanted to do was make his job even harder.

"I promised I'd get you to this wedding. I'll handle it." With his back to the other guests so none of them could see, Jack laced his fingers with hers and pulled her closer, speaking low enough so only she could hear. "Collin is right, you know. You're living very dangerously looking the way you do tonight, Cameron Lynde." He brushed his thumb over hers before leaving.

Cameron watched as Jack headed over to a bar table by the door where the two FBI agents from the Detroit office sat. She sipped her wine and took her time simply enjoying the view of him.

He'd brought her a drink and complimented the way she looked. This fake date of hers was starting to seem more real every minute.

She turned to Collin. "It means that I'm the stupidest person in the world, right? That I'm actually excited and happy despite having a psycho killer stalking me?"

Collin peered down at her. "I think you know what it means."

He clinked his glass to hers.

LATER THAT EVENING, Jack sat in bed, the pillow propped behind his back, while he talked on his cell phone. He'd called Wilkins to see if there had been any developments in the investigation, hoping that something had panned out with one of the Chicago cops his partner had spoken to. So far, unfortunately, none of them appeared to have leaked any information about Cameron's involvement in the case.

"How's it going on your end?" Wilkins asked. "You having any fun up there?"

Of course, Cameron chose that moment to poke her head out of the bathroom. "Hey—is there a trick to getting hot water in this place?"

"You have to let the faucet run for a good five minutes."

Jack turned back to his phone call.

"You're sharing a room with her, huh?" Wilkins asked.

Jack thought of how Cameron looked in that caramel-colored dress. He'd never seen her wear her hair like that before, nor that sultry thing she'd done with her eye makeup. She'd looked sophisticated yet incredibly beddable, and as a result, he'd been at half-mast all evening. Full-mast when he'd watched her eat the maraschino cherry from

Collin's drink. Thank God he'd been standing behind a table at the time.

He ended the conversation before Wilkins started asking those kinds of questions Wilkins liked to ask, questions Jack had no intention of answering. He was a private person to start with, and when it came to Cameron, even more so. He hung up the phone and rested his head against the headboard.

He knew what he had to do. It killed him, but he knew.

He grabbed his computer and tried to distract himself with work. He didn't have a whole heck of a lot of success with that, which was exactly the problem.

Cameron finished up in the bathroom and stepped out. The first thing Jack noticed was her outfit.

He frowned. "Don't you have anything less skimpy than that?"

Cameron glanced down at her sleeping attire, one of those velour tracksuit things. "I'm wearing pants, a T-shirt, and a zip-up hoodie."

Jack grunted his displeasure.

Cameron came around the side of her bed that was closer to his. "Somebody seems a little cranky."

Yes, somebody was. Because *somebody* was trying to do the right thing despite the fact that *somebody else* apparently wanted to torture him with—sweet Jesus she was bending over the bed right in front of him to adjust the pillows, and those velour pants stretched tight across her amazing ass that would fit perfectly in his hands as he licked—

"That's it, lights out. We have a big day ahead." Jack flicked off the lamp on the nightstand and the last thing he saw was Cameron's bewildered expression before the room went dark. He didn't care. If he so much as looked at her right then, he'd be done for.

"So I take it that means we're going to sleep now." Through the darkness, she sounded somewhat amused.

Jack debated over his next course of action. He got out of bed and went over to hers. His eyes had adjusted to the darkness and he could see her underneath the covers, outlined by the moonlight. He sat down on the bed next to her.

"I'm trying to stay focused here, Cameron. My first priority this weekend has to be to keep you safe."

"Of course—I was just teasing, Jack."

"I need to be extra vigilant tomorrow, especially now that I know the wedding is going to be outside. That changes the game—more than ever, I can't be distracted."

"I understand. Really, you don't have to say anything else."

In the moonlight, her eyes shimmered up at him like stones in a stream. Unable to resist, he reached out and touched her long, dark hair that fanned over the pillow. "I think I'll be glad when this wedding is over."

He could see her smile. "You and pretty much every person who's had contact with Amy over the last eight months."

"Good. I'm glad we're on the same page with this." Jack pulled the blanket up to her shoulders. "Now—no matter what happens next, keep these covers up. Think of it as the twenty-first century version of the Walls of Jericho."

She looked at him in confusion. "Okay . . ."

"Promise me, Cameron. No matter what happens."

"I promise. But why?"

"Because I'm going to kiss you good night." With that, he leaned forward and captured her mouth with his. She threaded her hand through his hair and kissed him back, meeting his tongue hungrily with hers. The next thing Jack knew, he was on the bed with her pinned beneath him.

Underneath the blanket, she spread her legs and he sank between them greedily. He was hard as a rock and throbbing being this close to her, and when she arched her hips against him, he nearly lost it.

"You're going to ruin me as an agent," he murmured huskily. "Once I get inside you, I'm not going to be able to think about anything else except doing it again and again." His hands went to the edge of the covers. Bullets hadn't stopped him, and this was a *blanket*. "I'll make it so fucking good for you. . . ." He kissed her neck, her throat, wanting to go lower, wanting to taste her everywhere.

Cameron exhaled unsteadily. "You are so not playing fair." But she didn't let go of the covers.

Jack buried his head in the pillow, struggling for that last shred of control. He lifted himself off the bed and grabbed his gun off the nightstand.

He handed it to her. "Take it."

Her eyes went wide, a mixture of surprise and amusement. "Okay. If I have to *shoot* you to keep you away from me, I think we should just throw in the towel and say screw it to the wedding."

"It's not for me. I want you to keep your eye on the door for the next five minutes. I'm going to take a cold shower."

Twenty-four

"WILL YOU JUST sleep with him already?"

Cameron looked around the salon. "Maybe you could say that just a little louder, Ame. I'm not sure everyone heard you over the hairdryers."

Thankfully, Jack was waiting up front, sparing her at least some embarrassment from her friend's comment. When they'd first arrived, he'd conducted a check of the entire spa and salon area, then had positioned himself by the door that was the only way in and out.

She and Amy sat next to each other, getting the finishing touches on their makeup. "There are a few things going on with us right now, you know," Cameron said pointedly. "Like that slightly sticky issue with me being attacked in my home by an armed intruder."

Amy immediately looked contrite. "You're right—that was a silly thing to say. You have a lot more important things to worry about than my wedding."

Cameron and Amy shared a look in the mirror.

"Wow. I even shocked myself with that one." Amy grinned. "Well, luckily, you'll be done having to put up with me in just a few hours. I bet you can't wait."

"Don't be crazy—there's no place I'd rather be this weekend than right here. Even if you have been a royal pain in the ass."

Amy laughed and wiped her eyes. "Stop, you're going to make me cry with all this mushy crap."

The makeup artist applying Amy's blush pointed sternly. "Don't touch your eyes. This is some of my best work."

The purple-haired, multi-tattooed and pierced cosmetologist doing Cameron's makeup chimed in with her orders. "Look at the ground."

Cameron obeyed, trying not to blink as the woman put a second coat of mascara on her lashes.

"That's waterproof, right?" she heard Amy ask her technician.

"Of course," he assured her.

"You can look up now," Purple Hair said when she had finished.

Cameron peered back up at Amy in the mirror. "Besides, I generally have this rule about not sleeping with a guy until he's taken me out on some kind of date."

"When he saves your life, I think you can bypass that part."

"He did have dinner delivered the other night, although I think the FBI picked up the tab. Do you think I can count that?"

Purple Hair stopped dusting blush over Cameron's cheeks. "Hold up. Are you talking about the dark-haired guy who came in with you? The one who searched me before I could do your makeup?"

Cameron grimaced. "Sorry about that."

"Don't be—it was the highlight of my month." Purple

Hair threw her a get-real stare. "That's the guy you're hold-ing out on? Sweetie, you need to grab that stallion and ride him like a cowgirl."

"I . . . don't really know you, but thanks for the advice."

Purple Hair winked. "Comes with the makeup. What do you think?"

Cameron checked herself out in the mirror. They'd left her hair down, with waves and a lot more volume than she could ever replicate on her own. And the makeup, which had felt like a lot going on, looked perfect and made her lips look fuller, her cheekbones more defined, and added a sparkle to her eyes. "It looks nice."

Amy snorted. "Nice? Give it a rest." She came up in the chair behind her, looking mismatched yet still elegant with her hair pulled back in an elaborate twist under her veil, and her jeans and white button-down shirt. She put her arms around Cameron. "You're lucky I love you so much, to let you look like that on my wedding day."

"You look gorgeous, Ame." No exaggerating there—minus the jeans and button-down shirt, Amy was the very picture of a blonde, fairy-tale beauty. "Aaron is going to be knocked off his feet when he sees you coming down the aisle."

"He better not be. That'll look terrible on the wedding video."

The two women shared a laugh, and Amy inhaled ex-citedly. "So? Want to help me get into my dress?"

Cameron nodded. "You bet."

"WHAT'S WITH AGENTS O'Donnell and Rawlings? Why couldn't we just bring Jack with us?" Cameron asked as she followed Amy outside. The two FBI agents walked a few paces behind them.

"Because I consider Jack a wedding guest, and *you* are

the only guest who gets the sneak preview. Besides, Jack needed a few minutes to get ready for the wedding."

Cameron stepped gingerly in her silver heels off the walkway and onto a white fabric runner. She followed Amy across the lawn to the enormous white domed tent that had been set up on a hill overlooking the bay.

Cameron took small, careful steps in her bridesmaid dress, although there probably wasn't much need to do so. The dress was fitted but had a slit on one side at her calf that made it easier to walk. Over the last eight months, the one part of Amy's pickiness that she didn't mind in the least had been her selection of the maid of honor dress— the same color and material as the bridesmaid dresses Melanie and Jolene were wearing, but different in style. Handpicked just for her, Amy had said. And when she'd said next that the dress was fuchsia, Cameron had nearly handed over her maid of honor badge right there.

Then she'd seen the dress Amy had chosen for her. Halter-style and pretty from the front, but that was nothing compared to the back.

Or, rather, the fact that there wasn't any back to the dress.

After that, Cameron had shut her mouth and vowed to never question Amy's judgment in anything bridal-related again.

"Are you sure you should be out here in your dress?" Cameron the Dutiful Maid of Honor asked Amy nervously. "What if you trip and get a grass stain on it or something?" Back when they'd gone dress shopping, she'd nearly choked at the price of the one Amy had chosen, a blush and ivory strapless taffeta Carolina Herrera with intricate ruffle detailing worthy of a nineteenth-century ball gown.

Amy shrugged. "Then I guess I'll just have to deal with it."

Cameron blinked. "Okay. Who are you and what have you done with my friend?"

Amy laughed as they came to the end of the runner. She waited as Agent Rawlings stepped into the tent to check things out. When he nodded, she grabbed Cameron's hand. "So when guests step inside the tent through this main entrance here"—she pulled Cameron inside—"they'll see this."

For a moment, Cameron was speechless.

It was breathtaking. There simply was no other way to describe it. They stood at the entrance of the tent, facing the altar. The fabric runner continued on, becoming a white center aisle across the grass that divided the silver and white Versailles chairs guests would sit on. Scattered across the runner were fuchsia and red rose petals and multihued leaves upon which Amy and the bridesmaids would walk. Along the aisle, all the way to the altar, were tall pillar candles that glowed softly. The altar itself was a site to behold, lit elegantly with additional white and silver candles and adorned with more red and fuschsia roses than Cameron had ever seen.

The most striking feature, however, was the thousands of tiny silver lights arranged in elegant tiers across the top of the tent. At night, she imagined, it would look just like a starlit sky.

Cameron stepped farther into the tent, taking it all in.

"And we'll have a harpist here at the entranceway, to play music as the guests take their seats," Amy was saying. "The ceremony is at six thirty, which will be right at sunset. Afterward, while we take our pictures and the guests have cocktails and appetizers back at that gazebo we passed, they'll set up the tables for the reception. The string quartet will be over there for the ceremony, which is where the band will go for the reception. They'll set up a dance floor over here . . . Oh, did I mention the heat lamps? See—hidden along the perimeter there? We had a hell of a time figuring out what to do with all the electric cords . . ."

Amy paused and looked anxiously at Cameron. "You haven't said anything. Do you think it's too much?"

Cameron shook her head. "No. You did it, Amy. It really is the most perfect wedding ever."

Amy smiled. "We used to come here every Labor Day weekend when I was a kid. I think I was nine years old the first time. I knew, even then, that this was the place I wanted to get married."

They both turned at the sound of a displeased voice coming up the path behind them.

"I told Amy she could have twenty minutes with you guys," Jack was saying to Agents O'Donnell and Rawlings, who stood attentively at the entrance to the tent. "It's been nearly twenty-five minutes and I—"

Cameron looked over her shoulder just as Jack stalked into the tent. He got his first glimpse of the back of her dress. Or lack thereof.

He stopped dead in his tracks.

"Wow."

His eyes lingered on her for another moment before he turned to Amy, gesturing. "This place looks great, Amy. You did one hell of a job."

Amy grinned. "Nice recovery, Jack."

Cameron walked over and touched Jack's face, unable to resist. "You shaved." She took in the classically handsome chiseled features he'd been hiding underneath the scruff, as well as how incredible he looked in his dark gray suit. It should've been illegal for a man to walk around like that without some sort of permit.

Jack grinned as she checked out his smooth jaw. "Don't worry—it'll be back in about two hours." He took his time looking her over. "You look stunning."

From behind them, Amy cleared her throat. "Not to break this up, but we have this wedding to get to . . . Cameron—you have your itinerary for tonight?"

"Yep. In my purse."

"Jack?"

He patted his blazer. "Got all six pages right here."

"As indicated on page two, I'll see you in the gazebo for bridal party pictures in five minutes." Amy pointed at Cameron. "Don't be late and make me regret choosing you for this position instead of Collin."

"Was he seriously in the running?" Cameron asked, slightly offended by this.

"Only briefly. But I figured his wedding toast would be filled with all sorts of lame sports references." Amy's expression was stern. "I'm expecting much better things from you." She left in a whirl of blush and ivory taffeta.

Jack nodded at Agents Rawlings and O'Donnell, who stepped outside for a moment, leaving them alone.

With a warm smile, he turned to Cameron and held out his hand. "So? Are you ready for this?"

She took his hand, lacing her fingers through his. "Definitely."

AMIDST THE CLAPPING and cheering, Jack escorted Cameron back to their table. He leaned in to congratulate her on a job well done when Collin raised his glass and beat him to it.

"Fantastic toast," Collin said enthusiastically. "A few laughs, a few tears—seriously, you smoked the best man."

Cameron shushed him as she took the seat between him and Jack, with a pointed glance in the direction of the other two couples at their table. Friends of the groom, she had whispered to Jack earlier—part of Amy's plan to encourage mixing and conversation amongst the various groups. He'd actually already known who they were, and who they were friends with, along with their full credit history and lack of priors, having texted their names to Wilkins for background checks as soon as they'd introduced themselves.

As Jack stood behind Cameron, helping her with her chair, he tried to focus on anything other than the bare satiny skin at his fingertips. It was quite artful, the way the dress covered her just so, right at the curve of her lower back. An inch lower and he might be able to see cheek . . .

He was going out of his damn mind.

"Aren't bridesmaids dresses supposed to be ugly?" he grumbled as he took the seat next to her.

"As if Amy would let any part of this wedding be ugly," Cameron said. Underneath the table, she rested her hand on his thigh and squeezed gently.

Jack sucked in his breath through gritted teeth. On the other side of her, however, Collin seemed wholly unfazed by Cameron's appearance. Jack kept one eye carefully trained on him, thinking things had better stay that way. Gay or not, best friend or not, no one with a dick was getting within a foot of Cameron while she wore that dress.

"My only criticism of the speech is that I didn't get as much airtime as I deserved," Collin complained.

Cameron brushed this off. "You got plenty of airtime. I talked about how the three of us lived together senior year, didn't I? I even mentioned how you used to make pancakes for me and Amy when we got home from the bars."

"We'd talk about the boys we'd met that night," Collin explained to Jack.

Jack was curious about this. Plus he needed something to keep his mind off Cameron in that dress. "How did the three of you meet?"

Cameron started to answer when Collin held up a hand,

cutting her off. "Ahem. Since no one asked *me* to give a toast at this wedding, I will handle this question. Besides, I tell this story better than you do."

Collin sat forward in his chair, lowering his voice dramatically. "It was a dark and stormy night."

Cameron rolled her eyes. "Oh boy."

Collin held up his hands. "What? It *was* a dark and stormy night. I should know—I walked you home that evening, remember?" He turned back to Jack. "It was our sophomore year. I was living in my fraternity house and had been having a rough time of things in college, struggling with the issue of whether I was gay. I was at Michigan on a baseball scholarship and homosexuality was not something one discussed casually within the athletic circles. Anyway, one night early in the year, my fraternity had an after-hours party and it was pouring outside. I was hanging out by the front door, drinking my usual—which back then was Jim Beam and Coke—when Cameron blew in, huddled under a red umbrella with Amy and another girl. They were all laughing, and when they closed the umbrella, Cameron stepped into the room and shook out her hair. It was like something out of a movie—she was the most beautiful girl I'd ever seen."

Jack toyed with his silverware. This story could go south very quickly . . . When his hand came to rest on his steak knife, this may or may not have been merely a coincidence.

"So I struck up a conversation with her and we hit it off right away," Collin continued. "We started meeting up after classes, on the weekends, and I knew that this was it: if it was ever going to work with a woman, she was the one. A couple weeks later, we were hanging out in my room on a Saturday night and I had it all planned out— that was the night I was going to make my move.

"We were sitting on my couch listening to the radio—it

was an eighties flashback night—and 'Bette Davis Eyes' came on. And Cameron sighed and rested her head against the back of the couch and said, 'I like this song.' "

Cameron cut in here. "Then you inched closer to me and turned your face to mine. And you said, 'I like this song, too.' "

"And I knew that was the moment," Collin said. "So I leaned over and kissed her."

Cameron took her hand off Jack's thigh and removed the steak knife that mysteriously had made its way into his grip. He threw her an innocent look. Like he would ever harm one precious hair on Collin's head . . . with witnesses around.

Nearing the climax of his story—for his sake, hopefully only in the literary sense—Collin continued. "The kiss went on for a bit, and I'm telling myself, 'Okay, maybe this is actually working.' So I pull back to see if she's into it, and she gazes up at me with sort of an amused expression and says . . ." He gestured to Cameron.

" 'I've licked stamps who were more excited than you by that kiss.' "

Jack burst out laughing.

Collin shook his head with a grin. "I know, right? Jack, I'm telling you—I was *crushed*. But only for a moment, because then she reached up and held my face between her hands and said, 'Collin—we're friends, right?' And I knew, even after only a few weeks, that this was a person who was going to be a very important part of my life. So I nodded yes, and she says, 'Good. Then listen to me: you need to get over yourself and just admit you're gay.' "

Collin looked at Cameron. "Hearing it said so matter-of-factly like that was liberating. So the next day, I decided to go to a very different type of after-hours party, on the other side of campus. And I kissed a guy for the first time."

"Patrick," Cameron said.

"You remember."

"Of course I remember."

Collin smiled. "And when I got home that night, she was the first person I called to tell about it."

Cameron covered his hand with hers. "You're right. You do tell that story better than me."

"I like it," said a voice from behind them. "I've never heard it before."

Jack instinctively rested his hand on the harness under his suit as the three of them watched a blond, athletically built man in a well-cut suit approach their table.

Collin, who appeared shocked, was the first to speak. "Richard."

Jack relaxed, recognizing the name. The ex-boyfriend who'd refused to come to the wedding.

"What are you doing here?" Collin asked him.

Richard's face momentarily filled with emotion at the sight of Collin, then he collected himself and checked out the reception. "So this is Michigan. Not bad."

There was an awkward pause as Collin remained silent. Richard shifted nervously.

Jack whispered in Cameron's ear. "Why don't we go dance?"

"I think that's a great idea," she said.

They said quick hellos to Richard before heading over to the dance floor to give them some space. Cameron glanced over her shoulder, and Jack's eyes followed hers and saw that Richard had taken the seat next to Collin and appeared to be doing most of the talking. Collin was at least listening, however, and at one point he rested his hand on the back of Richard's chair. Cameron smiled at the sight and turned back to Jack.

He led her toward the far corner of the dance floor, where he could be alone with her while keeping his eye on everyone else. Taking her hand in his, Jack pulled Cameron into his arms. He held her close with his other hand on her bare lower back as they began to dance. They fit perfectly together; in her high-heeled shoes, the top of her head came right to his chin.

"Thank you for this. For everything. I wouldn't have had this night if it wasn't for you," she said.

"I'm just sorry we couldn't be here under different circumstances."

"If there were different circumstances, you wouldn't be here at all." She shifted closer to him. "I'm glad you were the one who walked into my hotel room that night, Jack."

He smiled. "What a change—two weeks ago you hated pretty much everything about me walking into that room."

"That conversation would go a lot differently if we had it now. For starters . . . I don't think there'd be much actual conversation," she said in a throaty voice.

Jack's eyes bored into hers. "I'm at the edge, Cameron. Tread cautiously."

She shook her head, no. "I think it's time for us to leave this wedding."

"If we go now, there's no coming back. You're mine all night."

Her eyes flashed. "Promise?"

That was it.

Jack grabbed her hand and pulled her off the dance floor, toward the main entrance of the tent. He stopped before Agent Rawlings, who had been posted there all evening.

"We're heading back to the room," Jack said. "You and O'Donnell should keep watch over the Tower lobby—both the elevators and the emergency stairwell." He led Cameron out of the tent. The white runner went one direction, but he took her across the lawn toward the Tower. And their room.

Cameron threw him a look. "Nice. Rawlings probably knows exactly what we're going to do."

"Cameron, with the way you look tonight, every man at this wedding knows exactly what I plan to do with you."

"Wow, that may be the sexiest thing any man has ever— shit—I'm ruining my heels in this grass. I keep sinking in."

Without breaking stride, Jack lifted her into his arms and carried her.

"I could've just taken the shoes off," Cameron said with a smile.

"I'm not wasting time while you undo those damn straps."

He got her inside the Tower lobby, set her down, and led her into an elevator. He pushed the button for their floor. The minute the elevator doors shut, she reached for him. Jack caught her hands and spun her around, her back against his chest.

"Not yet, baby," he said huskily in her ear. "I need to get you into that room safely." He held her hands tightly, doubting he could take it if she so much as touched him. She pressed back and rubbed her just-out-of-sight ass teasingly against him.

Son of a bitch. Jack growled low in his throat. He thought about hitting the emergency stop button, pushing up her dress, and taking her right there in the elevator. And as much as he throbbed at the wanton image of her standing in her heels, bracing herself against the wall and moaning his name as he took her from behind, that was not the way things were going to happen for their first time together.

He bent his head and kissed the base of her throat, not trusting himself to get any closer to her mouth. He could feel her quick pulse underneath his lips. "Remember how I said I was in charge? That includes tonight, Cameron."

With a sly smile, she closed her eyes, tilting her neck to give him better access. "We'll see about that."

They would see, Jack agreed. The minute they got into that room.

The elevator sounded, indicating they had arrived at their floor. The doors sprang open and he smacked Cameron lightly on the ass to get her moving.

Twenty-five

AS THEY HURRIED through the hallway, Cameron's body tingled with anticipation. Jack had barely touched her, and she was already completely turned on.

He unlocked the door and let them into their room, tossing the key on the desk in the corner. As he did his usual check, Cameron noticed that housekeeping had turned down the beds and had left the lights on dim. She set her purse on the nightstand.

She turned to face him when he finished, thinking that if he didn't kiss her soon she might suffocate from all the sexual tension in the air.

She expected him to pounce and throw her onto the closest bed.

He didn't.

Jack folded his arms across his chest. "So I've been thinking about your Walls of Jericho. Actually not so much about the wall, but about the other part. Where I show you how a man undresses."

The temperature in the room rose so fast the glass on the television fogged.

Cameron exhaled. "All right. I'm watching."

First, Jack took off the jacket of his suit, exposing his gun harness. He quickly removed that as well and set it on the desk. His hands moved to his tie. He loosened the knot and pulled it off, and Cameron had to fight the urge to storm over and yank the rest of his clothes off him.

There was a glint in his eyes as he made no move to undress further. "Sorry, but this is the twenty-first century version."

"What happens in the twenty-first century version?"

"You lose the dress."

Well, then.

"There's not much underneath," she said. She'd had little choice with the way the dress was cut.

"I'm counting on that."

Cameron reached for the zipper that ran along one side and inched it down. Without dropping Jack's gaze, she then untied the halter around her neck. The dress fell in a pool at her feet. She faced him wearing nothing but her black silk thong panties.

And of course, her high heels.

Her nipples tightened in the cool air of the hotel room. Or maybe it was just Jack's look.

Lust clouded his eyes as he took in every inch of her, and she had never felt more sexy—and bold—than she did right then.

"Your turn," she said.

He undid the buttons on his shirt and peeled it off, revealing a tight white T-shirt that showed off his firm chest muscles.

Cameron was aching to get her hands on him. As if sensing this, he crossed the room. Her pulse skyrocketed as he approached, yet he still didn't touch her.

"Now you," he said.

She reached up and removed the antique-silver chande-
lier earrings Amy had picked for her, dropping them to the
floor beside the dress.

"That's cheating," Jack said.

"You have four times the clothing on that I do."

With one swift tug, he yanked his T-shirt over his head.
"Better?"

Hell . . . *yes*.

Cameron took her time, savoring the sight. The hard
muscles . . . the tight, six-pack abs . . . the light scattering
of dark hair on his chest. . . . She wanted to taste every
inch of him.

Then, briefly coming out of her daze, she noticed something else. Of course.

She had forgotten about the scars.

Three years ago she had read the files that contained a
very detailed report of the hell that Martino's men had put
Jack through during the two days they'd held him captive.
But she hadn't thought about the physical scars that kind
of hell would've left behind.

Her eyes took in the cigarette and electrical burns by
his right shoulder, moved to the knife wounds along his
side and under his ribs, then came to a stop on the quarter-
sized circular scar high on the left side of his chest—from
the bullet he had taken when making his escape.

Cameron raised her eyes to Jack's. He was watching
her carefully, to see her reaction.

She stepped forward and rested her hands on his chest.
She gently kissed the scars on his shoulder. She did the
same to the one on his chest, and after that bent down to
run her lips over the scars under his ribs and along his side.
Then, unable to help herself, she ran her tongue along the
soft trail of hair that started at his navel and disappeared
behind his belt buckle.

Jack pulled her up and stared into her eyes with a ferocity that would've scared her under any other circumstance. He guided her backward, and when she felt the edge of the bed against the back of her knees she needed no encouragement to lie down on top of it.

"You still have a lot more clothing on than I do," Cameron said, rising onto her elbows.

"I can fix that."

She watched as Jack undid his belt buckle, then the button on his pants. His eyes feasted on the sight of her lying on the bed before him as he unzipped his fly. She caught a brief glimpse of gray boxer-briefs just before he slid them off with his pants, socks, and shoes. Then he stood before her in all his glory.

She would never, ever compare him to a molten lava cake again. After seeing Jack's naked body, all other delicacies were henceforth ruined for her.

Of course, her eyes were drawn to *that* part of him, the part that was big and hard and raring to go. All for her.

Jack climbed onto the bed, and she lay back. His dark, fiery gaze made her shiver with anticipation, yet he still didn't touch her.

He nodded to her near-naked body. "You choose what's next."

Did he want her to beg? Because she was nearly at that point. "God, Jack . . . touch me . . ."

He smiled.

He was the devil.

"Choose," he repeated.

"I'll keep the shoes," Cameron said defiantly.

"I was hoping you'd say that." His hands moved to her hips and tugged her panties down her legs and over her shoes. Then his mouth started at her knee and slowly made the opposite journey, up her thigh, along her hip, her stomach, the V between her breasts, her neck, and swept down on her mouth. She moaned, finally able to kiss him. His arm slid under her back, and he pulled her up so that she was sitting on his legs, straddling his hips.

"You're so beautiful, Cameron," he said, running his finger along the side of her face. "Despite everything that happened, over the last three years there were so many times I would lay in bed at night, thinking about you."

"What did you think about?" she asked, sliding her hands up his chest.

"Doing this." He pulled her breast into his mouth. His tongue glided over the tip in a wet, silken caress, and he licked and sucked until she thought she'd go crazy. Then he moved to the other one, her nipple already hard and tight, begging for his touch. Gently cupping her breast, he drew the rosy peak into his mouth.

She started to rock on his lap, desperate for more. While his mouth continued its assault on her breasts, he slid his hands around her hips. One hand cupped her bottom while the other slid between their bodies. His fingers stroked their way to the core of her, opening the soft, wet folds. When he found the center, he teased her with his thumb, massaging back and forth until she was shaking. He slid a finger into her, and then another, and she gasped as his fingers slowly drew in and out, and again, finding a rhythm that nearly sent her over. She cupped his face and pulled him up, kissing him hotly.

As his tongue tangled with hers, she slid her hand down his chest, past his stomach and lower, where her fingers found him hard and throbbing. She wrapped her hand around the thick shaft, reveling in the sudden catch in his breath.

She began stroking him. "Did you think about this when you used to lay awake at night?" She ran her thumb over the engorged head in smooth circles.

He closed his eyes and groaned. "Fuck, yes . . ."

She slid her hand down to the base and cupped him as she whispered in his ear. "Did you think about me using my mouth, too?"

"Christ," Jack muttered, and before Cameron knew it she was on her back with him kneeling between her legs. He yanked off her shoes before she could protest.

"As hot as those pointy heels are, I've got enough scars on my body," he told her, his breath quick.

"I've got condoms in my nightstand," Cameron said, so ready she was practically panting.

"So do I. Many."

"Let's get one of them. Now."

Jack reached over and yanked the drawer open, nearly pulling it off the track. He quickly found what he was looking for, and the sound of a wrapper being ripped open was music to Cameron's ears.

"Let me put it on you," she said urgently.

"If you do, this might all be over before we get started."

The sight of him rolling on the condom got her even more worked up and she began arching her hips, needing him. "Jack . . ."

He moved over her. He grabbed her hands and pinned them over her head. "I'm right here," he soothed in her ear. She felt him between her legs, hot and hard and ready. He inched into her slowly, filling her.

"Spread your legs, baby—let me in," he urged. She did, and he moved deeper into her, then deeper still, and began a slow, tortuous rhythm. He held one of her hips with his free hand, gliding in and out as he pinned her to the bed. She took his achingly smooth thrusts again and again, and he brought her right to the edge, then backed away, holding her suspended there for what seemed like an eternity. She moaned his name, frantic to touch him, but he held her wrists against the bed. He slowed and withdrew from her nearly all the way, teasing her with shallow thrusts.

"Please, Jack . . ." she finally begged.

He let go of her hands, and when she looked up she saw that he was as close to losing it as she.

"Wrap your legs around my waist," he rasped.

She did, and he plunged all the way into her.

"Oh God, Cameron, you feel so good," he groaned.

She slid her hands up his back and tightened her legs around his hips, urging him deeper, needing him to fill her the way only he could. Her breasts crushed against his chest as he pounded into her, harder and faster, then he shifted his hips, hitting the spot that would drive her over. He slid his hands underneath her bottom, holding her against his thrusts.

He stroked her possessively. "I love being inside you, baby . . . For three years I've wanted to make you mine. Now I want to feel you come around me."

That was all it took. Cameron gripped his shoulders and cried out as she reached her peak and exploded, holding on to him as wave after wave of pleasure crashed over her. Jack pumped long and hard as the throes of her orgasm gripped him tightly, and he followed her over. She opened her eyes just in time to see the moment when he surrendered all control, her name a strained whisper on his lips as he shuddered and moaned and thrust deep one last time before crashing down on her.

They both lay there, trying to catch their breath. With his head buried in the pillow next to her, muffling his voice, Jack spoke first.

"Wow."

Cameron turned her head, pressing her cheek against his. "My thoughts exactly."

FOR ONCE, JACK was glad he had a hard time sleeping for more than a few hours at a time. He woke up, saw that it was still dark, and checked the clock on the nightstand. Not even 4:00 A.M.

Cameron lay on her side, curled against him. Both of them were naked. After their first round, she'd slipped on her underwear and his shirt, a look he'd found extremely sexy, especially when paired with her tousled hair. So sexy, in fact, that—well, he'd warned her what would happen if she wore those kinds of outfits around him . . .

He worried that he'd been rougher the second time around, although he held her mostly responsible for that, too. As if wearing his shirt and black silk panties hadn't been bad enough, after he'd stripped them off her she'd pushed him onto his back and used her mouth on him in what had to have been the single greatest torture he'd ever been subjected to. She had licked, stroked, and teased until he'd been so completely out of his mind that he'd flipped her over onto her knees and taken her that way, not stopping until she moaned and cried his name and collapsed onto the pillows.

He couldn't get enough of her.

It scared him a little, because he'd never before felt this way about anyone. Nearly thirty-five years old, he wasn't exactly innocent—he'd slept with his fair share of women, some he'd even met while working undercover. But all of his relationships had been casual—and he'd made that abundantly clear going into them. In the past, he'd always used his job as an excuse to avoid getting serious with anyone. Now he realized that with the right person, he wouldn't want an excuse.

Jack leaned in, whispering her name softly. He knew he was a greedy, selfish bastard to wake her up, but he loved the reassurance of their intimacy, what it said about their relationship without either of them actually having to say it. Not to mention, it had been a couple of hours and she was lying next to him naked. He could either sit there in the dark with a hard-on, or he could do something about it.

He said her name again, and she stirred. He rolled them both over and kissed her neck as they lay on their sides. His mouth wandered down the slope of her breasts, and he worked his tongue around one of her nipples.

Cameron woke up with a smile. "Hmm . . ." She ran her hands over him, sighing as she caressed his chest and stomach. Her hands dipped lower and found his achingly hard erection.

Her eyes opened mischievously. "We're there already?"

"It just seems to keep getting this way around you."

She slid one knee over his hip. "I like it this way."

Not needing any further encouragement, Jack reached back and got a condom from the nightstand. After he rolled it on, he grasped her hips and slowly sank into the warm, wet depths of her. He cupped her ass with one hand and rolled his hips back and forth in a smooth, unhurried rhythm.

When he heard her gasp, he paused. "Is it too much?"

She closed her eyes and moved her hips against him, urging him deeper. "It's perfect. Feel free to wake me every night like this."

Jack bent his head and kissed her.

He should be so lucky.

Twenty-six

AT BRUNCH THE following morning, Collin took a seat in the chair next to Cameron. Jack had left the table a moment ago to answer his cell phone.

"So," Collin said, getting comfortable.

Cameron set down her forkful of blueberry pancakes, ready to begin. "So."

Collin started things off with some not-so-subtle innuendo. "You look tired this morning," he said with a pointed look in the direction of Jack, who stood by the floor-to-ceiling windows while talking on his phone.

"You look pretty beat yourself," Cameron replied, nodding toward Richard, who had made his way over to Amy and Aaron's table to offer his congratulations.

"We were up all night, talking things through. That's it," Collin said.

"Oh. Well, I can't say the same thing."

"Alrighty then. About time. Let's hear it."

Cameron opened her mouth to answer—of course she'd

tell Collin about her night with Jack, she told Collin everything—then . . .

Nothing. She hesitated for a moment longer before shutting her mouth with merely a smile.

"That good, huh?" Collin said with a laugh.

Cameron blushed and waved this off. "Tell me how things went with Richard. Did you guys work things out?"

"There's some fine-tuning that still needs to be done, but I think we're going to try moving back in together."

Cameron was happy for him. If working things out with Richard was what Collin wanted, that's what she wanted, too. "So did you make him do some major groveling?"

"I didn't have to. He said plenty on his own—all I had to do was listen."

From their table, she and Collin watched as Richard shook Aaron's hand and hugged Amy. A few feet away, by the windows, Jack finished his call and made another, keeping one protective eye on Cameron at all times. He winked at her, and she smiled.

"You are so smitten," Collin said.

Two things happened then, in response to Collin's comment. First, Cameron realized just how right he was. Second, her thoughts turned strangely serious. Or, in light of current events, perhaps not so strangely.

As long as she was in danger with this investigation, Jack was, too. And everyone else close to her. Collin had already been hurt—what if something had happened at the wedding, to him again, or to Amy? She trusted Jack—and the FBI in general—to keep them all safe, but still. As long as Mandy Robards's killer was out there, she would always have a sense of dread hanging over her.

It was the FBI's investigation, and she would do whatever they told her to. But she'd been working an idea in the back of her mind, something that could possibly speed things along. For all their sakes.

Jack finished his call and came back to their table.

"How are the pancakes?" he asked as he took his seat.

"Delicious. How did your call go?"

"The security system at your house is set up and ready to go. Which makes me feel a lot better about being there." Jack grabbed his fork and stole a bite of pancake from her plate. "You're right. These are good."

His comments about the security system got Cameron thinking. "You know, having seen you in action this weekend, I'm surprised you felt comfortable being down the hallway from me that first night. While we've been here, you haven't let me out of your sight for more than a half hour." She caught the look on Jack's face. "What?"

"In the interest of full disclosure . . . I didn't let you out of my sight that night. I slept on your floor. Actually, more like against your wall." He mistook her silence. "I didn't say anything because I was trying not to scare you."

She shook her head. "No, I get it. I just . . . didn't realize you had done that for me."

Jack lowered his voice so Collin couldn't hear. "Don't look so serious. Trust me—you more than made up for it last night."

Cameron put on a smile, not wanting to ruin the mood. "Sorry. I'll just be glad when this investigation is over."

"It will be soon. I promise," Jack said.

She nodded in agreement.

Particularly if she had anything to say about it.

THEY GOT ON the road shortly after the brunch. Cameron wasn't eager to tempt fate—the entire weekend had been wonderful, and she wanted to keep it that way.

She had a lot of time to think during the drive home. She had some thoughts on a possible next step in the Robards investigation, but she didn't want to bring it up until they were back at her house. After Jack confirmed that the security system was working, and after they had settled in and unpacked from the wedding, she was hoping the two of them could sit down and talk through her idea. She had a feeling Jack wasn't going to be particularly receptive, at least not at first.

With the shorter fall days, it was just beginning to turn dark outside when Jack pulled the car into her garage. He told her to wait in the car while he checked to make sure the backyard was safe. Then he came back, grabbed their suitcases, deposited them at the back door, and escorted her to the house.

Coming out of her garage, Cameron noticed the new French doors on her upstairs balcony. "They look just like the old ones," she observed.

"I had our security team put them in over the weekend. We needed them with the new alarm system."

Jack unlocked the back door, left her standing outside for a few moments, then gestured for her to enter. To her, everything felt quiet and secure, but she followed him from room to room as he checked the house, waiting for him to confirm this.

"We're good," he finally said after finishing up with the third and last floor.

Cameron breathed easier after that, and even more so when Jack brought her over to the security keypad next to the door that led to the rooftop deck.

He pushed a few buttons on the keypad, then showed her how it worked. "We've got alarms on all the doors and windows, and glass-break sensors on every floor. You can arm the entire house by pushing this button right here. You should see this red light come on, and then you know you're good to go. You should always have the system armed. I've programmed in a short delay—you'll only have ten seconds after you enter the house to disarm the system before the alarm goes off. The security team put panels next to all the doors, so that should give you enough time. To disarm the alarm, you just enter the security code."

"What's the code?" she asked.

"You pick—any four-character combination that's easy to remember. Not your birthday or anything obvious like that."

He watched as she entered the code. "What's five-two-two-five?"

"It spells 'Jack' on the keypad. Should be easy enough to remember."

They headed back downstairs to the main floor. Jack had left her suitcase in the foyer, and Cameron grabbed it to bring it up to her bedroom to unpack.

Jack's arms came around her and turned her to face him. "Do you want to talk about whatever has been bothering you all afternoon?" His eyes searched hers carefully. "You were quiet during the car ride."

Of course he would pick up on that. "There is something I want to talk to you about," she admitted. "But I thought maybe we could get settled in first." She saw the stubborn set to his jaw. "I'm guessing you're not so keen on that plan."

He took her by the hand and led her through the kitchen and into the great room. "Good guess." He gestured for her to take a seat on the couch.

"How come every time we have one of these conversations, I feel like I should be in a room with a two-way mirror and a bright light shining in my face?"

"Then I'll spare you the usual interrogation tactics and get right down to it," Jack said. "Is it us?"

"Is what us?"

"Whatever's bothering you—is it about us?"

Cameron looked at him strangely. "Of course not—this was probably the most incredible weekend of my life. Why would I suddenly have a problem with us?"

She saw the tension drain out of Jack's face. He took a seat on the couch next to her. "Oh. Good." He grinned and threw his arm along the back of the couch, getting comfortable. "Me, too, you know. The most incredible weekend part."

"But you're still not going to like what I have to say."

Glowering ensued.

"Do I get the bright light now?" Cameron asked teasingly.

"I think I might skip the light and go straight to that paper clip technique we discussed earlier if you don't start talking."

"Just promise me that you'll consider everything I have to say before you answer."

Jack looked her over with his dark, predatory eyes. "All right," he finally agreed.

Cameron tucked her knees underneath her. "I'm obviously very worried about the Robards investigation. This is a strain on me, on you, and it puts everyone I know at risk. I know your team is doing all they can, but nobody's come up with anything so far."

She could tell from the way Jack's jaw twitched that he didn't like being reminded of this.

"I hate that the ball is all in this asshole's court, and that I pretty much just have to sit here and wonder if he's going to come after me again."

Cameron could tell from Jack's expression that he liked being reminded of that even less.

"But maybe there's a way we can control the situation," she said.

"How do you propose we do that?" Jack asked.

"That's what I was thinking about in the car. And I might've come up with something. We figured out that there's a leak—perhaps we can use that to our advantage. We know that the killer knew how to avoid the hotel cameras. But what if we spread the word that you guys have identified a guest who was using a camcorder in the Peninsula that evening—maybe for a vacation or a bachelor party, something like that. You let it be known that this guest caught on tape a man wearing a gray hooded T-shirt, blazer, and jeans, exiting the hotel shortly after Mandy's murder. You say that the FBI crime lab is trying to enhance the tape to come up with an image of the guy's face, and that you're hopeful you'll be able to identify him soon. Hopefully word will spread to the right person."

Jack got up from the couch. Odd that she'd ever found him hard to read—because right then she had absolutely no problem seeing how much he disliked this idea.

"You know as well as I do that a man exiting the hotel wearing a gray hooded T-shirt around the time of the murder means nothing by itself," Jack said. "*You* are the one who can tie that person to the murder. The only one. And the killer knows that. So what you're really suggesting is that we give Mandy Robards's murderer extra incentive to get you out of the picture."

"I'm suggesting we motivate the murderer to make a move that we will be prepared for."

"Cut the crap—you want me to use you as bait. You want me to provoke this guy into attacking you again."

"I think it's an option we need to think about, yes."

"No."

"You said you would consider everything before you answered."

"It's been considered." Jack stared her right in the eyes. "And I will spend the next twenty years sleeping on your floor before I ever willingly put you in danger."

Hearing that, Cameron got up from the couch and walked over. "After this weekend, I probably wouldn't make you sleep on the floor, you know."

But Jack wasn't in the mood for teasing. He moved away from her, over by the window. "I'm serious about this, Cameron."

"With you covering me, and a team of FBI agents who we'd set up in advance, don't you think I'd be safe? If you came to me as a prosecutor, this is exactly the type of operation I'd approve. Particularly with such a high-profile crime."

"If I came to you as a prosecutor, you would ask me about the risks. And I would tell you that no one, including me, can ever guarantee safety in an operation like this. I can take those risks with other people. But not with you."

His words hung in the air between them. Cameron finally spoke first.

"I agreed that you're in charge. So if you don't think this is a good idea, I'll drop it. For now," she added. She knew he wanted to be all moody and broody right then, but too bad—she wasn't going to let him. "I can't promise I won't bring this up again in the future, though. I can be kind of fussy about these things when I want to be."

She caught the glimmer of amusement in Jack's eyes.

"When did you ever actually agree that I was in charge?" he asked. "I think I missed that."

"It was more of an implied consent. I didn't reject the concept the two times you brought it up."

He shook his head. "You are such a lawyer." He looked out the window and sighed. "I do think it's a good idea, Cameron. And I want this to be over just as much as you do." He turned back to the window, gazing out as he thought things through. He ran his hand over his mouth. "I don't know, maybe if we could find a look-alike . . .

some female agent who looks like you, who I could station in this house in your place . . ."

He turned around. "Maybe if—" He stopped suddenly, presumably seeing the look on her face. "What? What's wrong?"

It was the thing he'd done right then. When he'd run his hand over his mouth.

It struck Cameron—the piece she'd been missing all this time about the night of Mandy Robards's murder. There'd been something in that moment when she'd seen the killer through the peephole as he'd left Mandy's room, something she'd never been able to put her finger on.

It was the way his blazer had pulled tight across his shoulders as he'd reached forward to push open the stairwell door. There'd been a faint imprint underneath his blazer, the same kind she'd just seen underneath Jack's blazer when he had reached up to rub his mouth.

Cameron stared at Jack in surprise.

"I don't know if this means anything . . . but I'm pretty sure the guy who killed Mandy Robards was wearing a gun the night he strangled her."

Twenty-seven

IT TOOK JACK a moment to process what Cameron had just said.

"A gun? What makes you think that?"

Cameron gestured to his shoulders. "There was a bulge under his blazer—I think he was wearing a shoulder harness. Working with FBI agents, I've probably seen it hundreds of times before but never consciously paid any attention to it. But when you moved your arms and rubbed your face like that, it looked kind of bulky right under your shoulders there . . ." She trailed off, as if unsure how to describe it.

"You could see my gun printing."

She nodded. "Yes."

"And you're sure you saw the same thing with the guy who left Mandy Robards's room?"

"Yes. I always felt like there was something I was missing, I just couldn't figure it out," Cameron said. "Does that mean anything, that he was wearing a gun?"

Jack's mind worked through this new development. They knew so little about the killer, *everything* meant something. And this piece of information could mean a lot. "I certainly find it interesting that he suffocated Mandy Robards when he had a gun on him."

"Guns make noise."

"Yes, they do. Although a professional could've brought a silencer to take care of that. I'm thinking more than ever now that this murder wasn't something that was planned."

"A jealous boyfriend, perhaps? Maybe he confronted Mandy about Senator Hodges and it escalated," Cameron suggested.

Jack shook his head. "We already looked into that angle. The shoulder harness is an interesting development. You might not have recognized it, but someone with a trained eye would've spotted the gun right away. That would be a sloppy, risky move, with the city's restrictions on handguns," he said, referring to the fact that Chicago citizens were not permitted to own or carry handguns. "Makes me think this guy is licensed in this city to carry a concealed weapon."

"Like a cop, you mean? Or an agent?"

"Maybe . . ." Jack mused over this for moment. Then something occurred to him. He strode over to the foyer and unzipped the duffel bag he'd left there earlier. He pulled out the case files he'd brought to the wedding— he'd made copies of everything and left the originals with Wilkins. He opened the file with the photographs of the people they'd interviewed in connection with Mandy's murder.

He located the photograph he was searching for and took a closer look.

Interesting.

He handed the photograph over to Cameron. She pointed.

"This is one of the photos you showed me the night of the bachelorette party."

"His name is Grant Lombard," Jack said. "He does private security for Senator Hodges. He carries a gun—I noticed it the night we interviewed him. He had the proper permits, and since Mandy had been suffocated the gun didn't jump out to us as a red flag. I remember him from the interview—sort of a cool, professional type. I also recall him being about five feet eleven and one hundred seventy pounds, so he matches the physical description of the guy we're looking for. I thought I remembered him having brown eyes, too, although I wanted to confirm that with the picture."

"The guy who attacked me had brown eyes," Cameron said.

"Yes, he did."

"By any chance does Grant Lombard have an alibi for the night of Mandy Robards's murder?"

"He says he was at home sleeping. Alone," Jack said.

"Given the time of murder, there's probably not too much we can make of that," Cameron said.

"True. But perhaps I need to ask him if he has an alibi for the time of *your* attack."

Cameron took a second look at the picture. "He can't exactly use the 'at home sleeping' excuse for four thirty in the afternoon. There's certainly enough here to make it worth checking into."

Jack pulled his cell phone out of his pocket and dialed Wilkins. His partner didn't answer, so he left a message on his voicemail. "Wilkins—it's Jack. I might have something in the Robards case—a lead worth looking into, at least. Call me when you get this message. I'll fill you in then."

Jack hung up, glad to finally have an actual lead to pursue after two weeks of hunting and pecking in the dark.

"We're not going to talk to anyone about this except Wilkins and Davis," he told Cameron. "Not yet, anyway. I don't want to take any chances that the wrong person could find out that you know more than we'd originally thought."

Although he didn't say it out loud, Jack knew that Cameron, as a prosecutor, understood that the gun could be a key piece of evidence. If Lombard did turn out to be the guy they were looking for, she had just inadvertently stumbled upon the link that could ultimately lead to his arrest.

The idea left Jack feeling very skittish.

"I'm sorry I didn't remember this right away," Cameron said. "That night at the hotel, you warned me not to be sloppy—I should've thought of this earlier." She looked annoyed with herself. "After all the times I've raked a witness over the coals for claiming to remember something after the fact. Now I've done exactly the same thing."

Jack reached for her. "I hate to break this to you, Cameron, but you're only human."

"Shh . . . I've been trying to keep that under wraps for years."

He smiled and kissed her forehead. "Your secret is safe with me."

She leaned into him, resting her cheek against his shoulder. "So where does all this leave us for tonight?"

Jack wrapped his arms around her. "Unfortunately, it means I have some work to do. There are a few things I want to check into."

Cameron pulled back, running her hands over his chest. "What kinds of things? And more important, how long will they take?" she asked with a coy smile.

Two days, Jack thought. For two days he'd been tortured by Martino's interrogators and had never broken once—not a single word. But this woman had him wrapped around her finger in one second flat with just a smile.

He knew he should probably run as fast as he could in the opposite direction.

Instead, he kissed her.

She kissed him back playfully at first, until he moved her against the counter. He wound his tongue around hers and slid his hands to her waist.

"I need to get to work," Jack said as he kissed the spot on her neck that he knew drove her crazy.

"You do," she agreed, as her hands wandered down his stomach. "And I need to unpack."

"I'll walk you to the stairs," Jack said. They kissed the entire way as he backed her through the kitchen and to the staircase. By the time they got there, his hands had some-how made their way underneath her shirt.

"So you'll come upstairs when you're done working, then?" Cameron asked.

"Yes. Shouldn't be too long." There was a lot of kiss-ing after that, and suddenly they were on the stairs and he was between her legs. He pushed her shirt up and scooted down, trailing his lips across her stomach.

She sucked in her breath. "Okay. I'm going."

"Yes. Go." Jack pulled himself up and kissed her—just one last time. Then he felt Cameron's hands unzipping the fly of his jeans. She reached into his boxers, and he groaned as she wrapped her hand around him.

He peered down and saw the sparkle in her eyes.

Work would just have to wait a few damn minutes.

"Do you have any condoms left in your suitcase?" he asked raggedly, at least having the presence of mind to think of that while she worked him over. The woman had the most incredible hands.

"Top outer pocket," Cameron said.

Jack stepped away, swore as he rummaged around, finally realized he was in the wrong pocket, grabbed a condom, and came back.

Holy fuck.

The little minx had taken the initiative of slipping off her jeans.

But she'd left the naughty-boots on.

"You know I feel naked without my heels," Cameron said.

Jack tossed the condom onto the stairs. He shrugged off his blazer, then took off his gun harness and set it on the stairs next to the condom.

"Slide up two steps," he ordered her.

She did. He spread her legs and knelt between them on a lower step. He watched her eyes widen as he slid one of her legs over his shoulder, then the other. He felt her tremble as he bent down and licked the top lacy edge of her panties.

"Jack . . ." she murmured, threading her fingers through his hair.

He hooked his finger around the waistband of her panties and pulled them down a few inches. He lowered his mouth.

Cameron moaned. "Oh god, you *are* the devil . . ."

Enough said.

Twenty-eight

CAMERON STOOD IN her closet, zipping her brides-maid's dress into a garment bag, when she noticed a figure hovering in the doorway.

"Were you just singing 'Bette Davis Eyes'?" Jack asked with a lazy grin.

Cameron blushed, not having realized that's what she'd been doing. Nice—a mind-blowing double orgasm and Jack literally had her singing.

"I might have been humming a little," she said noncha-lantly.

He cocked his head. "I thought that was your song with Collin."

She laughed at this. "I don't have a 'song' with Collin. It's just a song I like."

Jack appeared somewhat appeased by this. "Your Inter-net connection is too slow."

Thank God—he was cranky about something. *This* Jack she could handle. The Jack who cupped her face as he whispered the most romantic and sexy things anyone had ever said to her as he made love to her on her own staircase, on the other hand, was a force of a different nature.

"You mentioned that the other day," she said. "I've never had a problem with my connection before. Are you trying to run some super-fast secret agent program?"

"Yes. But it's slow even for that."

His teasing eyes made her stomach do a little flip. *So this is what it's like to fall in lov—hold on—not going to go there yet,* Cameron told herself. She'd been dating Jack for all of—what—two days?

"I hope you're not looking to me for answers about this Internet thing," she told him. "If there's a problem, I turn the computer off and then on again. If that doesn't fix it, I call Collin."

Jack folded his arms across his chest. "I think we need to talk about this Collin dependency. Because there's a new sheriff in town."

"Hmm. That's a little alpha for my tastes," Cameron said with a disapproving air.

She tried not to look totally turned on.

"I'm going to take a look upstairs at your computer," Jack said. "Maybe one of your neighbors is tapping into your wireless signal. It's easy to do in the city, with houses as close as they are. What's your password?"

"You won't need one. I leave the computer running and just let it go into sleep mode whenever I'm not using it."

Jack threw her a look that said this was a big no-no. "I think I now know why you're having Internet problems."

"What is it you're trying to do from your laptop, anyway?" Cameron asked.

"Just a few things I want to have ready when Wilkins calls. I can log onto the Bureau's network remotely—I want to take another look at Lombard's cell phone records that we pulled a couple weeks ago. Plus I've been think-ing about setting up a trace on his phone, although I'll need one of the tech guys to help me with that. Then we can track everywhere Lombard's been—at least with his phone—over the last few days."

Cameron put the bridesmaid's dress back into its spot on the rack behind the door. She glanced over her shoul-der. "Without a warrant, that sounds highly illegal."

"Legal, illegal, there are so many gray areas."

"I didn't hear that, Jack."

"Nothing to hear, counselor. I never said a word."

WHEN HE REACHED the third floor, Jack turned left and headed into the office. Cameron's desk faced the win-dow, overlooking her front yard and the street below. Jack went over to the desk and took a seat. When he moved the mouse, the computer sprang to life.

Possibly, he just needed to reboot the system since she'd left it running for who knew how long. Still, he wanted to be sure. He checked to see how many computers were linked to her router—as he'd said to her, maybe someone was pilfering her wireless connection and that was slow-ing everything down.

It took a second for the screen to open. What he saw threw him for a loop.

That can't be right.

There were *fifteen* devices using Cameron's Internet connection. Jack was aware of two—his laptop and Cam-eron's desktop computer.

So what the hell were the other thirteen? It was possi-ble that a neighbor could be stealing her signal, maybe even a couple, but thirteen neighbors using her Internet was extremely unlikely.

Then again, maybe it wasn't thirteen computers, but something else. That was what Jack checked next. He pulled up the data stream for the first device.

Strange.

It was transmitting an audio signal.

But Jack heard nothing. He turned up the volume on Cameron's computer. Still nothing. He moved onto the next device—this one was also transmitting an audio signal.

Again, nothing.

What the hell?

He quickly checked the other signals—all audio—and finally found something being transmitted through the eighth one.

It was the sound of a woman singing softly. A smoky voice he recognized well.

All the boys think she's a spy, she's got Bette Davis eyes.

Cameron. In her bedroom.

Jack could hear the sound of a drawer shutting, then a zipper, as she continued unpacking her suitcase.

Son of a bitch.

He deliberately began drumming his fingers on the desk—making enough noise for a test, but not too much— as he hurriedly checked the remaining devices. He knew what he would eventually find. When he got to the last audio signal, the sound of his fingers rapping against the wood echoed through Cameron's computer, clear as day.

Jack would've sworn out loud if he could have.

The goddamn house was bugged.

His mind raced, dozens of thoughts all at once. The masked man . . . Thursday afternoon . . . they had assumed he'd been waiting to attack Cameron when she came home from work. Jack realized now that Mandy's killer hadn't been in the house at four thirty in the afternoon to avoid police surveillance; he'd been there because he was after something else entirely. He wanted to listen.

He wanted to know what Cameron knew.

Nowadays, microphones used for eavesdropping were smaller than ever—less than the size of a button. And all one needed was a computer, a wireless network, and the IP addresses of the monitoring devices. Not much harder than setting up a nanny cam, particularly for someone who knew what he was doing.

Jack pulled out his BlackBerry—luckily, now that they knew what the guy was up to, they could turn things around. Assuming Mandy's killer was actively monitoring the bugs, they could back-trace the link to the IP address of the computer he was using to listen to them. And once they had that information, they could pinpoint the location of that computer—and the killer.

Jack started to type a text message to Wilkins— obviously, he couldn't call him or anyone else from the house with it being bugged. Then he stopped, realizing it would be faster to simply take Cameron out to his car and make the call from there. He'd have to slip her a note explaining the situation, of course, because they couldn't say anything that would tip the killer off—he could be listening to them right then.

Jack's stomach twisted into a knot.

The killer could be listening.

Assuming he'd been monitoring them, the killer would've heard every word he and Cameron had said that evening. Fragments of their conversations echoed through his head:

I'm pretty sure the guy who killed Mandy Robards was wearing a gun the night he strangled her . . .

His name is Grant Lombard. He does private security for Senator Hodges . . . He matches the physical description of the guy we're looking for . . .

By any chance does Grant Lombard have an alibi for the night of Mandy Robards's murder? . . .

Perhaps I need to ask him if he has an alibi for the time of your attack.

Then Jack recalled a separate conversation, an earlier one, and his whole body went cold.

To disarm the alarm, you just enter the security code.

What's five-two-two-five?

It spells "Jack" on the keypad. Should be easy enough to remember.

The killer knew the code to the alarm.

"Cameron," Jack whispered, his heart leaping into his throat. He'd left her alone . . . he couldn't hear her right then . . . the second floor was too quiet . . . Jack dropped his BlackBerry and reached for his shoulder harness—

"Don't make a fucking move," commanded a low voice behind him.

The distinctive sound of the slide of a gun chambering a round echoed through the room.

With his hand frozen at his harness, Jack looked over his shoulder. He took in the man standing in the doorway, aiming a gun right at his head.

"Lombard," Jack growled.

"You almost had it there, Pallas. Almost," Lombard said. "Now take the shoulder harness off. Slowly."

The first thing Jack noticed was that Lombard didn't have a silencer on his gun. Which meant that Cameron was still alive downstairs. Lombard had come after him first.

"I said take the shoulder harness off. Now," Lombard said quietly.

Jack read the look on Lombard's face and knew he wasn't bluffing. He unhooked the harness and set it on the floor. He'd be no good to Cameron if Lombard blew his brains all over the office wall right then and there.

"Kick it over here," Lombard said.

Jack complied. His eyes remained trained on the trigger of Lombard's gun. One twitch and he'd be out of that chair. *Dive to the floor, pull the desk over, and use it as a shield.* It wasn't the best plan, but it was something.

Then Lombard changed the game.

"Cameron Lynde," he called out loudly, his voice reverberating through the top floor. "I have a gun pointed at your boyfriend's head. If you're not on the landing in three seconds, I will kill him."

Jack forced himself to sound calm and controlled. "Get out of the house now, Cameron. Let me handle this."

Lombard didn't so much as blink. "Three seconds, Cameron. One, Two—"

"Don't."

The single, shaky word came from the landing a half a floor below them.

"Good girl, Cameron," Lombard said.

The three of them remained in a holding pattern. Lombard in the doorway, pointing his gun at Jack, Cameron out of view on his other side, halfway down the stairs.

"If I hear a gunshot, I'll run," she called up. "And I know it's me you really want."

"Neither of you has to get hurt—I know a way we can work this out," Lombard said.

"Don't listen to a fucking word he says, Cameron. Get out of the house now," Jack ordered her.

"I want to make a deal," Lombard said, talking over him. "That's all. You're a prosecutor, Cameron—you can make it happen. And this gun in my hand gives you one hell of an incentive to do just that. I know things—like the name of the person who told me about you. There's a mole—a big one. I can help you nail him. But we need to talk about this face-to-face. How do I know you're not standing there with a phone in your hand, calling the police right now? So come up the stairs slowly, with your hands in front of you. Do it now, Cameron. Or Jack dies."

It almost sounded convincing. Jack prayed she wouldn't fall for Lombard's speech. "It's a setup, Cameron. You come up those stairs, and we're both dead."

There was a pause. Cameron remained strangely silent. Debating her options, presumably.

Jack knew the time to act was now. In his mind, there was only one option, and that was getting her as far away from Lombard as possible. No matter what it took.

She'd said she would run if she heard a gun shot. He had to count on that. He would draw Lombard's fire and give Cameron a chance to escape. He wouldn't stop until he reached Lombard, no matter what hit him.

Other men had tried to kill him before. For Cameron's sake, he was willing to see if this asshole's luck was any better than the others.

Jack got ready to make his move.

Beads of sweat formed at Lombard's brow. He called down again, and his voice was strained and anxious. "You've got two fucking seconds, Cameron, so either get your ass up here or say good-bye to Jack."

"Okay! I'm coming," Cameron shouted up urgently.

But she wasn't on the landing anymore. There was the faint sound of a door opening—it came from the hallway on the floor beneath them. A hinge squeaked. Something metal rattled.

"She's getting a goddamn gun," Lombard hissed.

Fortunately, Jack knew the layout of the house a lot better than Lombard. Not a gun, he thought, realizing precisely what Cameron was up to.

She was fucking brilliant.

The door she had opened, the one closest to the stairs, was her linen closet. And while there wasn't a gun stashed in there—at least not one that Jack knew about—there was something else that could help them.

The circuit breaker.

Lombard snapped, having had enough. "Fuck you both." His eyes narrowed in on Jack. Everything happened at once. He pulled the trigger as Jack dove for the ground, knowing what was coming. There was a loud *CLICK!* from downstairs and—

All the lights in the house went out.

The gun fired in the dark, and the bullet whizzed over Jack's head. Not wasting a moment, he leapt up and ran for Lombard. Lombard reacted more quickly to the surprise of the darkness than Jack had hoped; he took off into the hallway. Lombard fired wildly behind him, and bullets hit the walls beside Jack. He kept going. Gaining on Lombard right before the stairwell, Jack saw his chance— he dove and tackled Lombard full-force. Grabbing for Lombard's gun, Jack pushed him backward at the same time, using all his strength to hurtle them toward the wooden banister. Jack braced himself—this was going to hurt—as they slammed against the banister and broke through with a loud crack.

Tangled together, both men plummeted thirty-five feet down the open staircase.

They landed hard on the first-floor foyer. Jack heard the sickening sound of breaking bone as he crashed on top of Lombard, who screamed out in pain.

Jack instinctively lunged for Lombard's gun, gritting his teeth at the flash of pain in his chest—he must have broken a few ribs. Fighting off a wave of dizziness from the shock of the fall, he pushed away from Lombard, stood up, and pointed the gun at him.

Jack caught his breath and wiped blood off his forehead with his sleeve. One of the bullets had hit the wall so close to his head he'd been cut by a flying piece of plaster.

"Almost had it there, Lombard," he panted. "Almost."

Jack heard footsteps above him. He looked up and saw

Cameron running down the stairs. Seeing him, she stopped on the landing between the first and second floors and sank against the wall in relief. Jack realized then that he and Lombard must've fallen through the stairwell right past her.

With a look of shock, Cameron peered up at the third floor, all thirty-five feet up, then back at him. "My God, Jack."

She caught sight of Lombard through the moonlight and swallowed. He lay on the floor before Jack with his right leg bent at a grotesque angle beneath him. Breathing heavily, he clutched his right arm to his chest and watched Jack warily.

With all the action, Jack had lost count of how many times Lombard had fired at him. He popped out the clip of the gun to see if it was still loaded. Three rounds left—more than enough. He slammed the clip back in.

He and Lombard had some unfinished business to discuss.

"Go upstairs to your bedroom, Cameron. Don't come out until I tell you," Jack said.

She nodded. "Right. I'll call for backup and an ambulance."

"Don't call anyone. Just go upstairs."

Her eyes widened. "What are you going to do?"

"You don't need to know. You're an assistant U.S. attorney—you can't be a part of this."

Lombard's eyes widened nervously.

Cameron hesitated on the landing, and for a moment Jack thought she wasn't going to listen to him. "Okay," she finally said. She left, and a few seconds later Jack heard the door to her bedroom shut.

He turned his attention to Lombard, who was sweating profusely as he lay on the floor at his feet.

"When we were upstairs, you talked about the person who told you about Cameron's involvement in the Robards case. I want to know who it was."

Lombard coughed, wheezing in pain. "Fuck you, Pallas."

"You might want to save that for later. I haven't even gotten started yet."

"Fuck you anyway."

Jack squatted down at Lombard's side. "You've been listening to Cameron and me this whole time," he said quietly.

Lombard tried to laugh, but it came out sounding hollow. "Almost every word. Loved the part where you wouldn't fuck her after I shot her. You're as weak as the rest, Pallas. All because of a woman."

Maybe Lombard saw him as weak because of Cameron, Jack thought.

But tonight she was his greatest strength.

"Since you've been listening, you know what she means to me. I would kill anyone who harmed her," he said with cold simplicity. "Give me a name, and I'll make an exception."

Lombard didn't say anything. But he didn't look so smug anymore, either.

Jack brought the gun in closer. "You shot her. I watched as you took this very gun and held it under her chin. Like this." He grabbed Lombard's jaw and shoved the gun right under his chin. Lombard flinched, breathing heavily through his nose.

Jack pushed the barrel harder, digging into Lombard's skin. "Give me an excuse to pull this trigger. I want to do it so badly I can taste it."

"I want a deal," Lombard blurted out through clenched teeth.

Jack nodded. "I believe you actually mean that this time."

He pressed the gun to Lombard's forehead. "Here's the deal: tell me what I want to know, and I won't have to tell the medical examiner that I shot you between the eyes in self-defense."

Lombard swallowed hard. He said nothing at first, but Jack saw it in his eyes.

Defeat.

Lombard sagged against the floor and finally gave Jack the answer he'd been waiting for.

"Silas Briggs."

LESS THAN TEN minutes after Jack called for backup, the house was teaming with people—some in uniforms, some not. He told the paramedics what had happened to Lombard, then spoke briefly to both Wilkins and the cops.

Jack stood side-by-side with Wilkins, watching as the paramedics placed a neck brace onto a handcuffed Lombard and slid a backboard underneath him. He glanced up at Cameron. She'd been sitting on the steps of the landing ever since the cops and FBI had arrived. He sensed she hadn't wanted to get too close to Lombard as he lay on the floor at the bottom of the staircase. He hoped she wasn't trying to avoid him as well.

"I'd like a minute alone with Cameron," Jack said to Wilkins. "Could you see to that?"

Wilkins nodded. "Of course. I'll make sure everyone stays down here."

Jack grabbed a blanket the paramedics had brought in, slipped past Lombard on the stairs, and headed up. He knelt down and wrapped the blanket around Cameron's shoulders. "Are you okay?"

She shook her head. "No."

Jack noticed she was trembling. He helped her to a

standing position, then led her up the stairs and into her bedroom. He closed the door behind them, took her by the hand, and sat her down on the bed.

"Say something, Cameron. Anything."

She sounded distant when she answered. "When he called down from upstairs, I was standing right here by this bed." She frowned. "I was trying to decide what underwear I was going to wear to bed that night, wondering if you liked black or red better." Her voice cracked. "Then this strange voice shouted down that he had a gun pointed at your head and that you had three seconds to live."

Jack knelt at the floor in front of her. "You did so great. Cutting off the power was the smartest thing anyone could've done in that situation."

She wiped her eyes. "Right, I'm such a hero. You dove off a thirty-five-foot staircase. I turned off a light switch."

"It . . . was a very key light switch."

She sniffed. Her nose was red and her mascara was smudged underneath her eyes. Jack thought he had never seen anyone look so beautiful. When he thought about what could've happened . . . how close he'd come to losing her . . .

"You're doing the serious face again." Cameron touched his cheek, looking him over with concern. "Are you hurt? You have to be, after that fall."

"I might've broken a few ribs," Jack said.

"What? We need to get one of the paramedics to check you out. You could have internal bleeding or something."

"It's fine. I'll have someone take a look later, when I'm finished with all this."

She shook her head. "Not later, Jack. Now. You're not invincible, you know."

"Shh . . . I've been trying to keep that under wraps for years."

That finally got a slight smile out of her. Jack got up and sat next to her on the bed.

She leaned her head against his shoulder. "I didn't go into my room, you know. I stayed in the upstairs hallway to listen."

"I figured as much."

Cameron turned her head to look at him. "Those things you said to Lombard . . . were you bluffing?"

Jack thought about his response to this. He'd said a lot of things to Lombard. But right or wrong, the man she'd heard down there was him. "Does it matter?" he asked her.

She paused for a moment before shaking her head. "No."

Twenty-nine

"THERE'S SOMEONE HERE to see you, Cameron."

Cameron glanced at the clock on her desk computer. It was after two o'clock, which surprised her. She'd been so caught up taking notes on the case files she'd been reading, she'd worked straight through lunch.

"Thanks, Elaine. Does this someone have a name?" She checked her calendar—she didn't have any appointments written down for that afternoon.

Through the speakerphone, the front desk receptionist's voice lowered to a whisper. "I'm not supposed to tell you."

After everything she'd been through recently, Cameron wasn't sure she liked the sound of that. She picked up the phone. "Do I at least know this person?"

"Yes. Definitely," Elaine said.

"Then why can't I know who he or she is?"

"I don't know—he just said I should ask you to come out here. Oh, he's looking over. I gotta go." Elaine quickly hung up.

Cameron set the phone back in its cradle. She considered the possibilities.

Jack or Collin?

Whichever of the two it was, he was taking her to lunch, she decided. She was starving.

She got up from her desk and headed out into the hallway, wondering what all the mystery was about. Her instincts told her it was Jack. He had dropped by her office frequently over the last couple of weeks, for both professional and personal reasons.

Thinking about him never failed to put a smile on her face. Since Lombard's arrest, Jack had spent nearly every night at her house—the only exceptions being the few nights she'd spent at his loft. They were busy during the week, each of them having been thrust back into work after the night of the attack, but they made up for it in the evenings and on weekends. Jack had decided to take on the job of repairing the stairwell banister, along with a few other renovations to her house, and Cameron had decided to assist him—which meant that she sat in the corner drinking wine and reading one of the hundreds of books from his collection that slowly seemed to be trickling into her house. She'd poke her head up every once in awhile and chime in with her two cents, and then somewhere around her second glass she'd start noticing all the ways in which Jack's muscles flexed under his T-shirt while he worked, and how delicious he looked getting sweaty and mussed, and uh-oh, suddenly they'd be on the floor getting sweaty and mussed in ways that didn't require a hammer and nails.

Best of all, though, she loved the way they talked—whether it was coming out of the movie theater, at a restaurant over dinner, or lying on the couch with her head against Jack's chest as he told about his former cases and she shared memories of her dad.

Luckily, the media attention surrounding them finally seemed to be dying down—something they both were looking forward to. The biggest story in the press for the last two weeks had been the indictment and subsequent resignation of the U.S. attorney for the Northern District of Illinois. All things considered, Cameron supposed, Silas's arrest had gone smoothly enough. The Monday morning after Lombard's attack, she had "happened" to be out in the reception area when Jack and Wilkins had arrived with their arrest warrant. There'd been a lot of yelling and swearing on Silas's part, particularly as Jack put the handcuffs on him. Standing off to the side with a few of the other assistant prosecutors, Cameron had watched as Jack remained calm and professional. He'd said something in a low voice only Silas could hear, and Silas nodded mutely, his lower lip quivering. Strangely, after that he'd been fully cooperative.

Closely following the scandal involving Silas had been the one with Grant Lombard—it wasn't every day, after all, that a U.S. senator's private bodyguard was arrested for murdering a call girl in one of Chicago's most luxurious hotels. This arrest, unfortunately, had put Cameron and Jack directly in the spotlight: after the attacks it became impossible to keep secret the fact that she had been a witness (sort of) to the murder. The media quickly linked her and Jack together from the apparently never-to-be-forgotten "head up her ass" comment of three years ago. Although the rehashing of Jack's remarks usually brought on another glowering session on his part, Cameron personally found it amusing to watch. She'd even slipped once—while he was trying to wrestle the remote control out of her hands to turn off the ten o'clock news, she'd teasingly said they should share the footage with their kids someday as evidence of their love at first sight. When Jack hadn't immediately scrambled off the couch to head for the hills, and instead had gotten quite amorous after her comment, she took it as a sign that she hadn't completely freaked him out.

Now, looking forward to Jack's unexpected visit, Cameron picked up her stride and turned the corner into the main reception area of the office.

He wasn't there. The entire waiting area was empty, in fact.

Over at the reception desk, Elaine held up her hands. "He told me he didn't want to wait out here—said he wanted to speak to you someplace private. I put him in Silas's old office since no one is using it right now."

Very odd, Cameron thought. More intrigued than ever, she cut across the waiting area and through the corridor on the opposite side. When she got to Silas's former office, she saw a tall, well-built man standing outside the door. He nodded as she approached.

"You can go right in, Ms. Lynde."

Keeping an eye out, Cameron cautiously opened the door and stepped inside. A stout man with neatly trimmed silver hair and an expensive suit stood before the window, looking out at the view of Lake Michigan. When she walked in, he turned around and smiled at her with a genteel air.

"Good afternoon, Ms. Lynde. Thank you for meeting with me on such short notice."

Cameron shut the door behind her. "Senator Hodges," she said with surprise. "It's a pleasure to meet you. What . . . brings you to our office today?" Despite their bizarre connection, and the fact that she knew far more about the senator's personal life than she had ever wanted to, they'd actually never met or spoken to each other.

Hodges crossed the room. "I think we both know this visit is overdue, Cameron. Is it okay if I call you Cameron?" He sat down in one of the two leather chairs in front of Silas's old desk. "Why don't you have a seat?"

Cameron nodded. "Certainly."

In light of everything that had happened that night at the Peninsula, it felt weird sitting in Silas's former office with Hodges. Really, though, it would've felt weird sitting with him anywhere.

"I'm greatly indebted to you, Cameron, and I wanted to thank you in person," Hodges said. "From what Special Agent Davis tells me, you single-handedly kept me from being arrested and undoubtedly saved my senate seat. Innocent or not, I never would've survived the scandal of being implicated in a murder. Let alone my . . . connections to Ms. Robards."

"I appreciate that, Senator. But honestly, the FBI team assigned to the case deserves all the credit. I just happened to be in the wrong place at the wrong time."

"You were nearly killed for being in that place at that time," Hodges said. "I can't tell you how sorry I am for that. How sorry I am for a lot of things, actually. I was a foolish man and my mistakes hurt others. In some cases, gravely so." His eyes clouded with sadness.

Cameron nodded, unsure how to respond. Talking to Hodges was sobering. Despite the fact that Mandy Robards's intentions toward the senator had been less than honorable—as Jack had confirmed now that Lombard had told him all about the blackmail scheme—the whole incident remained a sad testament to the lengths some people would go to for money. Or out of desperation.

"I've upset you," Hodges said.

"I'm fine. I'm just relieved it's all over."

"Actually, it's not quite *all* over," Hodges said. "Silas Briggs's resignation means I have an important task ahead. As the senior senator from Illinois, it's my duty to make a recommendation to the president regarding the person who should be named the new U.S. attorney. And I think I might know of just the right candidate." He paused deliberately.

Cameron pulled back in surprise. "Me?"

Hodges nodded. "You."

Cameron tried to decide how best to respond. "I appreciate the consideration, Senator. Truly, I do. But if I can be blunt, I don't expect you to offer me the job out of gratitude. Nor do I want you to."

Hodges smiled at this, as if he approved of her answer. "I had a feeling you were going to say that. So let me assure you that this has nothing to do with gratitude. After the allegations being brought against Silas, the last thing I would do right now is risk further potential scandal by naming a candidate who isn't fully qualified for the job. If anything, your connection to me counted against you."

Cameron remained skeptical.

Hodges laughed. "Do I need to convince you further?"

"If you're serious about this, then yes, you do."

"Good God, they weren't kidding when they said you were a tough nut to crack," Hodges muttered. "Fine—I'll give you the highlights, the facts that most convinced *me* when my vetting team came up with your name. You have the best trial record among all the assistant U.S. attorneys in this district. The judges—yes, we do talk to judges— say you're fearless and tenacious in the courtroom. After Briggs, frankly, that's what this office needs. You look good on paper: you come from a blue-collar background, you put yourself through law school, your father died heroically as an officer of the law, and the media already thinks you've got balls made of brass for surviving the ordeal with Lombard. But what most convinced me, Cameron— and I know you're being very humble and low-key about this—is that, per the request of the attorney general himself, you've been temporarily running this office since Silas's departure. Seeing how you haven't burned down the place yet, I thought I'd give you a real shot at the job. That is . . . unless you don't want it."

Cameron got butterflies in her stomach. Holy shit, this was really going to happen. No need to convince her further. "I would be honored, Senator, to be your nominee for the position."

Hodges looked relieved. "Good. Whew. I have to be honest with you—we didn't have much of a backup plan. I'm actually sweating a little under my jacket here."

Cameron laughed. "I'll try to be less difficult in the future."

Hodges smiled warmly as he shook her hand. "You do things exactly the way you see fit, Cameron."

They rose from their chairs and walked to the door together. "Funny you should mention that, Senator . . . because I hope you understand that, unlike Silas, I don't plan to be merely a figurehead in this position. I intend to keep trying cases."

"With your record, you try all the cases you want. Just make sure you win them." With a wink, Hodges opened the door and nodded to his guard outside.

Cameron watched them leave. She stood alone in Silas's office, trying to wrap her mind around the fact that there was a good chance it was going to be *her* office in the not-too-distant future.

U.S. Attorney Cameron Lynde.

That had a nice ring to it.

With a grin, she headed back to her soon-to-be-former office as fast as dignity and her three-and-a-half-inch heels allowed her. Once there, she shut the door for privacy, then sat down at her desk and picked up the phone.

He was her first call, of course, and she told him everything. When she had finished sharing her news, she could tell by his voice that he was smiling on the other end of the line.

"Congratulations, counselor," Jack said. "You deserve it."

She could tell from his tone that he was hiding something. "You knew already, didn't you?"

Jack laughed. "Okay, I knew. Davis let it slip that two agents in our office had been assigned your background check. I've had reservations every night this week at Spiaggia, waiting for Hodges to tell you. I figured you should finally get your dinner there, and this was the perfect reason."

Impossible man—being all sweet and everything. "I'm still trying to decide how I feel about the fact that you knew about this before I did."

"Don't be disappointed," Jack said. "The fact that I've been ridiculously proud of you for days doesn't change how excited you should be about this. Besides, I pretty much know everything. You should probably just start getting used to it."

"And on that note, I'm hanging up," Cameron said.

"Rushing me off so you can call Collin next?" Jack teased.

"*No,*" she said emphatically.

Damn, he really did know everything.

AND TWO WEEKS later, they had another occasion to celebrate. Albeit, one Jack was a little less enthused about.

"Happy birthday, Jack," Cameron said as they sat down at one of the bar tables to wait. She'd brought him to Socca restaurant that evening, a neighborhood bistro just a few blocks from her house. "Thirty-five. I think that merits a present or two."

Jack frowned. "Cameron, I told you not to get me anything."

"Well, I figured that was one of your seemingly endless supply of orders that I plan to ignore." She pulled two envelopes out of her purse and set them on the table in front of him. One was large and about an inch thick, the other small but with some sort of object in it. "Choose."

Jack picked up the larger envelope.

"Good choice," she said.

Jack opened the envelope and found a thick, multiple-page document. He slid it out and flipped it over. The names on the caption jumped out at him:

UNITED STATES OF AMERICA

v.

ROBERTO MARTINO, et al

It was a criminal indictment, signed by the U.S. attorney herself, charging thirty-four members of Martino's organization, including Roberto Martino, with over a hundred counts of federal and state law violations. It included everything from racketeering, drug, and firearm charges, to aggravated assault, attempted murder, and murder.

Jack paged silently through the indictment. When he was about halfway through, he slowed and read carefully through the counts pertaining to the murder of the DEA agent he had tried to warn, and his own torture at the hands of Martino's men. All of which was laid out, paragraph by paragraph, in graphic detail.

"I don't care if I don't get them on anything else. I'll hang them for that alone," Cameron promised quietly. "I'm going to file it next week. I thought I might as well kick off my new position with a bang."

Jack slid the indictment back into the envelope. It would be a bang, all right. He reached over and laced his fingers through hers. She knew what the indictment meant to him, but he needed to be certain she wasn't doing it for the wrong reasons. "Are you sure about this?"

"Definitely. I've wanted to try this case for three years."

"Things could get crazy," Jack warned her. "You need to be careful how you handle this. Lombard and Silas are nothing in comparison to taking on Roberto Martino."

"I've given a lot of thought as to how we should proceed," Cameron said. "I'd like to bring in all the agents from the Chicago office, ones from some of the other divisions as well, and execute the arrest warrants in a simultaneous strike. Grab Martino and his guys in one fell swoop so that they don't have time for a counter-move. I'll need someone I can count on to lead the task force. I was thinking that should be you. I also think you should be the one to arrest Martino himself."

Jack considered the implications of everything she had just said. Part of it had him slightly panicked.

Cameron cocked her head, misinterpreting his expression. "I thought you'd want the honor of taking down Martino."

"Oh, hell yes."

"Then what's with the look?"

"It just occurred to me that as U.S. attorney, you're now in a position of authority over me."

Cameron raised an eyebrow. "You're right, Agent Pallas. There *is* a new sheriff in town."

"Cute. How long have you been waiting to say that?"

She laughed. "About two weeks." She pushed the second envelope in front of him. "Don't forget about your other present."

Jack picked it up. "I'm thinking nothing can top my sworn enemy's head on a platter." He ripped open the envelope and slid out its contents.

He'd been wrong.

Keys and a garage door opener.

Momentarily caught off guard—a rare event for him—Jack looked up at Cameron. "Does this mean what I think it means?"

"I suppose that depends on what you think it means. If you think it means I'm asking you to move in with me, you'd be right." Her expression turned more serious. "If you also think it means that I wake up every morning wondering what I did to deserve having you back in my life, well, you'd be right about that, too."

Jack sat there for a moment, just . . . stunned. No one had ever said anything like that to him.

"Come here," he said huskily. He grabbed her chair and pulled it toward his. He kissed her, softly at first, then his hand moved to her back and pushed her closer as his emotions got the better of him. He pulled back to hold her gaze. "I love you, Cameron. You know that, right?"

She kissed him back, whispering the words in his ear. "I love you, too."

It took all of Jack's strength not to haul her out of the restaurant and drag her home right then and there. The combination of everything she'd just said, not to mention the black sweater, slim-fit skirt, and heels she was wearing, was driving him crazy. He threw her a sneaky grin. "I hope you won't mind skipping dessert tonight. I've got to get you alone. I'm dying here."

"My God, Jack—with a look like that, you two should just get a room. And try not to pick the one with a dead body next to it this time."

Hearing the familiar male voice, Jack swore under his breath. "Seriously, Cameron—your friends have the worst timing ever." He turned around and saw Collin standing before him.

"Happy birthday, buddy." Collin grinned, slapping him on the back. Behind him, Jack could see Wilkins, Richard, Amy, and her husband.

"I invited a few people to help celebrate your birthday," Cameron said sheepishly. She threw up her hands. "Surprise."

"We sort of come with the package," Collin explained. "Think of it as a collective gift from all of us to you: five bona fide annoying and overly intrusive new best friends."

"It's the gift that keeps on giving," Wilkins said.

Jack grinned. "I'm touched. Really. And since it appears I'm going to be moving in, let me be the first to say that all of you are always welcome at my and Cameron's house. Subject to a minimum of forty-eight hours prior notification."

When the hostess came by to escort them to their table, Cameron held Jack back from the rest of the group. "You're okay with this?" she asked.

"Yes. It's great." He kissed her forehead. "Thank you."

She wrapped her arms around his neck. "And in answer to your earlier question, I don't mind skipping dessert. In fact, I already have a dessert planned for when we get home."

Jack liked the sound of that. "Can I have a hint?"

"It involves me wearing your handcuffs."

Christ, full-mast. The thought of her naked and at his mercy threw his body into a tailspin. Jack pulled her into a corner where they were out of sight. "The hell with dinner— we're leaving now," he growled.

Cameron shook her head coyly. "We can't leave your party so early. That would be indecent."

In response to her teasing, Jack put his hands on the wall next to her, pinning her in. "So, Ms. Lynde . . . is that how it's going to be with you?"

Her eyes flashed devilishly.

"Always."

Keep reading for a preview of
Julie James's next romance

A Lot Like Love

THE CHIME RANG on the front door of the wine store. Jordan Rhodes came out of the back room, where she'd been sneaking a quick bite for lunch. She smiled. "You again."

It was the guy from last week, the one who'd looked skeptical when she'd recommended a cabernet from South Africa that—gasp—had a screw top.

"So? How'd you like the Excelsior?" she asked.

"Good memory," he said, impressed. "You were right. It's good. Particularly at that price point."

"It's good at any price point," Jordan said. "The fact that it sells for less than ten dollars makes it a steal."

The man's blue eyes lit up as he grinned. He was dressed in a navy car coat and jeans, and wore expensive leather Italian loafers—probably too expensive for the six to eight inches of snow they were expected to get that evening. His dark blond hair was mussed from the wind outside.

"You've convinced me. Put me down for a case. I'm having a dinner party in two weeks and the Excelsior will be perfect." He pulled off his leather gloves and set them on the long ebony wood counter that doubled as a bar when Jordan hosted events in the shop. "I'm thinking I'll pair it with leg of lamb, maybe seasoned with black pepper and mustard seed. Rosemary potatoes."

Jordan raised an eyebrow. The man knew his food. And the Excelsior would certainly complement the menu, although she personally subscribed to the more relaxed "drink what you want" philosophy of wine rather than putting the emphasis on finding the perfect food pairing—a fact that constantly scandalized her assistant store manager, Martin. He was a certified level three sommelier, and thus had a certain view on things; while she, on the other hand, was the owner of the store and thus believed in making wine approachable to the customer. Sure, she loved the romance of wine—that was one of the main reasons she had opened her store, DeVine Vintages. But for her, wine was also a business.

"Sounds delicious. I take it you like to cook," she said to the man with the great smile. Great hair, too. Nicely styled, on the longer side. He wore a gray scarf wrapped loosely around his neck that gave him an air of casual sophistication.

He shrugged. "It comes with the job."

"Let me guess—you're a chef."

"Food critic. With the *Tribune*."

Jordan cocked her head, suddenly realizing. "You're Cal Kittredge."

He seemed pleased by her recognition. "You read my reviews."

"Religiously. With so many restaurants in this city to choose from, it's nice to have an expert's opinion."

Cal leaned against the counter. "An expert, huh . . . I'm flattered, Jordan."

So, he knew her name.

Unfortunately, a lot of people knew her name. Between her father's wealth and her brother's recent infamy, rare was the person, at least in Chicago, who wasn't familiar with the Rhodes family.

Jordan headed behind the counter and opened the laptop she kept there. "A case of the Excelsior—you've got it." She pulled up her distributor's delivery schedule. "I can have it in the store by early next week."

"That's plenty of time. Do I pay for it now or when I pick it up?" Cal asked.

"Either one. I figure you're good for it. And now I know where to find you if you're not."

Okay, so she may have been flirting a little. For the last few months her family had been living under an intense spotlight because of the mess with her brother, and, frankly, dating had been the last thing on her mind. But things were finally starting to settle down—as much as things could ever settle down when one's twin brother was locked up in prison, she supposed—and it felt good to be flirting. And if the object of said flirtation just so happened to have polished, refined good looks, well, all the better.

"Maybe I should skip out on the bill, just to make you come look for me," Cal teased back. He stood opposite her with the counter between them. "So, since you read my restaurant reviews, I take it you trust my opinions on restaurants?"

Jordan glanced at Cal over the top of her computer as she entered his wine order. "As much as I'd trust a complete stranger about anything, I suppose."

He laughed at that. "Good. Because there's this Thai restaurant that just opened on Clark that's fantastic."

"Good to know," Jordan said pleasantly. "I'll have to check it out sometime."

For the first time since entering her wine shop, Cal looked uncertain. "Oh. I meant that I thought you might like to go there with *me*."

Jordan smiled. Yes, she'd caught that. But she couldn't help but wonder how many other women Cal Kittredge had used his "Do you trust my opinions on restaurants?" line on. There was no doubt he was charming and smooth. The question was whether he was *too* smooth.

She straightened up from her computer and leaned one hip against the bar. "Let's say this—when you come back next week to pick up the Excelsior, you can tell me more about this new restaurant then."

Cal seemed surprised by her nonacceptance (she wouldn't call it a rejection), but not necessarily put off. "Okay. It's a date."

"I'd call it more . . . a continuation."

"Are you always this tough on your customers?" he asked.

"Only the ones who want to take me to Thai restaurants."

"Next time, then, I'll suggest Italian." With a wink, Cal grabbed his gloves off the counter and left the store.

Jordan watched as he walked past the front windows of the store. She noticed that a heavy snow had begun to fall outside. Not for the first time, she was glad she lived only a five minute walk from the shop. And that she had a good pair of snow boots.

"My god, I thought he'd never leave," said a voice from behind her.

Jordan turned and saw her assistant, Martin, standing a few feet away, near the hallway that led to their storage room. He walked over, carrying a case of a new zinfandel they were putting out in the store for the first time. He set the box on the counter and brushed away a few unruly reddish-brown curls that had fallen into his eyes. "Whew.

I've been standing back there, holding that thing forever. Figured I'd give you two some privacy. I thought he was checking you out when he came in last week. Guess I was right."

"How much did you hear?" Jordan asked as she began to help him unpack the bottles.

"I heard that he's Cal Kittredge."

Of course Martin had focused on that. He was twenty-seven years old, more well-read than anyone she knew, and made no attempt to hide the fact that he was a major food and wine snob. But he knew everything about wine, and frankly he'd grown on her, and Jordan couldn't imagine running the shop without him.

"He asked me to go to some new Thai restaurant on Clark," she said.

"I've been trying to get reservations there for two weeks." Martin lined the remaining bottles on the bar and tossed the empty box onto the floor. "Lucky you. If you start dating Cal Kittredge, you'll be able to get into all the best restaurants. For free."

Jordan modestly remained silent as she grabbed two bottles of the zin and carried them to a bin near the front of the store.

"Oh . . . right," Martin said. "I always forget that you have, like, a billion dollars. I'm guessing you don't need any help getting into restaurants."

Jordan threw him an eye as she grabbed two more bottles. "I don't have a billion dollars."

"Sure, just a hundred million."

It was the same routine nearly every time the subject of money came up. Because she liked Martin, she put up with it. But with the exception of him and a small circle of her closest friends, she avoided discussing finances with others.

It wasn't exactly a secret, however: Her father was rich. Very rich. She hadn't grown up with money; it was something her family had simply stumbled into. Her father, basically a computer geek like her brother, was one of those overnight success stories *Forbes* and *Newsweek* loved to put on their covers: After graduating from the University of Illinois with a masters degree in computer science, Gray Rhodes went onto Northwestern University's Kellogg School of Management. He then started his own company in Chicago where he developed an antiviral protection program that exploded worldwide and quickly became the top program of its kind on the market. Within two years of its release to the public, the Rhodes Anti-Virus protected one in every three computers in America. (A statistic her father made sure to include in every interview.) And thus came the millions. Lots of them.

One might have certain impressions about her lifestyle, Jordan knew, given her father's financial success. Some of those impressions would be accurate, others would not. Her father had set up guidelines from the moment he'd made his first million, the most fundamental being that Jordan and her brother, Kyle, earn their own way—just as he had. As adults, they were wholly financially independent from their father, and frankly, Jordan and Kyle wouldn't have it any other way. On the other hand, their father was known to be extravagant with gifts, particularly after their mother died six years ago. Take, for example, the Maserati Quattroporte sitting in Jordan's garage. Probably not the typical present one received after graduating business school. Even Harvard Business School.

"We've had this conversation many times, Martin. That's my father's money, not mine." Jordan wiped her hands on a towel they kept under the counter, brushing off the dust from the wine bottles. She gestured to the store. "*This* is mine." There was pride in her voice, and why shouldn't there be? She was the sole owner of DeVine Vintages, and business was good. Really good—certainly better than she'd ever projected at this point in her ten-year plan. Of course, she didn't make anywhere near the hundred million her father may or may not have been worth (she never talked specifics about his money), but she did well enough to pay for a house in the upscale Lincoln Park neighborhood, and still had money left over for great shoes. A woman couldn't ask for much more.

"Maybe. But you still get into any restaurant you want," Martin pointed out.

"This is true. I do have to pay though, if that makes you feel any better."

Martin sniffed enviously. "A little. So are you going to say yes?"

"Am I going to say yes to what?" Jordan asked.

"To Cal Kittredge."

"I'm thinking about it." Aside from a potentially slight excess of smoothness, he seemed to be just her type. He was into food and wine, and better yet, he *cooked*. Practically a Renaissance man.

"I think you should string him along for awhile," Martin said. "Keep him coming back so he'll buy a few more cases before you commit."

"Great idea. Maybe we could even start handing out punch cards. Get a date with the owner after six purchases, that kind of thing."

"I detect some sarcasm," Martin said. "Which is too bad, because that punch card idea is not half-bad."

"We could always pimp you out as a prize," Jordan suggested.

Martin sighed as he leaned his slender frame against the bar. His bow tie of choice that day was red, which Jordan thought nicely complemented his dark brown tweed jacket.

"Sadly, I'm underappreciated," Martin said, sounding resigned to his fate. "A light-bodied pinot unnoticed in a world dominated by big, bold cabs."

Jordan rested her hand on his shoulder sympathetically. "Maybe you just haven't hit your drink-now date. Perhaps you're still sitting on the shelf, waiting to age to your full potential."

Martin considered this. "So what you're saying is . . . I'm like the Pahlmeyer 2006 Sonoma Coast Pinot Noir."

Sure . . . exactly what she'd been thinking. "Yep. That's you."

"They're expecting great things from the 2006, you know."

Jordan smiled. "Then we all better look out."

The thought seemed to perk Martin up. In good spirits, he headed off to the storage room for another case of the zinfandel while Jordan returned to the backroom to finish her lunch. It was after three o'clock, which meant that if she didn't eat now she wouldn't get another chance until the store closed at nine. Soon enough, they would have a steady stream of customers.

Wine was hot, one of the few industries continuing to do well despite the economic downturn. But Jordan liked to think her store's success was based on more than just a trend. She'd searched for months for the perfect space: on a major street, where there would be plenty of foot traffic, and large enough to fit several tables and chairs in addition to the display space they would need for the wine. With its warm tones and exposed brick walls, her store had an intimate feel that drew customers in and invited them to stay awhile.

By far the smartest business decision she'd made had been to apply for an on-premise liquor license, which allowed them to pour and serve wine in the shop. She'd set up highboy tables and chairs along the front windows and tucked a few additional tables into cozy nooks between the wine bins. Starting around five o'clock on virtually every night they were open, the place was hopping

with customers buying wines by the glass and taking note
of the bottles they planned to purchase when leaving.

Today, however, was *not* one of those days.

Outside, the snow continued to fall steadily. By seven
o'clock the weathermen amended their predictions and
were now calling for a whopping eight to ten inches. In
anticipation of the storm, people were staying inside. Jordan had an event booked at the store that evening, a wine
tasting, but the party called to reschedule. Since Martin
had a longer commute than she did, she sent him home
early. At seven thirty, she began closing the shop, thinking
it highly unlikely she'd get any customers.

When finished up front, Jordan went into the backroom
to turn off the sound system. As always at closing, the
store felt eerily quiet and empty without the eclectic mix
of Billie Holiday, The Shins, Norah Jones, and Moby she'd
put together for this week's soundtrack. She grabbed her
snow boots from behind the door, and had just sat down at
her desk to replace the three-inch-heel black leather boots
she wore, when the chime on the front door rang.

A customer. Surprising.

Jordan stood up and stepped out of the back room, thinking somebody had to be awfully desperate to come out for
wine in this weather. "You're in luck. I was just about to
close for the . . ."

Her words trailed off as she stopped at the sight of the
two men standing near the front of the store. For some
reason, she felt tingles at the back of her neck. Perhaps it
had something to do with the man closer to the door—he
didn't look like her typical customer.

He had chestnut brown hair, and scruff along his jaw
that gave him a dark, bad-boy look. Right off the bat, something about his demeanor, the way he commanded one's
attention, made her think he was a man used to getting his
way. He was tall, and wore a black wool coat over what

appeared to be a well-built physique. He was good-looking, no doubt, but unlike Cal Kittredge, he seemed rather . . . rough. Unpolished. Except for his eyes. Green as emeralds, they stood out brilliantly against his dark hair and five o'clock shadow as he watched her intently.

He took a step forward.

She took a step back.

A slight grin played at the edges of his lips, as if he found this amusing.

She wondered how fast she could make it to the emergency panic button underneath the bar.

The shorter man, the one wearing glasses and a camel-colored trench coat, cleared his throat. "Are you Jordan Rhodes?"

She debated whether to answer this. But the blond man seemed safer than the tall, dark one. "I am."

The blond man pulled a badge out of his jacket. "I'm Agent Seth Huxley, this is Agent Nick McCall. We're with the Federal Bureau of Investigation."

This caught her off guard. "The FBI?" The last time she'd seen anyone from the FBI had been at Kyle's arraignment.

"We'd like to discuss a matter concerning your brother," the blond man said. He seemed very serious and slightly tense about whatever it was he needed to tell her.

Jordan's stomach twisted in a knot. She forced herself not to panic. Yet.

"Has he been hurt?" she asked. In the four months he'd been in prison, there already had been several altercations. Apparently, some of the other inmates at Metropolitan Correctional Center figured a millionaire computer geek would be an easy mark.

Kyle, being Kyle, assured her he could hold his own whenever Jordan asked about the fights during one of her visits. But every day since he'd begun serving his sentence, she'd worried about the moment when she got a phone call saying he'd been wrong. And if the FBI had come to her store on the night of a blizzard, whatever they had to tell her couldn't be good.

The dark-haired man spoke for the first time. His voice was low, yet smoother than Jordan had expected given his rugged appearance.

"Your brother is fine. As far as we know, anyway."

That was an odd thing to say. "As far as you know? You make it sound like he's missing or something." Jordan paused, then folded her arms across her chest. Oh . . . no. "Don't tell me he's escaped."

Kyle wouldn't be so stupid. Well, okay, *once* he'd been that stupid, actions that had landed him in prison in the first place, but he wouldn't be that stupid again. That was why he'd pled guilty, after all, instead of going to trial. He'd wanted to own up to his mistakes and accept the consequences.

She knew her brother better than anyone. True, he was a genius, and assuming there was a computer anywhere within reach of the inmates, he could probably upload some code or virus or whatever that would spring open the cell doors and simultaneously release all the prisoners in a mad stampede. But Kyle wouldn't do that. She hoped.

"Escaped? Is there something you'd like to share about your brother, Ms. Rhodes?" Agent McCall asked in an amused, perhaps mocking, tone.

Something about him rubbed her the wrong way. She felt as though she was facing off against an opponent holding a royal flush in a game of poker she didn't realize she'd been playing. And she wasn't in the mood to play games with the FBI right then. Or ever. They'd charged her brother to the fullest extent of the law, locked him up at MCC and treated him like a menace to society for what, in Jordan's admittedly biased opinion, was simply a really bad mistake. (By someone with no criminal record, she noted.) It wasn't like Kyle had *killed* anyone, for heaven's sake, he'd just caused a bit of panic and mayhem. For about fifty million people.

"You said this is about my brother. How can I help you, Agent McCall?" she asked coolly.

He stepped farther into the store and leaned against the bar, seeming to make himself right at home. "Unfortunately, I'm not at liberty to fill you in on the details here. Agent Huxley and I would prefer to continue this conversation in private. At the FBI office."

And she would prefer to say nothing at all to the FBI, if they weren't dangling this bit about Kyle over her head. She gestured to the empty wine shop. "I'm sure whatever it is you have to say, the chardonnays will keep it confidential."

"I never trust a chardonnay."

"And I don't trust the FBI."

The words hung in the air between them. A standstill. Agent Huxley intervened. "I understand your hesitancy, Ms. Rhodes, but as Agent McCall indicated, this is a confidential matter. We have a car waiting out front and would very much appreciate it if you came with us to the FBI office. We'd be happy to explain everything there."

She considered this. Agent Huxley at least seemed to be somewhat more amiable than his partner. "Fine. I'll call my lawyer and have him meet us there."

Agent McCall shook his head firmly. "No lawyers, Ms. Rhodes. Just you."

Jordan kept her face impassive, but inwardly her frustration increased. Aside from her general dislike of the FBI because of the way they'd treated her brother, there was an element of pride here. They had come into *her* store, and this Nick McCall person seemed to think she should jump just because he said to.

So instead, she held her ground. "You're going to have to do better than that, Agent McCall. You sought me out in the middle of a blizzard, which means you want something from me. Without giving me more, you're not going to get it."

He appeared to consider his options. Jordan got the distinct impression that one of those options involved throwing her over his shoulder and hauling her ass right out of the store. He seemed the type.

Instead, he pushed away from the bar and stepped closer to her, then closer again. He peered down at her, his brilliant green-eyed gaze unwavering. "How would you like to see your brother released from prison, Ms. Rhodes?"

Stunned by the offer, Jordan searched his eyes cautiously. She looked for any signs of deceit or trickery, although she suspected she wouldn't see anything in Nick McCall's eyes that he didn't want her to.

A leap of faith. She debated whether to believe him.

"I'll grab my coat."